Courted

GATEKEEPERS OF THE GODS

JENNIFER CHANCE

Cover design by Dar Albert

0 9 8 7 6 5 4 3 2 1

 Created with Vellum

For Liz Bemis,
who lives Happily Ever After

A lone figure mounted the marble stairs, her hair lifting in the constant breeze that blew up from the sea.

She could hear the distant crash of waves far below, battering against the jagged wall of rock. Fortunately, this temple was safely set back from the cliff. A fall from this height into the Aegean would be certain death, even if you cleared the brutal rocks.

Still, whenever she lit the ceremonial fires this late at night, she couldn't help but think how many ships had foundered on that jagged wall, the line of enormous rocks breaking out of the water so violently they seemed to have been hurled out of the bowels of the earth by Hades himself. The wall extended for a quarter mile up and down the shoreline, with a single break in the center—a titanic natural gateway between land and sea.

To the world, those rocks were why Oûros was known as the home of the Gatekeepers of the Gods, an ancient seaside kingdom perched at the edge of Greece, protector of the divine pantheon and the path through which the gods could travel back and forth from Olympus whenever they chose.

The truth was a little more complicated.

She drew the long taper out from the traditional cloth satchel she'd slung over her shoulders, and approached the covered marble furnace that held the eternal fire.

This temple, one of the oldest in Oûros, wasn't on any of the tourist maps. It was unreachable except by ATV, and while it could be seen from the sky, a trick of the light and terrain hid it from any but the most targeted cameras. No one who wasn't looking would even know the temple was here. After all these centuries, no one looked.

The floor beneath her bare feet gleamed in the soft moonlight, swept clean by whomever the gods saw fit to tend their final temple on this earth. The gods of Olympus may have been barred from the world at large, but their long reach still extended throughout Oûros and deep into the Aegean as well. Another small detail that didn't make it into the glossy brochures.

As always, the fire burned within the temple's sunken furnace, fed by the gods themselves. A long-ago act of defiance and pride that had bound them to this land and its people. Defiance, pride—and love too, she thought. After all, romance remained the country's number one draw. That wasn't by accident. She leaned down and nudged the delicate wand of wrapped linen into the furnace, transferring the eternal flame to its tip. The taper would burn to the quick in a matter of a few minutes. But for her work this night, it would be more than enough time.

She turned and approached the open-air overlook, where the curving sweep of marble welcomed in the wind and sky. This night was cloudless, the moon shining its reflected light over the temple. The wind was low enough to ensure her fires would burn.

When she lit the first golden brazier, filled, as always, with bits of dried driftwood, it flared as bright and bold as the god who so fiercely prowled the seas. As always, the ocean responded with a mighty crash below, signaling it saw her. It recognized her act of fealty, of hope.

She smiled a little sadly. "Find him, Poseidon," she whispered. It had been a full year.

The second brazier was smaller and more delicate than the first, and its kindling was made up of twigs and dried flowers. Appropriate for the god of love, Oûros's divinely mercurial patron. But Eros hadn't been pulling his weight of late, and it was time she let him know it. Lighting the small pile, she murmured. "Eros, ever watchful, bring him love."

Then she turned to the third brazier. No kindling rested in its base, so she withdrew the sheaf of pages she'd written the night before, when her dreams had awoken her so forcefully. She placed the sheets in the golden bowl, then touched the taper to them, her lips curving as Morpheus's image came to her mind, cloaked in shadows. She didn't call out the god of dreams often, but he'd been sending her more than her share of nightmares these past several days.

"Through the slumber of the body, may our souls converse with the gods," she murmured. Maybe the shapeshifting god could help their kingdom heal. Maybe it was time to invite a bit more of the energy of *all* the gods back into this tired and troubled world. Well, some of them, anyway...

The flames crackled brightly, beacons in the darkness.

And a distant, murmuring laughter carried on the wind.

One

Em Andrews gazed out over the crystal blue water...

Forget that. If she was standing in the middle of an honest-to-God fairytale kingdom once consecrated to the Greek gods, this daydream was going to start off the Best. Way. Possible.

Emmaline Aphrodite Grace, stunningly beautiful princess and demigoddess of music, gazed out over her seaside paradise as sunlight danced over crystal blue water and members of her gorgeous, strapping guards trained in the crashing surf, preparing to protect her sacred temple from—

"Yo, Em! Where's the suntan lotion? I'm about to fry my face off!"

Em snapped back into focus and swung around, squinting as her best friend in the entire world ground to a halt in the sand beside her. Gasping for breath after the blurted demand, Nicki Clark braced her hands on her thighs, her reddish-gold hair and turquoise running tank plastered with sweat, her back heaving as she sucked in air.

"Red bag, side compartment," Em said, mentally picturing her packing list for the day's tote, everything neatly tucked into place. She would have grabbed the bag herself, except a tanned foot with perfectly polished toes snaked out of the shadow of the enormous hotel-monogrammed beach umbrella to kick it their way, the rasp following it as dark as death.

"Nicki, for the love of all the ancient gods... Silence."

"Lauren! You're up! You should have come jogging with me and Fran!" Nicki dropped to a squat and began rooting through Em's provision bag as a muttered curse floated out from under the umbrella. "Best thing in the world to knock out a hangover."

"Right after I finish icing my face. Promise."

"Where *is* Fran, anyway?" Em returned her gaze to the beach. It was filling up with tourists and sunbathers, but the last member of their group was nowhere to be seen. "You didn't lose her, did you?"

"Hardly. There was some sort of Farmers Market setting up. It looked awesome, but I wasn't going to stop my run for it." Nicki liberated the suntan lotion. "Fran found some sort of scarf thingy hanging from a rack and refused to move until she could buy it."

She sank onto the beach blanket, then grabbed a towel and a squeeze bottle of water to sponge herself off. "I'm here now, though, so if you wanna take a walk, feel free. I'll make sure nothing takes off on its own while Lauren is in recovery."

Em smiled, nodding her thanks. Nicki knew her too well— she *wouldn't* go wandering off to enjoy this beautiful day if Lauren might need her to go fetch food, water, or possibly a physician after she'd decided she could hold her own in a *tsipouro* drinking contest the evening before.

It had been their first night in this idyllic kingdom, the second and southernmost stop on their European tour. A tiny country carved out of the mountains of Greece and edged by the glorious Aegean Sea, Oûros was an anomaly in the modern world—a nation run by royalty, and apparently run well.

Regardless of any governmental prowess, what Oûros really excelled in was looking *amazing*. Em turned again to gaze out over the smooth, sun-kissed water of the Aegean, then headed for the shoreline, her feet sinking into the soft white sand. If she were Nicki, she'd come up with the perfect words to describe the water's particular shades of blue. Then again, if she were Nicki, she wouldn't be focusing on the pretty picture the Aegean Sea made at all. She'd be analyzing riptides and undercurrents, trying to set up the perfect scenario for an impromptu wind-surfing competition.

Em wasn't interested in cataloging their European odyssey for some extreme travel blog. She wanted to *immerse* herself in it, diving into the inherent escape it provided, if only for a little while. Floating on the Aegean, she could forget about the letter she'd received before she left Kansas City, the rich, creamy stationery, the crisp typed words. *Final scholarship deferment... Decision needed...sincerely hope you will consider...*

No. She didn't need to think about any of that. Not yet, anyway.

Now she needed simply to revel in the glittering waves that had been beckoning to her all morning. She wasn't totally used to swimming in open water, but she couldn't resist the lure of the gorgeous, jewel-like azure sea. It already seemed to hold her in its shifting grip, drawing her out, pulling her deep...

"Watch out!"

Em didn't have time to react as a pair of large, powerful hands planted themselves on her upper arms, then lifted her off the sand a good two inches and thrust her to the side as if she were some sort of toy. A phalanx of the training navy guys, or whatever they were, pounded past, but as soon as they hit some imaginary mark in the sand, the fastest one of them turned and sprinted back to her. He wore long scuba-style tights and a gray tank emblazoned with Cyrillic writing she couldn't make out.

Still, it looked close enough to Greek that the guy could have been any US frat boy—creating a whole new meaning to the term "Rush."

He was just...beautiful. There was no other word for it. Muscles bulged out of his tank top and indented deep into his deeply tanned skin. Even beneath his thick tights, his legs still managed to look wickedly cut. His dark hair was just long enough to curl, and as Em stared, he raked a hand through it, pushing it back from sun-bronzed skin as his golden eyes swept over her, flashing with concern. She got a vague sense of perfect cheekbones and a strong jaw, then her own gaze settled on the guy's absolutely criminal mouth. *Holy Mother of—*

"You're all right?" Somehow, that mouth was moving now, spouting fluent if heavily accented English, and Em had to force herself to stop looking at the guy's lips and actually process his words.

"What? Ah. Yes, sorry." She shook her head, waving her arm to encompass him, the beach, the passing gulls—anything that would deflect his attention away from her. "I didn't mean to get in your way."

"Footrace. Unscheduled." He grinned, and her heart almost stopped. "You're going swimming? Be careful of the undertow. It can sneak up on you."

"Oh." She glanced out at the water. *Undertow?* She'd read about the currents off Oûros's Royal Beach in her tourist guidebook, but neither it nor Nicki had mentioned any sort of serious water hazard. Still, the man was looking at her with concern, so she nodded confidently at him. "I'm a strong swimmer. But thank you."

His expression was skeptical, but he did her the courtesy of not challenging her. At five foot two with a slender frame, Em suspected she didn't look like a powerful anything, but she knew how to *swim*, for heaven's sake. Before Hottie Greek Guy could say anything more, however, a shout sounded from the men up the beach. He looked toward them, which gave her a view of his chiseled profile. Em took the moment to gape, imprinting the image in her memory. Seriously, the man could have been Odysseus standing there, his face wind-hardened and sun-baked but as yet unlined except right around his eyes. His jaw tightened as he called something back to his friends, and those gorgeous lips—

Navy Adonis Man turned and clearly saw her staring, and there was no way Em could stop the blush this time. "Be careful," he said again, and he bowed—actually bowed to her!—before turning to lope off.

Polite, protective, AND sexy as hell. Maybe not the best ad for Oûros's military, but it certainly worked for her.

Em continued down to the edge of the water, slipping out of her beach cover-up and folding it neatly on the soft sand past the tide line. Surely no one would think she was littering if she folded her clothing carefully, and she wouldn't be in the water long. Besides, the cover-up belonged to the hotel, technically. She dropped her glasses—cheap five-dollar tourist models, nothing she couldn't afford to lose—on the pile as well.

There, it looked very tidy. She'd always been one to cross every t and dot every i, but she'd become even more OCD since she'd returned home to care for her parents, with her mom now prone to drifting away from wherever she was sitting and her dad locked in his own bitter thoughts.

Her parents.

Don't go there, Em.

Shrugging off the sudden surge of guilt, she stepped resolutely into the water. It was exhilarating, but nowhere near as chilly as she'd feared it would be. She moved deeper until the water lapped at her thighs, bracing for her modest one-piece suit to be covered. That was always the worst. Still, she plunged in as quickly as she could, willing the Aegean Sea to wash away her negative thoughts.

What was the point of taking her first vacation in a year if she just beat herself up during it?

She needed to follow Fran's advice and relax—really relax—while she had the chance. Her parents were fine, she knew they were fine, and she needed to accept that they would *continue* to be fine for the next few weeks while she was traveling with her friends.

She would be back before they knew it.

And then she'd...carry on. Send her reply to Northwestern one way or the other and make her decision work.

Somehow.

Ignoring the deep pang in her chest, Em resolutely turned her face toward the far wide sea, letting her mind drift into daydream, the only solace she really had anymore, what with the interminable hours of caring for her parents, working with the doctors and counselors and insurance experts, even praying in the small hours of the morning when her parents finally slept and she allowed herself the grief that surged up to overwhelm her.

In many ways, her father should already have been far along the road to recovery from the accident. But it was as if he couldn't take a step forward without looking back, while her mother could barely take any steps at all, her brilliant, beautiful brain still so damaged and frail.

When they were awake, it was all Em could do to distract them both.

But when they were asleep, she could escape too—if only for a little while. Escape into the ridiculous, over-the-top daydreams that had so colored her childhood as she'd listened to her mother read from her classroom literature and mythology; drift into the wild, brilliantly colored fantasies that had been her lone companions for hour upon hour of her own studies, her chin bent, her arms raised, her eyes on the sheets before her, but her mind off and racing through an entirely different landscape with a music all its own.

And now she was inside one of those miracle landscapes as she slipped deeper into the water and let the soft waves lift her up, her arms reaching out as she gloried in the beautiful sea. She wasn't a landlocked princess anymore, but a sea nymph frolicking in the Aegean—maybe even Aphrodite herself. Today, Em instantly decided, today her daydream would be that she was swimming out to meet her former sea nymph friends, and their reunion would be filled with pure and ridiculous joy.

She struck out across the waters, glorying in the feel of it sluicing over her back. The current did feel a little strange to her, odd pressures cutting across her body as well as head-on, but she had so much energy pent up inside her that she relished the opportunity to work a little harder than she expected.

Enjoy this, she ordered herself, as her heart began to surge harder and her muscles stretched. She more than most knew that the music would always come to an end before she was ready. The better she took advantage of these glorious strains of happiness, the better she would be able to savor them when the harsh dissonance of reality came crashing back down on top of her.

Two

"**K**ristos!" The bark of laughter made Kristos Andris, crown prince of Oûros, turn back to his captain of the guard, his gaze leaving the flashing red suit of the woman who was now too far out in the water for his liking. "What, you think that you can ignore your friends for the first pretty American of the day? The beaches will be crawling with them in a few hours."

"You're questioning my authority?" Kristos grinned and pushed out his chest. "How dare you challenge the heart of our beloved country!"

Without further warning, he launched himself at Dimitri Korba, not surprised the soldier was prepared for him. The guy wasn't just captain of the guard, after all—he was a straight up demigod, a half-son of Zeus many times removed. He could handle an unexpected attack.

Now Kristos and Dimitri crashed to the sand as the other soldiers sent up a cheer, then were up again quickly, circling each other, ready to fight.

Kristos lived for these brief and no-holds-barred clashes between them, the same way he lived for the rough work and brutal training of the Oûros National Security Force, the most delicate way the Council of Ministers could come up with to describe the country's fiercely dedicated military unit, so it didn't unnerve their neighboring countries with words like "army." Kingdom or not, however, Oûros was more than a fairy tale nation-state at the edge of nowhere. Its soldiers were strong; its defenses sound. They'd had to be, to protect the world from the gods who stood on the other side of its gates.

No one knew the true charter of the nation of Oûros, founded by one of Hercules's own descendants to guard the entryway to Olympus. No one needed to know. It was enough that Oûros had remained strong for centuries, that it had withstood both military takeover and political merger attempts, that it had even sent its highly trained forces all over the globe to support its allies. Their sacred nation would hold for a little while longer.

He didn't have to lose everything quite yet.

Even as Kristos was about to lunge forward, though, Dimitri froze, then stood taller. Everyone had worked too long with the preternaturally instinctual captain of the guard to miss the move. The other team members, who'd been surrounding the fighting circle in a loose, heckling group, swiveled as one to see what Dimitri was staring at, then they stood straighter too.

Kristos didn't need to turn to see who it was, but he did anyway. He quickly wiped his face with his tank top, then squinted to take in the new contingent of men that approached on both a rolling ATV and on foot.

The few tourists who were out at this hour didn't seem to notice that the second most important man in the kingdom was in their midst, flanked on either side by men in military uniform, their sleek guns holstered but at the ready. The defenses of Oûros might be solid, but they were also almost invisible to both visitors and nationals alike most of the time. It was how the country had managed to make tourism its number one national product, enjoyed by travelers from all over the world.

Council Minister Cyril Gerou wasn't looking for photo ops today, unfortunately. "Prince Kristos," he launched in without fanfare. "You were due at the palace an hour ago."

"We're working out a new training regimen."

"A task that will now fall ably to your second in command as you take on your family duties. Finally." Cyril's tone was sharp, far sharper than Kristos had ever heard it.

His heart sank. So this was it, after all. He'd been granted a year, they had told him. One fucking year, then he'd be called up for official royal duty as crown prince. They'd been counting down the final days even as he'd been racking his brain for any assignment that would take him to the air, the ocean, the mountains—to anywhere but here in the seat of the kingdom. But every attempt he'd made to escape the Crown's reach had been pointless, and secretly he'd known there was really no escape.

Had a full year already passed?

As it always did, a rush of anger and misplaced outrage shot through him as he thought about his older brother Ari, and the wreckage of the plane in the rolling waters of the Aegean that had never been confirmed as his, not completely or definitively enough for Kristos.

Still, he was alone in holding out hope, it seemed. The royal family had a missing crown prince, and they had a partially-recovered plane. There was no way anyone could have survived that crash, and the entire country had gone into mourning when the news had been made official. The glorious crown prince of Oûros, the darling of the international glitterati, had been pronounced dead at twenty-eight years old.

It was beyond a tragedy, for many reasons. Not the least of which was that it meant the younger son, Kristos, must take up his glorified duties as the new crown prince.

Which made him want to hurl.

Now he looked at the long-suffering Cyril, mentor to the princes of Oûros and a chief advisor in his own right to the Crown. Cyril stared back at him, equally resolute. Kristos could have told him not to worry. He wasn't going to argue the point in front of his men. Least of all Dimitri, who had been one of Ari's closest friends until that fateful day a year ago. That day, the demigod captain of the guard had been assigned elsewhere. Ari had left to pilot his aircraft on his own. There was no doubt that he'd been tinkering with some new gadget or another that apparently had been too much for the small plane. It was just something Ari did.

Prince Ari died by his own hand, some might suggest, if they actually knew the truth.

Which, of course, they didn't. The political machine of the royal family of Oûros would never allow anything to besmirch the name it had so carefully cultivated over the long centuries of its existence. As his grandfather liked to say, Oûros had survived twelve centuries of guarding the gods. It would survive this.

Whether due to a shift in his gaze or some peculiar sixth sense, Cyril seemed to realize he'd won. He turned and gestured for Kristos to precede him.

Still, maybe holding on a bit too desperately to his one fleeting last view at freedom, Kristos glanced to the ocean, and searched for the bright flash of red against all that crashing blue.

He froze. "Where is she?"

"Where is who?" Cyril's voice was testy, but he looked out to the water as well. "There's no one out there."

"There was." Beside him, Dimitri was looking too. "The American swam well, it appeared. She looked to be in no danger."

"Well, she sure as hell wasn't wearing scuba gear." Kristos took a few steps toward the water's edge, when suddenly his focus was rewarded. A white-skinned body burst up out of the water as if she'd held her breath long enough to explore the bottom of the sea. She whirled around toward shore, clearly getting her bearings—only she chose the absolute worst time to do so.

One of the famed Oûros cross waves swelled against her, causing her to turn, then turn again in alarm. She hadn't been prepared for the undertow, no matter what she'd said. Now, caught where she was, she couldn't easily strike out toward land, which left only open water as an option until the currents eased and she could once more head toward shore. Given the panicked fluttering of her legs and arms as she took again to the sea, that wasn't going to be an ideal situation for her for long.

"Send one of your men. You'll be spotted instantly, and we don't need the distraction." Cyril was long used to tourists running afoul of the waters of Oûros, and he wasn't going to let this one die either. But, given his sharp glance to the villas surrounding the beach, he also had a healthy understanding of the paparazzi that trolled the area, looking for anything that might earn a quick euro. Kristos suspected his own picture had probably been snapped a half-dozen times already, but he'd been dealing with photographers long enough that he'd stopped giving a shit years ago.

Besides, it was only going to get worse, not better, if Cyril had his way...which it looked like he would. Kristos was demanded in the palace, so to the palace he would go.

"I'll get her—" Dimitri began.

"No!" Kristos said, snapping the word. He could feel the press of royal obligation weighing down on him, but he refused to let it take hold quite yet. The pretty American woman wasn't in danger so far, no; but that didn't mean she was safe. "She's my responsibility," he said, causing Cyril to stare at him, patent shock on his face. "I'll get her."

"Your what? Kristos!" But the advisor's words were lost behind him as Kristos dashed forward and entered the waters that he knew and loved as much as he loved every rock and tree of his country. He had explored Oûros's crescent of the Aegean in every season and in almost every weather condition. He knew exactly when the woman would begin to flag, and he would be there for her.

And if it helped him put off reality for that much longer, then so much the better.

He dived deep into the rolling sea.

Three

This was starting to seriously suck.

Em struck out again with more force, hitting the water at an angle, gratified that she seemed to be making some headway, though all too aware of how far she was being drawn out into the deeper water with every surge of the strange current. She wasn't scared, not really. There were boats emblazoned with the Oûros coat of arms that patrolled the far edge of the bay, specifically to ensure no swimmers strayed far enough into open water to be struck by larger craft, or, God forbid, get dragged by the currents out to sea.

Still, she wasn't really in the mood to be plucked out of the water in some sort of fishing net. For one thing, she'd never live it down. For another, she was grateful enough for her *own* friends taking care of her. She didn't need anyone else to join that particular refrain.

Nevertheless, it was becoming painfully clear that she also wasn't in anywhere near as good a shape as Nicki was. And though she'd always loved swimming, her college intramural swim team suddenly seemed like a lot longer ago than a year. It didn't help that she'd devoted most of the past several months to standing over beds and pushing people in wheelchairs, not to her butterfly stroke.

She seemed to recall that the beachfront curved around to a sandy point to the right of the white stucco and red-tiled villas. Perhaps if she could reach that area, there'd be shallower waters and less current.

If I make it that far. Her arms felt like leaden weights as she slogged through the water slowly—too slowly, her brain was beginning to chime. And her failsafe might not be so fail proof either. Was she even far enough to catch the attention of the patrolling boats? Should she stop swimming now and tread water, waving as much as she could to catch someone's eye?

The thought of waving anything sent a surge of dread through her. *Why was she so tired?*

Maybe she should try to head closer to shore.

Em plunged forward, focusing on her strokes, but she gradually became aware that the problem rested less with her technique than with the continually shifting current. *Undertow*, Hot Navy Guy had said. But there was more than an undertow going on here.

She knew how to swim against a current. It wasn't fun, but it was manageable. As she'd noticed when she'd first set out, however, this current seemed to have two thrusts, one directly at her and one that cut across her body, immediately taking her every effort and spinning her off course, so that she wasn't taking one stroke forward to make up for two back, but two back and one to the side.

It had seemed charming a few minutes ago, but now it was getting downright obnoxious. She was getting spun around, unsure of her destination, and the unfamiliar strain was dragging on more than her muscles. *How am I going to get to shore?*

Suddenly all the weight of the past year pressed down on her. Her parents' horrific crash had come out of nowhere, seeming like a nightmare from which she could never, ever wake up. She'd dropped out of grad school to come home. She was an only child, after all, and her parents had no family close, certainly no family who could take care of such intimate and often harrowing details as personal care for both broken bodies and minds.

Her father should have bounced back more quickly, but he hadn't, and her mother's progress seemed to come in completely unpredictable fits and starts. So Em had quietly told her grad advisors that she wouldn't be able to continue her studies for the foreseeable future. They'd said all the right things and had been so gracious. They understood her need to care for her parents. They'd extended her scholarship offer for a full year, in fact.

Dear Ms. Andrews... Decision needed...

But who was she kidding? She hadn't played her violin seriously in over a year, and every time she tried her original audition piece, she flamed out. She might not be able to cut it at Northwestern anymore. Even if she could by some miracle still make the grade, the likelihood of her joining a major orchestra had been slim anyway.

And if she lost the people who'd given her music in the first place, what did any of that matter?

Even this trip had seemed like a bad idea, despite Lauren doing all the work up front—arranging the live-in care for her parents, refusing to accept any money. She'd come in with guns blazing the way she always did, offering to whisk Em away on a whirlwind European girls trip, and before Em could protest, her mother had seemed to come to life in front of her. She'd turned her soft, quiet eyes on Em and had whispered that she should go. That they would be okay, that she needed to "enjoy being young."

At those words, her father had closed his hands over her mom's shoulders and had just held her, his face racked with guilt. Her mom had patted his hands the way she always did, exonerating him of his role in their shared tragedy moment by moment, day by day, even if she didn't realize she was doing it.

Her parents, such a loving and tight unit in health, were like two stars who'd moved too close together in infirmity, the strength of their gravitational pull sucking Em into their constantly shifting cycles of grief and pain and love.

The accident had taken so much from both of them. How could Em not do everything in her power to help them get well?

I can. I probably will.

What little energy she did have was quickly seeping out of her. She redoubled her efforts, cresting the water's edge only to see another wave strike at her from the wrong direction. *Enough with the freaking current already!*

Suddenly, an entirely different force struck her broadside, causing her mouth to open in shock and seawater to fill it as panic swamped her. Then strong arms were around her hips, lifting her high, past the cresting waves. Still, too much water had gone down her lungs and she coughed and spluttered, her chest seared with pain.

"I've got you! I've got you." The thickly accented voice rolled over her with sharp command. Beyond recognizing it as belonging to the man she'd spoken to on the beach, Em accepted it on an almost visceral level as the voice of authority. Of safety. "You're closer to the beach than you think. I need you to let me do the work without interfering. You hold on. Don't fight me."

The pressure in her lungs was almost unbearable now. "Can't—can't—"

"I'm turning you. I said, don't fight me." The man's hands pivoted her in the water, and without warning, she felt a strong smack between her shoulder blades. As she coughed and gagged, seawater sluiced from her mouth, making everything burn. Then she sucked in another great lungful of air, only to begin coughing again.

"Come on, spit it out. You're strong," his voice rang out again. "You can do this."

No sooner had she drawn in another rasping pull of air than the man shifted her against his body, and she felt the strength of him surround her, keeping her buoyant as he changed direction. The way he hooked her, with his powerful arm crossed over her chest and his hand gripping her high on her waist, she was almost in a back float, but her waterlogged brain couldn't compute how he could move his own body while hauling hers along.

Em tried desperately not to cough, not to slow him down in any way, but it took her only a second to realize she didn't need to worry too much about that. The guy practically exploded through the water, carrying her like she was a pool toy. More quickly than she ever expected, she felt her flapping feet connecting with sand as he hauled her upright, his arm around her waist. He lifted her more than actually helped her walk as she stumbled out of the surf and up onto dry land. Her eyes swam, and she felt dizzy, then the coughing started again as he got her to her knees, helping her retch the last of the water free from her lungs.

Just as she caught her breath, warm hands were wiping away the water from her eyes. She realized too late she was staring at a chest, a chest that might as well be naked, given that the soaked shirt stretching across highlighted pecs and abs that practically rippled with muscle. Oxygen seemed to lodge in her throat again, and her entire body spasmed, which earned her a startled curse and another flat-handed smack on her back.

"You're safe, *koukla mou*, I've got you—"

"I'm fine, I'm fine!" Em tried to wave off her rescuer's ministrations, but he turned her to face him, his beautiful golden eyes now directly in front of her. Eyes that stared at her with worry that showed he had no idea of her true source of distress.

Can he seriously be this gorgeous?

"You're breathing well, yes, but you're not fine. What's wrong?"

"Nothing—nothing is wrong. Thank you. I can walk." Still, she didn't try to stand, and he made no move to let her. And the shaking only got worse. She knew it would get worse. The shock, the surprise, the exhaustion, and the weight of everything she was trying to escape out there in the water seemed to all let go at once, and her body seized again despite her best efforts to control it.

When the man looked up and shouted something she didn't understand, yet another wave of mortification crashed through her. *Oh God, we've drawn a crowd.* Why hadn't she realized there were people around them? Of course there would be people. It was a public beach. With people on it.

"I'm so sorry, I'm fine," she managed, though she could barely understand her own words, she was shaking so much. "If you'd let me get up—I just need to walk around. I'm sorry."

"Don't apologize. You have done nothing wrong." The man's words were harsh with the crack of command, but Em was beyond responding to any more orders. "I am calling for my men, *koukla mou*. You're frozen." And with another curse, he pulled her into his lap, surrounding her with his heat.

His men? Was he in charge of that little group of navy guys?

"Why are you so cold?" he continued, and though her brain seemed to be on the verge of shutting down, Em knew he thought she was going into shock. "It is a warm and sunny day. We have only sunny days here in Oûros, didn't you know that? It is a kingdom of sunshine and joy."

He was talking to her like she was a child, and Em closed her eyes in humiliation. Seriously, this was not happening.

"I just—I get the shakes sometimes. It's okay, I—get cold, it's —" Now didn't seem to be the best time to talk about poor blood circulation, but Em couldn't help her rat-a-tatting teeth as the man's rough arms encircled her, his thick biceps and corded forearms covering her chest and waist. He dropped a soft kiss on the crown of her head, as natural as if they'd been dating for years, and murmured something else to her.

Wait, what? Had he seriously just kissed her?

Warmth snaked through her now, all right, but that was mostly because a man was actually *holding* her. She hadn't had that happen in so long that she'd practically forgotten what it felt like to have someone pressing against her, skin to skin, chest to back, lips to ear, surrounding her so completely that she had neither time nor breath to think about anything else, anyone else, anywhere else...

Whoa, there, girl. Dial it down a notch.

Only now the man who was making such insane, impossible images dance through her head was speaking again, his voice rich with Mediterranean sun and spices and, *God*, his arms around her felt amazing. "You get cold, yes, I can see that," he murmured into her ear, his breath fanning through her wet hair.

Despite herself, Em shivered again, and he held her yet closer. As her heart pounded thunderously, his next words were soothing, gentle, and once again in a language she couldn't understand. He was trying to help calm her down—not rile her up. *Settle down!* She implored her newly reawakened libido, which was beginning to thrum with anticipation at a real, live man holding her real, live body in his real, live arms...

Her newly reawakened libido was apparently not to be deterred.

"The water is treacherous," Sexy Navy Adonis said. "I tried to warn you, but I didn't do a good job. For that, I am sorry."

He kissed her hair again, and Em gave up thinking any more

rational thoughts. Instead, she closed her eyes, wishing the world away while she stored up all these memories for the next however many years it would be until she could feel a man's body against hers again. "I didn't—you didn't—"

"Shh. All is well." He rocked her into him and she became aware of other parts of his body too. His broad, flat chest, his knotted abs—and even lower, as his groin snugged up against the drenched backside of her suit.

Em's eyes popped open, though the man couldn't see her. Nevertheless, while she might be the one trembling, she wasn't the only one affected by their tight embrace.

Oh my God.

"What can I say, *koukla mou?*" Hot Rescue Guy's thickly accented English whispered against her ear. "I am but a man."

And when she turned to apologize, his mouth was right there, his lips soft and warmed by the sun, his expression open and sure. It was the most natural thing in the world for her to lift her face that little bit as well and touch her lips to his.

Sunshine. That was the first coherent thought that raced through Em's mind. Her rescuer tasted like sunshine and salt and sand, like blue skies and possibilities. Something shifted in her that made her trembling stop for a second, her heart lurching with surprise into completely unfamiliar territory. *What—how?*

Oblivious to her confusion, her gorgeous Greek adonis kissed her back, hard and firm, but only for a moment. Then he lifted his head, his rich laughter rolling forth as someone pounded up the beach.

Four

Kristos held the American a little closer than he needed to as Dimitri reached them.

Of course Dimitri would be first on the scene, and carrying the lightweight blanket that was part of the specialized kit they were testing that morning. The blanket was intended to guard against hypothermia for weather much colder than this day had any hope of being, but Kristos was not about to argue. For whatever reason, the small American woman had reacted completely out of proportion to her time in the water.

As he'd come up to her, he realized that she'd actually been swimming strongly enough, making adjustments in the water to combat the current, though he didn't doubt she was tiring. But once he'd gotten her to dry land, she'd seemed to become somehow more exhausted, as if the gorgeous blue-green seas had pulled more out of her than she'd been willing to give. Even now, her full-body reaction was concerning him. Despite the heat he was willing back to her body, not all her trembling was due to her female awareness of him—though *enough* was, certainly. More than enough was.

Still, the part that wasn't chilled him to the bone. Was the American suffering from shock? Was she sick?

He didn't think so, but he couldn't deny an intense desire to understand more. To take this woman into his care in a way that he had never been tempted to by the parade of lovely, long-legged beauties who'd been drawn to him despite his surly attitude and battle-worn body. His own countrywomen were the most gorgeous in the world, of course—but Oûros drew worthy competitors for that status from every nation on the globe, and he'd always had his pick. Never once, however, had he felt *protective* about his conquests. Never once had he wanted more than the pleasure of a stolen kiss or a passionate, sun-soaked interlude before duty called again.

This little American, however, shaking in his arms... She was different.

And he wanted to know why.

She felt so right, lying here with him, submitting to his hold though he sensed she wanted nothing more than to dart away. He'd gotten but a taste of her when he'd almost run into her on the beach a bare hour ago, and he'd be lying if he didn't admit that he'd wanted to take her into his arms right then. She'd seemed almost wounded, her eyes large and smudged with worry, her skin too pale for full summer.

And her kiss...

He definitely wanted to explore more of that.

Dimitri tossed him the blanket, and Kristos used the excuse to shift the woman off his lap and into more appropriate cover. Probably not a moment too soon, as he suddenly became aware of the line of people that now surrounded them. His gaze shifted up to the villas edging this section of the beach. Were there watchers in those windows as well? Probably. It had been a slow morning so far on the quiet beach.

Kristos also didn't miss the fact that Minister Cyril was

scowling with severe censure as his men surrounded him, shielding the woman from the view of most of the tourists. His gaze said what his words would not. Had not ever, though throughout Kristos's life, he'd certainly deserved the admonition: *I told you so.*

"She is fine, just a shock to her system—" Kristos began, only to be interrupted by an imperiously feminine command for everyone to *go*, to *get out of the way*, to *stand aside*, to *move.*

"What's happening here?" A tall, ponytailed blonde in an elegant bikini top and micro-sari strode into their tight circle, pushing even Dimitri out of her way. Dimitri gaped at the willowy woman, and Kristos could understand why. Beyond the fact that she was stunning, if also a little pale for summertime, the blonde spoke Greek with the flawless dialect of Oûros. If it weren't for her clearly American demeanor and fair coloring, she could pass for a native as she pointed a long, manicured finger at Kristos. "What's wrong with Em?"

"Shock." At his words, the woman huddled in front of him seemed to gather all her energy together, as if the sudden scrutiny was all she needed to snap her back into place. She scrambled swiftly to her feet, swaying only a little as she clutched the blanket around her.

"It's fine, Lauren, truly," she said, and her voice was stronger too—clear and feminine, but not overloud. "I was out swimming and—this man..." She turned to smile gratefully at him, and Kristos felt like he'd been sucker punched. "He saw I was in trouble."

"This man?" The woman named Lauren sniffed. She turned her narrowed eyes on him, then jolted in recognition as well. The effect of her undivided focus was impressive, but not in the same intensely personal way that he'd been affected by the woman he already wanted back in his arms. The blonde spoke again in the lilting tones that characterized his native tongue. "Well, I thank you, Prince Kristos, for coming to Em's aid. She is usually a very good swimmer, I assure you."

"She *is* a very strong swimmer." Kristos switched back to English for the benefit of the young woman named "M." He quirked a glance at her. "You are feeling better, Em?"

"Emmaline," she said. Then she blushed, as if she'd just admitted an embarrassing secret. "Everyone calls me Em, though. And yes, I am feeling much better. The current did get the best of me, and you did warn me." Her flush deepened, but she met his gaze, apology filling her eyes. "I'm sorry for causing you any trouble."

"It's no trouble at all," he said. He watched emotions flood across her expressive face a moment more, then gestured to Dimitri. "We can have a doctor check—"

"No doctors, thanks," Lauren said, still speaking in Oûrois. She stepped in front of Dimitri when he would have helped guide Emmaline forward. "We'll get one if we need one."

She dismissed the royal bodyguard with a wave of her hand, never mind that he towered over her in both height and breadth. "Thank you again for your help, Prince Kristos."

Dimitri stared at the imperious blonde, clearly surprised and more than a little annoyed, and Kristos hid a grin. It was good to see the burly demigod flummoxed by someone, especially a beautiful woman. All too often, members of the fairer sex fell at Dimitri's feet, completely unaware that he had the blood of gods in his veins, but sensing it all the same.

Kristos nodded again to Lauren, speaking in English. "You are staying with us long? I hope you find the remainder of your visit to our shores more relaxing."

The blonde's shrewd gaze shifted to him. "A few days, yes."

This announcement earned her a startled glance from Emmaline, who shrugged out of the ultralight blanket, tidily folding it up with the manner of someone used to packing things away neatly and efficiently. She offered the blanket to Kristos, but Dimitri reached out, taking it from her while preventing her from touching Kristos again. Though Emmaline said nothing, a blush swept once more up her cheeks. She clearly realized she'd gaffed, but didn't know how.

"It was a pleasure to meet you, Emmaline," Kristos said, pushing past Dimitri to pick up one of her hands. It was small and still ice-cold in his own, the fingers trembling. "I hope I may do so again during your stay here."

"Of course," she murmured, but her expression was only polite now, her face a mask of deference. Not because she'd guessed his royal station, he suspected. It simply was her natural way.

"If you're quite through, Your Highness? There's much we have to accomplish today." Cyril had appeared again at his side, speaking in their native tongue, and Kristos fought the groan. He turned away from the vision of the American Emmaline as his men formed a loose phalanx around them.

It was all part of the act, he knew, an act that he suspected greatly surprised Emmaline, if not her savvier friend. Even now he saw the two of them step back, their heads together.

He resolutely looked forward and swung into the waiting ATV, not wanting to see Emmaline's reaction when she realized that she'd been rescued not by a respectable member of the Oûros National Security Force, but by some spoiled and pampered prince.

He scowled at the men falling into ranks around him. Just that quickly, he'd gone from protector to protected. He didn't like it one bit.

So much of it was for show too. There was rarely any threat to the royal family of Oûros. They didn't mine oil or rare minerals here, they didn't harbor criminals from the international community, and their palaces, though fortified, were not positioned as strategic strongholds so as to make them desirable for other countries. More importantly, Oûros kept its success and riches close to the vest, held back to assist its own people in wartime, should wartime ever come again.

And as to their work in protecting the world from a wholesale return of the Greek gods, well... Zeus and most of his court had been content to stay on their side of the gates between Earth and Olympus for more than twelve hundred years. No outsiders needed to know of that part of the Oûros royal charter.

Still, that didn't mean that the Crown was going to take any chances with the only remaining heir to the throne. If Kristos was truly about to take on the mantle of royal responsibility, he knew that meant taking on the tedium of royal security as well.

"I'm scheduled to fly out again tomorrow on maneuvers, you know. It's been planned for weeks," he warned Cyril as the advisor joined him in the ATV, though he knew it was an empty challenge. Cyril didn't bother looking back at him. This battle had been decided in the throne room of the king. Cyril was simply the messenger.

"Not anymore. Your cousin Frederick will now be called up to serve in your place."

"Frederick." Kristos allowed his disgust to register in his tone. "Then we really are doomed. I should warn my men."

Cyril's lips twisted, but he didn't disagree with Kristos. The advisor had spent nearly twenty years in the royal armed forces, and he knew Frederick well. "He will learn."

"Not likely." Still, Kristos turned his gaze forward. "I assume there's been no word of any further discoveries."

Cyril didn't have to ask him what he was talking about, but his reply was more measured when it came, almost kind. "None," he said. "Your brother is sorely missed by the entire family, Kristos. The search has been exhaustive to reclaim his remains for proper burial, and your mother has spent far too many nights in the Temple of Winds, praying to any god who will listen for his safe return. But it's been a year. We must move forward now, for the good of the country. You understand that more than anyone."

"I understand it." And he did. If his parents had seen fit to have other children besides himself and his brother, he would have gladly abdicated his role to a younger sister or brother so he could continue doing the work he was meant to do. But they hadn't, and now his role was clear. His father was nearing sixty years old—still more than capable of running the kingdom—but to assure the proper succession, there had to be a prince by his side until the Crown officially changed hands.

That prince was supposed to have been Ari. Instead, Kristos would have to take up the kind of duties for which he'd never been prepared. He would sooner take a bullet than answer a reporter's prepared question; and the idea of dancing attendance on a host of coddled diplomats made his stomach churn.

"So what's on the agenda first, then? I haven't exactly been paying attention to your memos, I'm afraid."

"The gala reception to celebrate your official accession as crown prince is in three days' time," Cyril said, his relief apparent that Kristos had apparently turned the corner. "Your mother and father have put everything in place. Now that it's been a week since they've returned from France, we will make the official announcements." He hesitated. "It would be best if we also announced your engagement at the gala or shortly thereafter."

Not this again. "No." There was a limit to his patience with royal tradition. "We talked about that six months ago, Cyril. My position hasn't changed."

"And you agreed that you would consider the weight of your responsibilities."

"Which I have. And *after* that consideration, I've decided

that every tradition makes sense when it serves a purpose." They had left the sand and laughter, turning down cobblestoned streets lined with the small businesses and restaurants that made Oûros such a picturesque destination for tourists. Here, they abandoned the ATV and continued on foot, so the security detail surrounding them could ease back, allowing the prince and his advisor more privacy as they wound their way through the old city. "However, catering to dictates set down centuries ago, when the average life expectancy was thirty-five years, no longer serves a purpose. I'm not going to die before having a *child*, Cyril. Give me a chance to live a little first."

As soon as the words escaped his lips, a chill iced his bones. How many times had his own brother said the same thing to Cyril, to his parents, to anyone who would listen? Kristos had proven his worth to the Crown in combat, but his brother had had to face an entirely different scope of responsibilities as the eldest son.

And now he was gone. Kristos pictured the faces of the mourners who had filed past his brother's empty coffin at the official state funeral months earlier, the look of blank sorrow in his parents' eyes. Other than ensuring that the gates of the gods stayed strong, he and his brother cared little about tradition. But that was perhaps beside the point, now. Kristos had a kingdom full of people who did care, and parents who were still so filled with grief that their decisions had begun to seem weak, ineffectual in the eyes of even their closest advisors.

Perhaps Oûros needed its traditions for a little while longer.

But Kristos was *not* the man they needed to fulfill them.

Cyril had the good sense not to comment, allowing Kristos to stew in his own thoughts. They reached the lower gate of the palace, a simple affair cut into the cliff rock, looking more like the entry of a storage vault than a passage up to the premier royal residence. Still, the illusion of the bored guards stationed at the entrance was just that: an illusion. Developed over long years to keep the royal family out of sight and mind of all but the most diligent tourists, except in ways that were carefully orchestrated by the Crown.

The residential palace of Oûros was a simple affair to the outside eye, an sturdy aerie perched at the top of Mount Nazar overlooking the city and beach, unassailable from the ground due to the sheer cliff walls, and well protected by the thick forests and rising mountains surrounding it from the other three sides. The palace was more fortress than fairy-tale castle, and generations of Oûros royalty had wisely kept it that way. The Visitors' Palace across the city was used for state events and celebrations, and it had all the ethereal charm the country could wish for, without any need for the protracted security measures required in a permanent residence.

A residence he would one day share with a *wife*, Kristos thought suddenly—sooner rather than later, if Cyril had his way.

Wincing, Kristos wondered who the advisor had picked for him, if anyone yet. What daughter of the aristocracy had earned the right through the Crown's unofficial selection process to be presented to him as a candidate for royal bride? He'd have to be polite about whoever it was, and who knows? Maybe she too would be open to a long, *long* engagement, at least long enough to give Kristos time to get out of this mess.

His mouth tightened. Or maybe she would take one look at his battle-ravaged body, and simply let him go.

He had to return to the military. It was the only place he could truly belong at this point.

But for now, he had to bide his time, and play the role expected of him. He could only hope that word of his arrival at the castle today hadn't made it to the media, or the circus would begin in earnest. Would it be so much to ask for him to have one more day of relative normalcy before any chance at personal freedom was wrenched away from him?

Kristos thought fleetingly of the young American: *Emmaline.* A name as unexpected as she was. A name he suddenly wanted to speak again, now that he was losing her behind walls and gardens and layers of expectations too thick for anyone to battle through without creating lasting damage.

Maybe far too much damage.

The gates of the royal palace closed behind him.

Five

"What do you mean we're not all going zip-lining? I thought we'd agreed to get our adventure on today! We can't just lie around the beach the whole time!"

Em looked up from her tour book as Nicki and Lauren approached. Beside her, Fran snapped her attention away from her copy of *Psychology Today*. "We're canceling zip-lining? I may not actually die in the jungles of Oûros? Praise God."

"You and I are still going zip-lining, yes," Lauren said to Nicki, her voice holding a note of authority that Em knew well. It was her *please don't make me kill you* voice. Zip-lining actually seemed kind of fun, but there was no mistaking the set to Lauren's jaw. "But Em is touring the Visitors' Palace with Fran."

Fran looked at Em. "What's the Visitors' Palace? Is that where your prince lives?"

"I have no idea."

When Lauren had ushered Em back to the safety of their brightly colored beach ensemble, they'd found Nicki and Fran waiting for them, so Lauren had promptly recounted the tale of Em's rescue by the crown prince of Oûros. Em was still having a hard time processing the whole thing.

How could she have missed out on the fact that she was being kissed by a *prince?*

She'd known vaguely about the death of the older brother, Aristotle Andris—it had made international news a year ago on all the entertainment channels. But she hadn't ever really thought about the younger military-focused brother beyond seeing him as part of the royal family, dressed in mourning colors for the state funeral. The story had slipped away in a blink, and the world had churned on. Yet here she was, halfway around the world, starring in her own fairy-tale story where she'd gotten *kissed* by a *prince.*

Now she could only shake her head as Nicki swung her gaze between Lauren and her. She wasn't going to lie. If she saw the inside of Oûros's ceremonial palace, it would only make the story better, giving her images and details that she could carry back home, maybe even helping her come up with a story to delight her mythology-loving mother.

Frannie lifted her champagne drink and toasted Lauren. "You know what? It doesn't matter—this is the best news I've had all day. Here's to the Visitors' Palace!"

Lauren strode over to them, dangling two tickets in front of Em. "The next tour isn't until two p.m., siesta time for most of the city, except for lunatics who like to imagine they are jungle monkeys."

"It'll be fun!" Nicki protested, but Lauren waved her off.

"It'll be suicidal. Meanwhile, I have it on good authority that Em's Prince Charming is starting to take up his royal duties as of *today.* Which means he'll be meeting local bigwigs this afternoon at the Visitors' Palace. Which means..." She waggled her brows.

Em stared at her even as she reflexively took the proffered tickets. "Which means what? You want me to stare at him through a window like some kind of stalker? I've already embarrassed myself enough today, don't you think?"

"Embarrassed! Hardly. The way he looked at you was epic, Em. Like stop-my-heart epic. Besides, Frannie will be with you, and she's not tagging along for her health." She pointed at Fran. "She's officially on duty for any and all photo ops."

"Photo ops."

Lauren rolled her eyes. "Come on! Wouldn't you want to have a picture with His Princeliness to keep the memory for good?"

"Oh, geez, no. I—" Then Lauren's words caught up with her, and Em couldn't deny the traitorous lurch to her heart. *A picture.* "You think he'd let me take a photo with him?"

"Absolutely. They do that sort of thing here all the time." Lauren's words were final. "His older brother and the royal parents did, anyway. They're the most tourist-friendly royals on earth, I'm telling you. You get yourself in front of Prince Hottiedom, there's no way he won't let you do a selfie with him." She winked as Em faltered, knowing she'd won the day. "But don't go breaking his heart, okay? He's going to be king someday."

"I'm sorry, did I hear you correctly?" Frannie demanded. "We *so* need to break his heart, and he's already halfway there, I bet." She turned to Em. "He's seen you half-drowned and was moved enough to kiss you. *Now* he's going to see you at your best. And I know exactly where to get started. I found it after I managed to ditch Nicki this morning."

"You did *not* manage to ditch me!"

"Semantics." Fran grabbed Em's hand. "C'mon. We need to get you cleaned up."

Three hours later, Em found herself at the public entryway to the Visitors' Palace, both she and Frannie clutching their tickets like kids at Disney World. They wouldn't be able to get all the way to the heart of the palace designated for the royal family and their most favored guests, but she'd see the rooms where the first family of Oûros entertained foreign dignitaries and hosted royal balls. She'd bought a guidebook specifically focused on the palace that detailed each of the rooms and their fabulous artwork featuring the Greek gods as well as the celebrations held there for the past half century. More fodder for her developing story. Both the real one and the one she'd embellish for her mother's enjoyment.

As Lauren had predicted, Em already had enough to make that tale far exceed her wildest imagination. Even now she was making up twists and turns, trying on different options for size. The prince could...see her across the courtyard before she reached the Visitors' Palace, then stride toward her to sweep her up into his arms. Or, he could...see her from some perch inside and send her a small box wrapped in gold paper and tied with a silver ribbon, a keepsake of Oûros that she could cherish forever. Or maybe even...she'd see him first, only he'd be followed by men in masks, and she could alert him to the danger...

Em suddenly felt lighter than she had in months, the effects of this impossible European vacation finally taking hold. She smoothed her hand down her simple, cream-colored shift, then shook her wrist a bit as the heavy gold cuff caught the light. Frannie had insisted on taking her shopping—with Lauren's money, Em had a feeling—and having her hair and makeup styled at one of the city's walk-in beauty parlors. Though she could never match the exotic beauty of the Mediterranean women of this town, she *did* feel prettier and more confident. Her shoulder-length hair, so often skimmed back into a tight, serviceable ponytail, now hung in loose curls, and she was actually wearing makeup for the first time in forever.

"You're beautiful, Em. You remember that. There's a reason why Prince Kristos couldn't keep his hands off you."

"You didn't even see him!" Em protested. "His hands were nowhere near me. You're going off what Lauren told you, and she *lies*."

"She wasn't lying this time, though, was she?" Fran shook her head at Em's reaction. "God, I wish all my coaching clients were as easy to read as you."

"Oh, great. Just what every girl wants, to be completely and utterly obvious."

"It works on you, though. Still, try to throw me a royal cousin or something, after you're done wowing the first family in here, okay?"

"They may not be out—oh." Em looked up as they rounded the corner and got the entire view of the plaza. "Oh, wow."

"This is so much better than zip-lining," Fran breathed.

Beyond a busy clutch of bistros and open-air cafés, the dazzling splendor of the Visitors' Palace rose above the plaza in three domes of glass. It was a triple solarium, the center dome soaring highest until it seemed to become part of the sky. In front of the building was the famed palace garden, something else Em had read about in her book, but even that was about a million times more impressive in person than on the page.

Laid out nominally like the gardens of European mansions in tailored, lush squares, the similarities to traditional formal landscaping stopped there. Each plot was luxuriously over-grown, with pathways and bridges crisscrossing the space, bordered all around by broad walkways. The guidebook had detailed how the garden was first installed in the Victorian age to lure the English monarch to visit Oûros during one of her trips to Greece. They were unsuccessful in getting Queen Victoria to venture along the Aegean Sea, but the gardens were such a hit with the residents of the country that they were allowed to flourish and expand until they practically overran the place.

Even now, Em could see children of multiple nationalities darting in and out of the trees and along the cobblestoned walkways, nannies or parents hurrying after them. The entire courtyard had more of the air of a festival than a royal residence, and she and Fran stared around like wide-eyed tourists, gaping at the colors, the energy—and the noise.

"You can't tell me that people actually live here," Fran murmured, surveying the crush of people. "I'd go insane inside a week."

"They don't, not anymore. Not ever, I don't think," Em said, holding up her book to explain the source of her new knowledge. "They use it exclusively for meetings, dances, and receptions." She looked back up and sighed, taking it all in. "But it sure is pretty."

"That's the first authentic smile I've seen on your face this week," Frannie announced. "You need to relax like this more often."

"So you keep saying."

"Well, it's true. The world doesn't need you to keep spinning it, Em. You can take some time to simply be." Her gaze shifted to the small line of people queuing up in front of the marble steps leading to the Visitors' Palace. "I think that's where we go."

They moved to the line of gawking tourists, arriving as the tour set off. Their guide, a smartly dressed young woman, trotted up the steps, even as another couple bumped into Em from behind.

"Oh! Sorry, *scusi*," a feminine voice said hurriedly. When Em turned to smile at her, she noted the woman's sharp eyes— and the enormous camera held on her companion's shoulder. Wasn't there some sort of rule about camera sizes inside the Visitors' Palace? That thing looked like it could see to outer space. "You're enjoying your visit to Oûros, yes?"

"Oh yes, it's lovely here," Em said, not caring that she was practically gushing as the woman's gaze sparked with interest. "It's like some ancient Greek myth come to life."

"Okay, girlfriend, look sharp." Em felt her elbow tugged as Frannie urged her along, and together they hastened up the steps to keep up with the crowd.

Six

"Pay attention, Kristos. These are serious matters."

"Then turn off the damned monitors. I don't know how you can focus on anything with those all cued to different channels." Kristos scowled as he turned away from the bank of video screens that lined the conference room. They were in an interior chamber in the Visitors' Palace, the place his father and brother had always referred to as the war room, though Oûros hadn't officially been at war for over half a century. At the front of the room, seated around the edge of the gleaming wooden conference table, sat Cyril, two additional aides, and his half-cousin Stefan, the Crown's current diplomatic envoy of choice.

But Kristos's attention was focused only on his father. King Jasen Andris was still well in his prime, his graying hair the only indication that he wasn't still a robust man of thirty-five. Well, perhaps not the only indication. Deep lines etched his face now, where a year ago, Kristos would have sworn his father was ageless, invincible.

Then again, a lot had happened in the past year.

Now his father studied him as he approached, but offered no comment and certainly made no move to shut down the monitors. And Kristos knew better than to ask again. His father's mantra was *Vigilance First*, believing that with enough time, most catastrophic decisions could be avoided altogether.

Too bad that for Kristos, catastrophic decisions had already been made for him. Still, he approached this calamity like he had every lost cause in the field: head-on. "I've agreed to take up my ceremonial role, Father, but let's get a few things clear. There's a limit to what that role should entail in the twenty-first century." Limits such as no forced marriages, he thought grimly. And, ideally, fewer parades.

His father shook his head. "Not so ceremonial as that. Oûros's success depends on maintaining a strong position on the world stage."

A small knot of worry lodged in Kristos's gut at his father's grim expression, but he pushed it away. "A position you are more than capable of continuing to hold."

"Capable, yes." His father didn't dispute the assertion, and some of Kristos's tension eased. Still, he looked at his father a bit more closely. Did he look more tired than he should? Paler? Granted, his parents *had* just returned from Paris, and that city could take the fire out of anyone. But still.

His father's next words made him refocus. "Nevertheless, that doesn't mean you're *also* not completely capable of making decisions by my side. The people would be glad to see a young man on the throne and to know that the Andris line is continuing."

"Which brings me back to my original point. The line does not need to continue in the next three days," Kristos protested. "I haven't even hit thirty—you didn't have children right away, and no one seemed to care."

"Oh, they cared. Just not enough to ever force the question."

"Exactly." Kristos pressed his point home. "There's a limit to what's reasonable these days, and I think we've now identified one of those lines. Being a prince of the realm is a job, and I'll do the job to the best of my ability. But no one will expect me to pop up with an heir and a spare anytime soon. It's not remotely necessary."

His father's shrewd glance swept over him. "There are other reasons for you to show interest in marriage, Kristos, beyond the traditions you seem so quick to dismiss. The death of your brother was a terrible shock to the country."

Kristos forced his jaw and his tone to stay steady. "The country has seen worse." He shot a glance to his half-cousin, but as usual, Stefan Mihal's face was completely unreadable. Light-eyed and light-skinned in a country with its share of swarthy men, he was the consummate chameleon and probably held more secrets in his little finger than Kristos ever planned to in his entire life. He was also, like Dimitri, a demigod, only Stefan traced his heritage back to the fast-thinking and faster-talking Hermes.

Ever the diplomat, of course, Stefan kept his thoughts to himself.

"Worse, yes," King Jasen continued. "But we aren't striving to make 'the best of a bad situation' here. We are striving to present a front of inviolable strength. Both to reassure our own people and to serve as warning for any who might think we are flagging. There has been a long stretch of international turmoil at or near our shores in recent years. Surely you know that more than anyone, given the role you've played in maintaining our defenses. We must show strength, not weakness."

"Then why don't we show strength with a military that doesn't hide its true nature under a veil of handshakes and publicity shots." Despite his sincere intentions to be level-headed in all dealings this day, Kristos felt his hands tighten into fists. It was a long-held bone of contention with his father that Oûros's diplomatic strategy of private preparation and public downplay had succeeded perhaps a bit too well, for a bit too long.

In a world where military prowess was no longer determined by the size of your force but by the sophistication of your weaponry, Oûros's role in international matters could quickly take on meaningful weight. If only anyone knew about them other than their closest allies. And, of course, the gods of Olympus.

They certainly had more than enough money to get the word out. Kristos hadn't ignored *all* of Cyril's e-mails over the past year in regards to his new role of crown prince. He was well aware that the country was flush with cash, so flush that their charitable efforts had begun spilling out of the region and onto more distant shores. But beyond humanitarian efforts, Oûros could do more. They could afford to completely overhaul their security force and make new allies—who in turn could come in handy when it came to decisions with international ramifications. It was a win-win.

As if following his line of thought, Jasen's eyes hardened. "If you wish to contribute to those conversations, then you must show your commitment to your role as crown prince, Kristos. It is not a role you can play at when the mood strikes you, nor one you can resist forever, no matter what you might believe. Your brother had all the same objections that you did, yet he also knew it was time for him to step into his duties as heir."

"Yeah, that worked out really well for him." Kristos didn't hide the bitterness in his voice, and his father, to his credit, didn't flinch.

"Even the gods can't rule death," he said calmly. So calmly that Kristos wanted to shake him. "Life, however, allows us to choose our path. Yours is clearly laid before you."

"And you're telling me that it's somehow my royal *obligation* not only to give up my work in the military—which is where

I belong, and you know it—but that in addition to being forced to play nice with the press, an effort I despise, I also need to find a wife in the next week in order to ensure order in the kingdom? Why? Who could possibly care? And *don't* say the gods."

He waved an irritated hand at Stefan, who remained impassive. "We've got Dimitri and Stefan here representing said gods on the daily—I can't turn around without running into either of them. Then there's, what—another thirty or so demigods stationed at various levels in the military and royal staff—plus nomads who could be called in at a moment's notice? And don't tell me that demigods are in short supply. Every generation there's enough descendants whose recessive Olympian genes flip to dominant to trigger their status if they choose to embrace it. I know that because you're the one who taught it to me. We have *plenty* of godly strength to carry the day."

"Royal strength is just as important," his father countered. "The demigods in service to the Crown need an actual *Crown* to give their sacrifice meaning. Or maybe you've forgotten that their tireless dedication is an act of loyalty to the gatekeepers of the gods? If the royal line falters, the gates to Olympus will too."

"Yeah, well, it's not going to falter in the next three *days* if I don't knock up some pedigreed princess. I can't even believe we're having this discussion."

"Ah...Gentlemen." Stefan's quiet interruption sounded from the corner of the room, but Kristos didn't have time for the well-spoken aristocrat right now. In many ways, Stefan was more royal than he was, never mind his specialized lineage. But while his half-cousin might hold the floor on matters of international intelligence, today's issue was substantially closer to home. Kristos focused on his father, who at least had the grace to meet his gaze.

"The financial unrest among our nearest neighbors has not gone without notice of the Council, Kristos." King Jasen said.

"Oûros is stable, but we're stable because we are intentional in all we do. Our people feel differently about us because we do *not* endure high unemployment, and we do *not* send all our young soldiers to die upon battlefields we did not choose. Our financial strength is not undervalued or overvalued, or subject to the vagaries of the international market. We live in a bubble, and bubbles are fragile and require constant vigilance. We have higher obligations than a typical kingdom, as well you know. The illusion we project of being little more than a carefree tourist destination is one that generations of monarchs have worked hard to uphold. Would you be the one to change that?"

"I still fail to see how me getting married can matter one way or another in that discussion." Kristos's gaze narrowed. "Our finances are strong, you said. We aren't facing bankruptcy. Our military may not be adequately equipped, but the ranks are full to bursting with willing men and women, unless I have misread the reports."

His father gave a short laugh. "No. Those are not our concerns."

"Gentlemen." Stefan's voice was more insistent. Kristos continued to ignore him.

"Then what's this truly about, Father? Is there some Oûrois family you owe a favor to? Someone you already have picked out for me once I agree to the wisdom of your plan?" He saw the flicker of surprise in his father's face, and his back went rigid. "Then *no*. Just no, no, and no. I don't care who she is. I don't care what you promised. The answer is no. I'm not going to be shoved into a forced alliance with someone I don't know, not even for the good of the country. That's the stupidest thing I've ever heard of in my life. And if you think—"

"Kristos!" Stefan's voice was like a gunshot. Kristos turned, then saw his half-cousin's gaze wasn't fixed on him at all but on the infernal bank of monitors at the back of the room. Monitors which now were all tuned to the national media service of Oûros—and an eerily familiar-looking man and woman struggling out of the water to collapse on the white sands of the country's famed Royal Beach.

"What the hell? Turn that up!"

Kristos strode several steps toward the screens as the images zeroed in on him pulling Emmaline tenderly into his arms, rocking her on the beach as he stared down at her with abject adoration. Where had the cameraman been to get such a shot as that? Across the bottom of the screen, a caption read: "Aphrodite emerges from the sea for the crown prince?" and the reporter, a sharp-eyed woman he instantly disliked, spoke about the "prince's heroic rescue of a woman who clearly holds a special place in his heart—as well as his arms. A woman we were lucky enough to speak to briefly on the steps of the Visitors' Palace this—"

"What?" Kristos whirled, scowling at Cyril, who was already in motion, pushing his way past Stefan with a phone at his ear and signaling for the aides to follow him. "What is she talking about? Why is Emmaline at the Palace?"

His father stared at him wide-eyed, and damned if there wasn't a smile playing around the old man's face. "You could have told me you were dating, Kristos."

"I'm *not* dating."

Stefan snorted. "You are now. At least she's pretty, I'll give you that."

Kristos turned back as the newscast resumed, with the reporter approaching a woman with soft, shoulder-length brown hair. She turned, and Kristos stood rooted in place as Emmaline's lovely heart-shaped face filled the screen. He hadn't really focused on any one element of the American when he'd practically bowled her over in the sand, though he'd remembered her pretty face, her startled eyes. Later, when he'd held her in his arms, she'd been coughing like a drowned rat and trembling all over, but she'd still been attractive on almost a soul-deep level, someone he simply didn't have the strength to resist.

But this Emmaline wore some kind of filmy white dress and enormous gold jewelry, her hair long and soft, and her eyes…

"Kristos."

Kristos waved off whoever was speaking, focusing on the screens. He could barely make out what the female reporter was saying, but Emmaline's expression was radiant, and her words sounded like something out of a Oûros tourist guide. "—some ancient Greek myth come to life," she said, and her voice and eyes were so earnest, her emotion so clear, that Kristos found himself half wishing he could meet her…and he *had* already met her. He'd had her wrapped in his arms, in fact, or at least an earlier version of her.

Then he paid attention to the words crawling across the bottom of the screen, and his eyes sharpened. "Who's writing these captions, and how can they make these statements? Who are these people?" He whirled on Stefan. "Make a call. Get this *off the air*."

Stefan looked at him with real amusement. "We're way beyond that, I'm afraid. This has already been piped halfway around the world."

Cyril stuck his head back in the room, distracting him from the wall of monitors. "We've located her. She's on the official tour of the Visitors' Palace." He scowled at Kristos. "You want me to let her know she's about to make international headlines as your bride-to-be?"

The curse that followed Cyril out the door could be under-stood in any language.

Seven

"I could probably get used to this royalty thing, you know," Frannie said dryly as they walked into the grand atrium of the Visitors' Palace. "I'm sure that says something not very flattering about my self-identity, but I thought I'd put it out there."

Above them, the soaring glassed-in roof showed a flawless summer-blue sky, and Em sighed, looking up at it, imagining what it would be like to dance beneath a starlit night. Surely that had to be the number-one use for this space.

The tour guide confirmed it, detailing the recent balls hosted by the royal family, all of them to benefit one or another of the queen's favorite charities, or to honor visiting dignitaries who had helped soothe issues or broker agreements among their war-torn or financially bankrupt neighbors. How did little Oûros manage to keep hold of its money when no one else did?

She snorted. Probably because barely anyone knew it existed. Though a popular European destination, the country was too far east to tempt most Americans, even those looking for the quintessential Mediterranean escape. In fact, they were among the only Americans in the entire tour, most of the guests hailing from Australia, Italy, or England.

They'd lost the couple with the enormous camera almost immediately, and she imagined them roaming through the palace unchecked. Maybe they were invited magazine people or something like that, photographing décor for *Royal Living*. She wondered who the typical reader would be for such a magazine. Not her, certainly, but for the discerning multibillionaire, she was sure that the Visitors' Palace's gracious furnishings might inspire at least a few redecorating touches—such as the Waterford crystal chandeliers, the deep-pile Persian rugs, and the vases that she hoped weren't Ming, given their size and the fact that they weren't sitting behind thick velvet ropes, but probably were.

"It really is perfect here, isn't it?" She shook her head. "Lauren was right, this is going to be one of my favorite memories of this trip."

"Well, hello, it's about to get more perfect. Prince Charming and his posse of hotties are at your twenty."

"My what?" Em looked up, startled at Frannie's suddenly tight words. Then she saw him too. Kristos Andris had been unbelievably beautiful on the beach, no question, but he'd also been just a man, a soldier—not a Greek prince. And he'd been soaked to the bone in a scruffy tank top and scuba pants, his hair matted to his head and sand streaking his wet skin.

That wasn't the case now. As he strode out of a large doorway at the back of the grand ballroom, the crown prince of Oûros looked positively regal in a gleaming white shirt open at the collar and a sharply tailored black suit, the jacket unbuttoned, a glint of silver at his wrist and polished loafers on his feet. His expression was open and relaxed, and Em's heart surged as their gazes connected and his smile deepened further. She gripped Fran's arm to keep herself standing upright. He didn't seem like he was annoyed that she'd played the tourist card by showing up here, thank heavens. In fact—

"Girl, for those who are keeping score, Lauren was completely dead-on about this guy. He is way into you."

"He's just being polite." Em turned to Fran. "You have your camera, don't you? Do I look okay? Lauren thought he'd be willing to do a photo. Do you think she's right?"

"Oh, she was so right. He's coming your way." Still, Fran's eyes widened as she glanced again over Em's shoulder. "And the attending guard isn't slowing down either. They look a little too purposeful, honestly. There's something a little...off about this."

"What?" Em turned around and blinked, startled at how close Kristos already was. Close and coming fast. He gazed at her with unquestionable warmth, and Em immediately felt herself going stiff, wary, despite his welcoming expression. *Am I supposed to curtsy or something? Is that what you do?*

The prince—before she'd known he was a prince—had *bowed* to her after he'd almost tackled her on the beach. Was bowing a common practice? Was that what she should do? What was proper Oûrois royalty etiquette and *why don't I already know?*

"Um, here's what I think," Frannie murmured beside her. "He's acting a role here, and you're a very important part of it."

"Acting," Em managed without changing her expression. She watched Kristos approach, as if they were some kind of long-lost friends. "Why would he be acting?"

"No idea, but he definitely is." Frannie spoke quickly. "So he needs you to be delighted to see him as well, delighted and *not* stiff, *not* freaked out. Whatever his lead, you go with it, okay? At least until we can figure out what happened to set him off."

Em nodded as she surveyed the crowd, the other tourists in the great atrium. They'd noticed the prince as well, of course. Cell phones were up, photos were being taken, and a sudden buzz of conversation swept through the room like an eager rise of bees. What were they talking about? Em wondered. A few of the tourists and then more glanced her way, and she felt their interest like a physical touch. Suddenly, it seemed like there were people all around her—too close, too intense.

"No, you don't, Em. I'm serious, chin up." Fran's hand was firm on her elbow. "You're allowed only one near-drowning experience a day, and you already punched that card."

"But there are so many people looking at us."

"Too many, yeah," Frannie agreed, her eyes sharp on the crowd. "Which means *something* happened, something that everyone knows about except—" Her face suddenly cleared, a mixture of understanding and surprise, with a touch of dismay chasing over her features. "Oh shit."

"What?" Em tore her eyes away from the prince and his suit to stare at Fran. "Oh shit what?"

"Paparazzi. Why didn't I think of that?"

"What are you *talking* about?"

"You were seen, honey." Fran gave her another hard squeeze. "Someone took your picture out there on the beach with your royal rescue committee. The prince here is clearly about to do damage control by acting like you two are old friends. You got it?"

Em got it, but she didn't have time to respond to Frannie, because Prince Kristos was suddenly right there, saying her name as if it were some sort of magic charm.

"Emmaline." He walked the last few steps without his men, who fanned out in a watchful semicircle, a move that simultaneously guaranteed they wouldn't be attacked by the crowd—but also that they'd fully captured everyone's attention. The solarium had gone completely silent as well, something that would have been unheard of in the States, but here it seemed that the event of a royal prince speaking to a commoner whom he'd just called by name was enough of a moment to merit listening closely. "This is a wonderful surprise. You should have told me you wanted to see the Visitors' Palace, I would have taken you around myself."

"Ah…" Em scrambled to keep her expression equally relaxed. "I didn't want to interrupt you."

"Nonsense." Kristos's warm tone indicated to her that she was playing her role well. His eyes were encouraging, and his hand, when he brought hers toward his mouth, squeezed her fingers gently. He brushed his lips across her knuckles, and Em couldn't help but freeze, trying to fix the image in her memory so diligently that she would never forget it. "You are always welcome in my home."

His eyes crinkled at the corners, and she got a glimpse of the man he would one day be: weathered and happy, always ready to take on the world. Her very own prince to fill a thousand daydreams.

Kristos was saying something else, though, and she blinked at him. How had he moved so quickly to be so near? And what in the world was he thinking, looking at her that intently? Even if photographers had captured images of them on the beach, as Frannie suspected, it wasn't as if they'd been having sex out there or anything.

That thought practically scrambled her brain, and she offered Kristos an apologetic and what she suspected was a completely dazed smile. "I'm sorry?"

"Never be that," he murmured, and before she could make sense of his words, he leaned forward the final inch and pressed his lips against hers.

Despite herself, Em drew in her breath with a sharp gasp, her fingers tightening compulsively on his and her knees practically buckling, such that the prince's other hand snaked around to the small of her back, anchoring her to him. She let her eyes drift shut for one beautiful, glorious instant, then the sudden raucous sound of laughter and applause broke through her bubble of perfection, and she jerked back sharply, trying to straighten, to draw away.

But Kristos wouldn't let her. He pursued her as she shifted back, his mouth claiming her anew, and suddenly, caution fled Em. This was her moment, damn it, *her* memory, and if she didn't take it for all it was worth, she was going to regret it for the rest of her life.

She loosened her fingers from his grip and lifted her hands to either side of his face, cupping it gently, tenderly, as if they weren't virtual strangers in the middle of a crowd of tourists, but a prince and his long-lost lover, reunited on the shores of some windswept beach, transported by their impossible passion for a moment more.

Then Kristos shifted, firmly and decisively, looking down at her with surprise but also with approval, satisfaction—and something else too. Something she wasn't too certain about that chased through the depths of his golden eyes like a predator in full pounce.

"That," he murmured for her ears alone, "was perfect."

Eight

Kristos straightened, intrigued to see the relief brightening Em's face. She hadn't known. She clearly had been in the Visitors' Palace the whole time, and hadn't seen the images on the screen.

His men had now gone into full-tilt royal-ambassador mode among the crowd. The people were dispersing—still gawking, many of them, but politely. Surreptitiously. This was Oûros, after all. There was a sense of decorum lacking in some of the other major cities of Europe, with their constant crush of people and the media monster that had to be fed.

Em seemed to sense his withdrawal and shifted away as well, which only made him want to grab her close to him again. For as much as she'd been acting the role he'd needed her to, he couldn't shake the idea that she hadn't been altogether present... like she'd been caught between reality and a daydream. Still, now she appeared firmly grounded in the present once more.

"Kristos, I'd like you to meet my friend, Francesca Simmons," she said as she turned to the pretty, faintly Greek-looking woman standing next to her. "She was kind enough to come with me here—" Em hesitated, and Kristos knew without turning that a blush was climbing up her cheeks. "I guess—well, I sort of wanted to get a picture with you, if you happened to be here."

"A picture!" Kristos snorted. "I don't think you'll have to search too hard to find pictures of us anymore."

Emmaline frowned at him, then understanding flashed in her eyes. She glanced to her friend. "Fran said there had probably been photographers on the beach."

"There are photographers everywhere." Kristos fought a sigh, instantly regretting his actions, or, more to the point, his *re*actions. He had walked out here with a defined plan to rescue Emmaline from further scrutiny. Then he'd reached her, touched her hand, and that plan had gone up in smoke.

Now there would be more pictures of the two of them together, which meant more gossip and more news reports. The situation was already ridiculous, and he'd made it worse. "But come. I intended to *free* you from this crowd and to determine what we can do to restore some sense of privacy to your lives while you're staying in Oûros. Unfortunately, I seem to have done exactly the opposite. Francesca, would you join us?"

"Of course." The woman's voice was low, almost sultry, and it fit with her dark hair and eyes. She might not be of Greek descent, but she had Mediterranean blood in her somehow, he would swear it. There was a definite cast to the shape of her face that he couldn't quite place. Recognizing such things had never been his strong suit.

Ari would know, he thought, a sudden pang jolting him back to the task at hand. Because of Ari, he was in this mess to begin with. He needed to focus.

They stepped back into the phalanx of guards, but Kristos's exit was hampered by requests from the crowd—autographs, photos. Ruthlessly, he forced himself to remain gracious with the press of people and to be glad that there weren't more, since they were still inside the Visitors' Palace.

Cyril had warned him about this in more than a few of his countless missives about Kristos's impending role of crown prince. He was going to be a celebrity, and with that status came responsibility. And of course, it wasn't the first time he'd ever been singled out for this attention. But what was new was that he wasn't being "singled out" at all.

"Could I take a picture of you both?" A matronly woman with an Australian accent clutched her camera—a real camera, he recognized instantly, but not such high quality that he suspected she was a member of the press.

No longer caring if she was or not, he drew Emmaline closer to him. "Of course," he said, earning him a startled glance from Emmaline. "If it turns out well, you can send it to the palace PR department through our website. We'd love to have a copy."

"Oh, well, of course! I'd be happy to do that!" The woman lifted her camera, and Kristos could see the slight tremor in her hands, probably from excitement. If that picture took at all, it would be a miracle. Still, he leaned close to Emmaline, reveling in her nerves, her heat, and he realized that he was eager to kiss her again.

The embrace they'd just shared had not been what he was expecting, exactly. After all, he'd already kissed her once, so he knew what she should feel like. The attraction between them was easy to understand, but this newest kiss with Emmaline had seemed almost special. Like she was bottling up the moment, somehow afraid to breathe.

What had been going on in that busy mind of hers?

The tourist fairly bounced as she thanked them, then Kristos motioned to the closest guard as a surge of other tourists pressed forward. "He'll get you safely away," he said as Emmaline shot him a questioning look.

"What about you?" she asked, her worry plain. As if she could somehow help him out of this tight spot, when she knew nothing about his world.

Kristos's smile felt almost odd on his face as he handed her off to the waiting aide. "It's part of the job." Watching his guard usher her out ahead of them made him feel uneasy, though, and he focused on the people around him while he tried to collect his thoughts.

What was he going to do with Emmaline now that he'd helped perpetuate the rumors that Cyril had assured his father would be featured on every entertainment "royals watch" within the day? And could that actually be true? Was there really so little going on in the world that anything that happened to his family was news?

Then again, this was the story of a strange American woman who'd appeared out of nowhere and had landed in a prince's arms. If he didn't know the key players in the drama, he'd probably be curious too.

He twisted his lips. Now that this media distraction *had* happened, though, he should turn it to his advantage. His father wanted him to announce a bride—and here a potential bride had shown up, completely unwittingly. Even better, there was no way Emmaline would think his actions were sincere.

Unless, of course, she watched the news and believed what she saw on TV.

Hmm.

It still didn't matter. Emmaline was an American, with a life halfway around the world, who had no idea that her presence was giving him a much-needed out to satisfy his father and the general public and their desire for "royal tradition." He could create a sham relationship with her easily enough, then send her on her way after he'd figured out a more permanent solution to get him off the throne and back into the line of fire with his fellow soldiers.

Time. That was what he needed. Just a little more time.

And, in particular, a little more time with Emmaline. That was a definite requirement.

"Sir?" A guard was at his side, one of the men he'd trained with, and the soldier's eyes were deferential but also apologetic. "We should get you inside as well," the guard said. As if Kristos could not adequately protect himself in a room full of tourists in thick-soled walking shoes and nylon money pouches.

Still, he nodded, allowing the protocols of his new position to guide him, even as he reinforced his decision to use the opportunity Emmaline's presence provided.

He simply couldn't imagine this as his future. He hadn't been born to be cooed at and feted and dragged along from place to place, nodding earnestly and signing photographs. It wasn't possible.

Had Ari seen this as his future too? He and his older brother hadn't much discussed their differing roles over the past few years. After nearly two decades of life pretty much on equal terms, they'd both diverged sharply in their mid-twenties—Ari to become the prince he was born to be, Kristos to rise higher in the ranks of the military. It was the way things were supposed to turn out.

Now Kristos frowned, stepping out of the buzzing glass ballroom and into the hushed quiet of the corridors beyond. The short hallway opened into another chamber, this one also outfitted with a conference table and the requisite wall of video screens. Emmaline stood at the edge of the room, snugged up against her exotic-looking friend, staring at the screens as if they were a horror movie that wouldn't shut off.

"Aphrodite from the sea?" ran one caption as pictures scrolled through—these starting out earlier than the first feed, showing Kristos on the shore with his men as Cyril drove up, then diving into the water. The camera followed him the entire way, until he lifted Emmaline free of the current and tugged her to shore. Then came the pictures that had everyone in a lather, with him cradling her on his lap. At the time, it hadn't seemed like such an intimate act, so brazen and possessive. At the time, it had simply felt...right.

But now, watching himself on screen, he could maybe see what everyone else was seeing. It certainly didn't look like he and Emmaline had met each other that day.

He came up to her now, and she turned to him, her face a mask of mortification. "I'm so sorry that I've caused you all this trouble," she said.

Kristos frowned at her. Did she really hold herself responsible? "You didn't cause it."

"Well, I didn't do anything to stop it. And then I came *here*, dear God." Emmaline winced, waving her hand at an image of her on the steps of the Visitors' Palace. "That woman standing behind me. I mean, her camera was enormous. I should have known she was from the press."

"Honey, you didn't say anything you shouldn't have." The woman beside Emmaline—Francesca?—sent Kristos a piercing, accusatory glare, again, so much like Ari's that he blinked. "The prince knew what he was doing."

Kristos nodded, but his next words were cut off by Cyril's sharp voice.

"He's right." Emmaline jumped as the advisor joined them, then rubbed her arms as if she was cold. "Prince Kristos could have sent one of his men to ensure you made it to shore safely, Miss Andrews, but he didn't. And we're very grateful you are both well after your adventure." Cyril slanted him a look. "The rest was completely out of your control, as his highness is also well aware. The developing story is now taking on a life of its own."

Emmaline grimaced, but though she wasn't schooled in managing the media, she knew enough to guess what was to come. "The pictures taken in the glass ballroom. When you came out to talk to me." She frowned at Kristos, her brows drawing together. "Why *did* you do that if you knew we'd been seen earlier?"

Cyril kept talking, neatly skipping over Emmaline's question. "Photographers were gathered outside, lying in wait for the tour attendees, many of whom recorded your entire encounter with the prince. The pictures were uploaded quickly from there. Subsequent spreading of the story via text, instant message, and various forms of social media has begun but has not traveled far. We are still on the other side of the world from America, and we do not expect them to start picking up the story until their next news cycle, although we should have a statement prepared for that." He smiled, looking almost human. "American cable television networks are the engine that truly drive international media."

"America!" Emmaline blinked, her voice swinging back toward disbelief. And maybe a little bit of shock. "You've got to be joking. I understand it here in Oûros—I mean, he's the prince—you're the prince." She turned to Kristos, as if he had any doubt about whom she was talking. "But surely this isn't an actual story-story. It can't be."

Cyril's lips thinned. "Well before he married, England's young Prince Harry getting drunk at a bar was a story-story that lasted in the international media for five days, Miss Andrews. Here we have a crown prince about to take on his royal duties as monarch-in-training, and one of those duties is managing generations' worth of traditions among a people known for their long memories." Cyril stopped short of betraying the worst of those traditions, thank the gods, but the old man's wry expression told Kristos that he knew he was doing him a favor. "Don't think your father didn't try the same thing." He nodded curtly to the Americans again, but his gaze never left Kristos. "Miss Andrews has advised us that she and her friends will be departing our shores tomorrow afternoon."

"So soon?" The urgency in Kristos's voice rang loud even in his own ears. Still, he could be excused for being desperate. He needed Emmaline *here* if she was going to appear to be a legitimate potential bride-to-be. She couldn't flee the country. Not yet, anyway. "Surely we could convince you to stay longer."

As Emmaline blushed, Cyril continued, his voice now a shade more exasperated. "For the duration of your stay, Miss Andrews and Miss Simmons—and perhaps for the duration of your travels until you return to America, we would like to offer the protection of the ONSF—Oûros's National Security Force. To ensure your safety."

"A security force!" Emmaline exclaimed, and even the more jaded Francesca's eyes went wide. "Surely that's not necessary."

Cyril's face was grim, but he didn't say anything for a long moment, and, like a smack to his forehead, Kristos suddenly realized the full impact of his rash actions both at the beach and now, in the Visitors' Palace. In his simple enjoyment of having Emmaline in his arms—and, far worse, his *continued* interaction with her in the grand ballroom—he'd effectively painted a target on the woman's back. Now she would be pointed at, harassed, photographed, and even stalked because of him.

Cyril's offer of the ONSF seemed to be simply a gesture of royal *politesse*, but the fact that he thought such measures were remotely necessary drove Kristos's guilt further home. He should man up and face his responsibilities, dammit, even though the prospect of having Emmaline for a little longer was so tantalizing, it was all he could do not to reach out and grasp it with both hands.

Only to stave off the future, of course. Not for anything more than that.

But still…

"I'm so sorry, Prince Kristos." Emmaline's confused gaze met his. "I should never have kissed you on the beach—and certainly not here. It was irresponsible of me. But we can make it right."

Cyril snorted, but Emmaline was already shaking her head. "No. No, this is silly. We can leave now, before anyone realizes I'm gone. You can make a statement that we're old friends, that we met in college study abroad, whatever. We'll slip away as quietly as we can, and you won't see us again."

"That won't be necessary."

"No," Emmaline said again, her voice firm. "If I stay, it will ruin everything, and I…I would hate that." She turned and focused on Cyril again as Kristos stared at her. *Ruin everything? What is she talking about?*

But Emmaline had clearly made up her mind, and now faced Cyril directly. "Tell me what we need to do."

Cyril's words were direct and to the point, but Kristos found his own gaze turning to the TV again. Every channel now had something on the "American princess-to-be" sighting, and a few had devolved into generic video taken of him while in ONSF uniform, looking like he wanted to be anywhere but in front of the camera. Talking heads were already speculating about how long his relationship with "the unknown woman" had lasted and what would happen next.

Another wave of guilt rolled over him. Emmaline and her friends were now in danger because of him. *What had he been thinking?*

"Double the security team," he said, his hard voice overriding Cyril's. He glanced at Emmaline, then waved to one of his men. "Phone." The man gave him his cell phone without hesitation, and Kristos swiped it on, scrolling to the contacts. He pressed a button, and an instant later, his own phone sounded in his pocket. Cutting off the call, he handed the device to Emmaline. "Take this. Call me the moment you get safely into your room, and we'll make arrangements for your transport to wherever you're headed next. I've put you in danger, and I apologize for that."

She was shaking her head, but he could see the beginning edge of distress settle over her as her gaze strayed again to the bank of TVs. He turned her toward his security detail, worry already knotting his gut.

"Just go," he said.

Nine

"You're tougher than you look, babe."

"Like that would take much." Em grimaced as she and Frannie made their way back through the streets of Oûros's capital city. With the assistance of the ONS-whatever group, they'd received new clothing, including the kingdom's traditional brightly-colored scarves that effectively covered their hair and draped down over their shoulders.

Told to walk hunched over and quickly once they reached the streets of the city, they'd been taken along a series of passageways that the guards had explained were cut into the very rock of Mount Nazar, where the royal residence was located. They'd ended up about a quarter mile away from the Visitors' Palace, and once they'd made it into open territory, the guards had fallen back to a respectful distance. Deciding to play it safe, she and Fran had steered well clear of any TV monitors, at least until they'd made it to their hotel.

There, an unusually large number of people—many of them with the kind of real cameras that marked them as professionals—milled around the airy open foyer. Frannie and Em hunched further, muttering into their makeshift disguises. They'd worked out what they would say if they were caught, but no one so much as looked at them.

Em felt like she was walking through some kind of dream landscape. They were actually doing it—evading the paparazzi, people with phone cameras and sharp eyes who were all here in this hotel because they wanted *her* picture. It was almost exciting if she ignored the roiling nausea in her gut.

Fran squeezed her arm. "Hang in there, girlfriend. This honestly is going to be the best vacation story ever. Focus on that." A cry went up outside of the hotel's front entryway as they reached their elevator bank, and Em glanced that way, noting that the gawkers had caught sight of one of the guards.

They'd discussed this in advance too, that having the guards enter the hotel would be a clear indication that Emmaline was on-site, so it was better to create a distraction outside, so she and Fran could more quickly return to their rooms. After all, they weren't *officially* in any danger, just unduly popular for the moment.

Worked for her. In front of them, the elevator door swished open, and she bolted for it.

"Hold the doors, please?"

Frannie's startled laugh turned into a cough, and Em didn't trust herself to speak, so they both crowded into the elevator, practically shrinking into themselves to keep quiet as Nicki and Lauren breezed into the elevator car. The door slid shut, and Frannie straightened first.

"About time you guys got here." As Nicki and Lauren jerked back in surprise, she pulled off her scarf, then shook it out like a pillowcase.

Nicki recovered first, her eyes bottle-cap round. "Oh God! *That's* what you bought shopping? You were supposed to make her look hot, Fran, not like some sort of Greek grandma."

Em pulled her own scarf free as Frannie kept talking. "Did

you not have your phones? Because we totally just caused an international incident."

Em winced. "Really, Fran?"

"What are you talking about?" Lauren's brows shot up. "You were photographed? Today at the beach? I thought something like that might happen, but then when no one said anything, I figured you made it out of there without being noticed. Then my phone ran out of juice."

"I shut mine off because I didn't think roaming charges in the middle of the mountains would be such a hot idea," Nicki put in. "And I gotta tell you, you guys won't believe how much fun we had!"

"Seriously, what happened?" Lauren's words carried over Nicki's as they exited the elevator and turned left toward the room. "And I want *every single minute* from the moment you arrived at the palace, which I know Em has memorized. But I also know Fran will add the juicy details that Em didn't notice. So Fran wins."

Em's laugh bubbled up in her throat as Frannie started talking. She felt like hugging her friends, despite all the craziness. Without them, she wouldn't be in this paradise. Without them, she wouldn't be soaking in this sunlight, roaming these streets—

Kissing a prince.

Now that they were safely out of range of the paparazzi, she allowed herself to relax. Not bothering to try to wipe the silly grin off her face, she pulled out her key card first, the others standing back because she was *always* the one to have the key card ready, just as she was always the one with the lists, the printed research pages, the multiple copies of directions. After only a couple of days, they'd developed a pattern in hotels, restaurants, even taxi stands. A pattern that was eerily similar to how they'd interacted as college friends, and yet different. Richer.

Wanting to gather all her memories close to her heart, Em heard the locks give way and pushed inside—then stopped short, Nicki almost running her over.

"What in the *hell*?" Lauren herded them all into the room, closing the door quickly behind her.

"What the fuck happened in here?" Nicki pushed past Em, picking up speed.

Em could only stare, all the tension returning to her body, just that quickly. The room was in total disarray—suitcases pulled out and unzipped, papers spilled out over the ornate coffee table that was the centerpiece of the tiny suite, everything upended.

"Who's in here?" Nicki yelled, bounding through their small suite to one of the bedrooms. "I will kick your sorry ass, is what I'll do!"

"Check the safe," Lauren ordered, but Em was already on it. She and Frannie rushed into the second bedroom, and Frannie went on to the bathroom, calling the all clear to echo Nicki's shout. But Em didn't have to crouch down at the foot of the bed to know something was terribly wrong.

"Empty." She reached inside the safe to swipe her hands in the empty space. "Passports all gone. Everything's gone." She rocked back on her heels.

She needed to call Kristos. She knew she needed to call Kristos. But right now, she couldn't resist a completely irrational spurt of anger at the man. They had been simply Americans enjoying a beautiful day at the beach before he'd run into her. Since then, they'd become some sort of weird media sideshow that was turning seriously scary. "There's nothing left in here." She searched all around the safe, picking up the clothes that had been pulled from the hangers and tossing them on the bed. "Nothing in the safe, I mean. I think the only thing we had in there was our passports, though."

"Money?" Lauren asked sharply.

"Carrying it," came a chorus of responses, which meant they all had their driver's licenses too—not that those would do them any good.

"Good. That's a start." Lauren looked around, as if this wasn't the first time she'd returned to find her hotel room ransacked. Somehow, that made Em feel even worse. Why had she let herself kiss Kristos at the beach? And why in God's name had she gone back for *more*? "We're going to have to call the embassy in Greece. Oûros isn't big enough to justify having one here. For fuck's sake. Our passports." Lauren kept muttering as she strode over to the phone. She picked up the receiver and punched the button for the front desk, but Em's attention was on Fran.

Frannie looked as shocked as she felt. *This is all my fault.*

She didn't realize she'd said it out loud until Fran's gaze snapped to meet hers.

"It most certainly is not your fault," she retorted. "You didn't ask to get rescued by the freaking god of the seven seas. You went for a *swim*. The rest is on him, and believe me," she said resolutely, moving over to sift through her dresser drawers, "that boy is going to pay."

"You've got that right." Nicki strode back into the suite, her scowl deepening. "Rifled every single bit of our clothes in there —bathing suits, underwear, you name it. We're going to have to wash everything in bleach. Nothing else except our passports seems to be taken, though. Thank God Lauren warned us about not bringing jewelry."

"They weren't after money," Frannie confirmed, hefting an ornately beaded bag and waving it at them. "There's still five hundred dollars left in here—and it was sitting out. They only took our passports. They didn't even try to make it look like a normal theft."

"But why? To steal our credit information?" Nicki scowled. "Seems like an awful lot of hassle to go through to cap some random Americans."

"Except we're not random Americans, not anymore." Em wrapped her arms tightly around her waist. Her eyes went to the television screen, but she couldn't bring herself to turn it on. Instead, she pulled out her phone, stiffening her resolve to make the call. "We're the evening news."

Her phone rang in her hand, surprising her so much, she dropped it.

"What the hell!" Nicki growled. Lauren turned around at the unexpected ringtone and spied the device, narrowing her eyes as Em snatched it back up. Em swiped on the phone and held it to her ear.

"Hello?" she managed.

"Oh, good." Kristos's rich voice sounded even more foreign over the phone, and the lurch of her heart warred with the anxiety spinning through her stomach. "You hadn't called, and the men—"

"Someone broke into our room!" Em blurted, gripping the phone. "They took our passports. We can't travel anywhere without them."

There was the shortest of pauses on the other end of the line, then Kristos was back in her ear. She could hear the sound of his footsteps, striding quickly, then breaking into a run.

"Stay on the phone with me, Emmaline. All your friends are there?"

"What? Yes," she said, nodding as three pairs of eyes stared at her. "Yes, we're all together."

"Then stay in the room. If you aren't dressed for walking, do that now. I'll have the security detail meet you at your rooms in five minutes to get you out. All of you."

"But we can't *go* anywhere, Kristos," Em said, shaking her head though he couldn't see her. "They took our passports."

"Passports can be arranged," he said tersely. "In the meantime, pack whatever belongings you have, get into clothes you all can move in, and do not open the door to anyone but the ONSF." She could hear him draw in a long breath, then let it out, clearly trying to manage his temper. "Allow me to welcome you as guests of the royal family of Oûros."

Ten

"Go now," Kristos barked, his phone still at his ear. "And keep me posted." The on-site detail at the Grand Hotel Oûros would get the women to the garage without issue, but they still needed to get them safely to the palace.

He turned, scowling at Stefan and Cyril. "Their passports were taken. Security at that hotel must be completely nonexistent."

Stefan lifted his brows, apparently unconcerned. "'American Princess' trumps any news story this week. The people looking for more information were eager, and money was easy to come by. I'll alert my contacts in the media that the news will break. I don't think it's reasonable to try to keep it off the air. Too many outlets. It will get out no matter what we do. We can only manage the story from this point further." His gaze slid to Kristos, and something approaching irritation did flash across his face then. "You had to go and kiss her again. You couldn't leave well enough alone."

Kristos rolled his eyes. "Like *you're* the poster child for restraint."

"Enough." Cyril raised his hand. "I'll discuss their situation with the US embassy in Athens. Expedited passports will not be a problem, I'm certain." He flattened his lips. "A few days, at most. Less, if possible." He slanted a look at Kristos. "Have you decided upon a story?"

Kristos blinked, surprised at being offered the chance to craft his own spin instead of Cyril and Stefan taking the lead. For the first time, he felt the tangible weight of his new responsibilities sit a little more easily on his chest. "Simple is best. Emmaline is a friend, someone I met while I was in school, both of us touring France. We dated, broke it off, and her visit to Oûros was an unexpected but very pleasant surprise."

"Not bad. Doesn't cover the kiss here this afternoon, though." Stefan stood aside as their car arrived. He waved Kristos and Cyril inside. "Go on ahead. The first ping on the passports has hit." He touched his hand to his earpiece. "Story will break inside of five minutes, you can guarantee it. Better hope none of these women is in the US witness protection system, or we're going to have a very busy night."

Kristos and Cyril had reached the long drive to the royal palace within five minutes, Kristos taking in the looming structure as they approached. What would it look like to an American who'd just endured her room being ransacked, her belongings stolen? Would she see the quiet ramparts and feel safer, or less so?

Nothing he could do about that now.

He winced as he saw his parents standing at the top of the stairs, waiting to greet them. He'd not even had a chance to see his mother today, yet here he was bringing an international incident straight to the castle doors within three hours of taking up the royal reins. They should have left him to his men and their missions. At least he knew how to behave there.

He exited the car almost before it came to a rest, leaving Cyril behind. His father looked grim, which was his father's usual look, but to his surprise, his mother simply beamed at him as he bounded up the stairs. She held out her hands to gather him into a hug before he could say anything, then stood back to look at him with an adoring gaze, every inch the doting queen.

"Mother," he started in, not sure for a moment if she had seen the television reports. "I'm sorry that—"

"Sorry!" Her eyes widened, and she looked from him to his father with irritation. "*Sorry*, he says. And you're just as bad, Jasen, with your long face and tense jaw. You two are hopeless."

"Catherine, now is not the time." Jasen Andris wiped a tired hand over his brow. "This is a serious matter."

"No." His wife's expression was firm and resolute, but her eyes sparkled. "Godless mercenaries crossing our borders and terrorizing mountain villages is a serious matter. Zeus threatening to foment a revolt of the naiads is a serious matter. This isn't even a *halfway* serious matter." She turned to Kristos. "The young women have had their passports stolen, Jasen told me. Stefan should have that set to rights in twenty-four hours or so. But given the celebration at week's end, it would seem rude to turn them out so soon, now that they're already going to be staying an extra day or two. How are you framing the story? You don't really know the girl, do you? She seems very nice."

"I don't—*enough*, slow down." Kristos forced himself to laugh, catching his words in time. He needed to puzzle through the situation on his own before he tried presenting it to his mother. "Right now, we have to make sure they're safe. I'm sure you can find out everything you need by grilling them on your own."

She patted his arm. "I fully intend to."

Cyril had joined them on the short staircase, his attention on the king. "In the meantime, the breach of security at the Grand Hotel Oûros is troublesome, Your Highness. With tourism our most valuable commodity, stolen passports is a less than ideal development."

"How are the news stations handling it?"

"They'll be silent on the matter of how the passports were obtained, Stefan assures me. The first story will break shortly, however, and as we're hosting the Americans at your private residence..."

"Of course," Jasen said to Cyril's unspoken question. "Perform all the usual checks."

"What? No!" Kristos protested, stopping Cyril with a hand. "Background checks aren't necessary. These are our guests, not a band of insurgents."

"We perform checks on the *pope*, Kristos," his father said, waving Cyril on. "The sooner you get used to how things work at the castle, the better for all concerned."

"It will be delightful, you'll see," his mother said, tucking her arm into his. "Now tell me all about your American friend while we wait. I am not going to lie, this is the most fun I've had in well over a year."

Kristos hesitated, then caught the suddenly intent look in his father's eyes as he gazed at his wife. His father seemed...old again, a cast to his face that Kristos was simply not used to seeing, and one he didn't care to see. But his mother's bright smile was infectious, and she did seem genuinely enthralled by the idea of the mysterious American who was now being splashed across screens throughout Europe and soon across the Atlantic as well.

He hadn't seen her look so happy in—well, in longer than he could remember, honestly. What harm would it do to extend the illusion that he was a young man in love for a few more days, while the women were under their roof? And, once again, at the very least it would throw a wrench in his parents' plans to have him married off by Sunday.

As with any good lie, however, he knew he needed to start with a liberal dose of the truth to make this work. "You should know how it really happened, Mother. I met Emmaline for the first time today, down at the beach while doing maneuvers with the aquatic crew. 'Met' is perhaps an understatement. I ran into her when she stepped into the path of our footrace."

"Ran into her!" His mother's perfect eyebrows lifted. "She wasn't harmed?"

"Not at all." This was the part of the story that would be the illusion, but he'd lived his entire life in his mother's household. He knew her weak points. "But when I came back to make sure she was okay, there was something about her. I don't know. She was pretty, definitely, but she seemed almost familiar."

"Oh boy," his father said dryly, and his mother elbowed the king in the ribs.

"You're the least romantic man I know. This is outstanding. Kristos, I command you to continue."

At that point, Kristos's earpiece crackled. "We've got a problem." Stefan's voice was clipped, sharp. "The news broke while the women were still in the hotel. All exits are blocked, unless we elect to escort them under armed guard."

"Too much show of force." Both Kristos and the king spoke at once, the latter sending him an approving glance.

"Agreed. Next option?"

"Where are they now?"

"They're all in the limo, still secure, idling in the garage."

Kristos nodded, then bowed to his parents before turning to dash back down the stairs, pulling his cell phone from his suit jacket as he went. "Keep them there, Stefan. I need ten minutes."

Eleven

"Who actually smokes anymore?" Nicki continued to fiddle with the various compartments inside the limo, including a sleek silver ashtray built into the door. "Do people do that in Europe? Is that still a thing?"

"I swear to God, I'm not taking you anywhere," Lauren groaned, while Frannie giggled, buried in one of the lush pashminas that had been folded up on the smooth leather seats of the limo.

"Take *me*, then," Frannie said. "I promise not to play with the taxis." She glanced outside the idling limo. "Although if this one takes any longer to get going, we might as well walk."

Em stared out the window as well, her fingers gripped around the phone that Kristos had given her. She had to return it to him first thing, before she forgot. Not that she usually was the type to forget those things, but she also wasn't usually the type to have her picture on TV. Lauren had switched on the in-limo device as soon as they'd all piled in, and the first thing they'd seen was a teaser for the official news broadcast, that would "reveal" the identity of the mysterious woman who'd captured the prince's heart, the so-called Princess Aphrodite.

Worse, it had let drop that she was staying at the "prestigious" Grand Hotel Oûros.

Nicki let out a low whistle. "No wonder we're getting the official escort to the castle."

"We've got to already be too late, though," Lauren said. "That's why we're cooling our heels. How many exits out of this place will allow for a limo to sneak past? Not many."

Em shook her head. "Guys, they're going to put our passports up on the media, you know they will. Is that even legal? Shouldn't there be some sort of repercussions for that?"

"Who knows what's legal here?" Frannie put in grimly. "If anyone has any interesting arrest records floating out there, though, now would be a good time to mention them."

Nicki snorted. "I've been too busy blogging to get arrested for anything interesting. And Em, you cannot tell me that you have."

"Like you wouldn't have been my first call." Em immediately sobered, though, her eyes going wide. "My God—my parents. I have to contact them."

"That can wait until we get to the palace," Lauren said. "Let Oûros pay the long-distance fees."

At that moment, there was a sharp knock on the car door. Everyone jumped, but the door opened quickly, and they were suddenly being glared at by a man Em recognized, dressed in a perfectly cut suit. "The hotel is surrounded. We're taking you out a different exit. You'll split up to distract the crowd."

"Split up!" Nicki's alarm rang loud. "No way."

"Yes." The man lifted his hand, his voice like a whip crack. "Miss Andrews will depart by way of motor van, the rest of you in the limo. Otherwise, I fear far more pictures will find their way to the Internet and international media than any of you want. Once the crowd realizes their prey is not in the limo, you'll reach the castle that much more quickly."

"It's okay. I know him," Em said to the others, and Fran nodded too. She suspected they'd both recognize that intelligent, shuttered face again anywhere. "He was with Kristos in the Visitors' Palace, briefly."

He nodded. "We don't have much time."

"Will they be safe?" Em was already turning for her bag.

"They'll be safe. Leave your things. You'll be reunited with them shortly."

"Okay, so…I'm not saying goodbye to any of you," Em said as she forced her voice to remain steady. "Not until I see you next. Which will be in about thirty minutes, so don't miss me too much."

Before any of them could respond, she was being helped out the door by the man in the suit. Without even a bag to hug to herself, she tucked her elbows tightly to her waist and hurried beside him. He walked in long strides, down another level of the parking garage, and straight across the wide expanse to an open delivery truck.

"You're seriously putting me in a delivery truck, like I'm a drug shipment or something," Em said, her eyes rounding. "This is that big a deal?"

A man emerged from the shadows at the back of the truck. "It's that big a deal, Emmaline."

"Kristos!"

Her escort's surprise was plain as Kristos hopped down. "You're *not* supposed to be here. You were to command the trucks, nothing further."

Kristos, for his part, merely shrugged. "You haven't been watching the news, Stefan. The girls' identities are being shot around the world; we have reports of flights being booked into the city from all parts of the globe, probably more media people. Cyril advises that it's going to get worse before it gets better, at least for the next few days. It's time for a new strategy."

Stefan shook his head, peering into the back of the truck. "You can't tell me Jasen has approved this."

"He has no idea." Em watched as Kristos strode forward, gripping Stefan's arm in a way that seemed almost ceremonial. "Take care of her friends. Keep them safe and out of sight, and we'll let all this die down. I had no idea how much damage I could cause in the first few hours of taking on my official duties, and it needs to stop."

Em peered into the back of the truck. As her eyes became accustomed to the gloom, she could see what had set off Stefan. A motorcycle. She snapped her gaze back to the two men. "We're not going to the palace, are we?"

Kristos looked at her, and something odd chased over his face, something fierce and proud and—possessive. Then it was gone, and his expression became warm again. Almost comforting. "Not at first," he said. "We'll be besieged with media, tourists, even the public of Oûros if they think I've somehow chosen you for my bride. It's a headache we don't need. Let the story die, the media disperse, then we'll return."

"How long will that take?"

Stefan pressed his finger to his earpiece. "The crowd is starting to shift. We need to move."

"Then by all means." Kristos turned and waved Em into the back of the truck. "Ladies first."

"This is safe?" she asked, but her words were directed at Stefan, who stared at them both with exasperation.

"Not even remotely," Stefan said.

Em thought about it for another second, but she felt Kristos's gaze on her. She was the one who *always* played it safe, after all. Made lists. Double-checked. This was all completely off the rails.

And yet somehow, deeply right.

"We should probably get going, then," she said.

Twelve

Kristos felt Emmaline trembling beside him in the dark, but he couldn't deny his own surge of excitement. The plan was a simple one. Three trucks would leave from the loading bays of the hotel in quick succession after the limo, along with cars streaming out of the hotel that had been delayed by the management-imposed garage lockdown.

Emmaline could arguably be in any of those vehicles, and most probably the limo, so everyone would disperse and they'd continue to the outskirts of the city. And then the fruit truck he'd chosen would slow enough to let them out the back.

The plan also met his primary need: get out of town with a beautiful woman. Check and check. Fortunately, Emmaline was dressed in a tank top, khakis, and tennis shoes. She'd handle the ride easily, even if it was longer than she expected.

They exited the hotel, Emmaline stiffening as the sound of many hands pounded along the sides. "What are they doing?" she whispered.

"Showing us that they expected this maneuver. But they can't be certain, right? Not with so many vehicles leaving at once. It's the perfect shell game." He quirked her a glance, peering through the darkness. "You good?" He turned toward her, but as he did, she straightened.

"I'm good," she said, her voice sounding stronger than he would have given her credit for.

And even thinking that gave him pause. How much did he really know about Emmaline Andrews? He hadn't taken the time to get the download of information from the Crown's security check, and, despite his words to his father, he knew that was a precaution that was wise to take. What if he was harboring an escaped convict?

His lips quirked up at the idea. It wouldn't be the first time.

"One thing, though." Emmaline glanced at him in the gloom. "Wherever we're heading, I will need to make some calls. Will that be possible?"

"Oh yeah," he said, satisfaction rippling through him. "Where we're heading, you'll be able to do whatever you want."

She didn't respond to that, and Kristos turned his attention to the feel of her hand in his, the warmth of her body next to him. And more too. The rumble of the truck wheels on the asphalt. The sound of traffic rushing around them, of city noise gradually diminishing to a low, distant rumble. The truck slowed at last, and he gestured to the motorcycle strapped to the inside wall of the truck. "You've ridden before?"

Emmaline nodded tightly when he offered her his helmet. "Where's yours?"

"I couldn't explain my plan to my parents, so a second helmet would have been suspicious. They'll find out soon enough from Stefan, if they haven't already."

Any additional conversation was halted as the truck slowed, then turned sharply. "That's our cue." He moved toward the unlatched door and hauled it open, blinking against the bright light. A few paces took him back to the bike, and Emmaline slid onto the seat behind him.

"Um, I haven't exactly ridden a lot."

"Put your feet on the spokes. We won't be on the road long."

"How long is long?" She sounded dubious, but she gripped his waist easily enough. "And how hard is it going to hurt when we land without a ramp?"

Kristos smiled, remembering her own words earlier that day. Had it really been just this morning that he'd seen this woman for the first time? "It'll be an adventure."

They shot out the back of the truck and hit the dirt lot, and even Emmaline's bitten-out curse made him happy. She yelped and grabbed him more tightly, her head pressed against the back of his jacket. This far away from the city—traveling in the opposite direction of the castle—no one was still following the truck. They'd made it out. He felt marginally bad about leaving Stefan to clean up his mess with his parents, especially his mother, who had images of fancy dresses and balls dancing in her head, he was sure. But then he felt the warmth and excitement of Emmaline against him, and couldn't bring himself to care very much about anything else at all.

The trip to the chateau was a winding one. The place itself was private, yes, and fortunately not one of the family residences but the home of a friend who could be counted on to lend it for royal business. Still, Kristos had to time his arrival carefully—quickly enough that he would draw no attention, but in a roundabout way so that his final destination wasn't immediately identified, if anyone should be tracking his motorbike.

Emmaline didn't once complain and finally straightened on her seat, daring to look out over the lush forests that lined the roadway. An hour into the journey, however, she tapped him on the shoulder. She leaned forward as he turned toward her.

"Any chance we're going to be stopping soon? I'm going to need a break, um, soon."

Kristos nodded and gunned the engine. He didn't want to

stop before they reached the chateau, but he also didn't want Emmaline to spontaneously combust behind him. So the answer was simply *more speed.*

Thirty minutes later, they turned off the main road. He wasn't sure if Emmaline's sigh was in reaction to the imminent shot at a bathroom or relief that they'd made it through the last twenty miles alive. She hadn't even screamed after the second or third turn, and it had been all Kristos could do not to push the bike harder, just to get a reaction out of her.

Fortunately, this far from the capital city, no one seemed tuned to the entertainment channels. They cruised past the gatehouse without incident, the guard familiar with his face. Another bonus of not wearing a helmet. When they finally glided up to the entrance of the chateau, however, Emmaline let out a small gasp of appreciation.

Kristos stopped the bike. "Easy off, watch the sides. The pipes will be hot."

"What *is* this place?" Emmaline dismounted a little shakily, but a second later, he was there, his hand on her shoulder, to steady her. He couldn't seem to stop touching her, he realized, especially here, where there was no one around to see. And now, with an entire chateau at their disposal...

"The home of a friend, who's currently summering in New Zealand." At her startled glance, he shrugged. "He wanted to go skiing."

"You've got to be kidding."

Emmaline pulled the helmet from her head and held it out to Kristos, her gaze still on the house. It soared above them, traditional Greek architecture matched with timber-and-glass construction to make the most of the expansive views. His friend Theo had spared no expense in creating this idyll in the forest, and Kristos had spent many weekends here on leave, reveling in the beauty of Oûros that lay beyond its coasts.

Now he reached for Emmaline's hand, and she let him tug her along for several steps before seeming to remember herself. "Kristos, I don't have any more clothes. How long are we going to be here?"

"A few days, maybe—less if the story dies down quickly." He amended his statement on the fly, seeing the alarm flash across her face. "And I called ahead and alerted them about our arrival. They had enough time to get to the local town for some changes of clothes for both of us."

"Of course they did." But she said nothing further, allowing him to draw her up the stairs to the chateau. They were greeted at the door by Theo's housekeeper and butler, to whom Kristos spoke in the rapid language of the countryside, his fingers entwined with Emmaline's, who was looking more and more like she wanted to bolt. He squeezed her hand reassuringly when he was through. "First, you should call your...parents, yes? Siblings?"

Boyfriend? He wondered silently, but Emmaline nodded, her confusion dissipating. "Yes, my parents. What time is it in the US?"

"About nine a.m." After she'd decamped to a small guest bathroom, he led her to a small room that served as Theo's guest office. It was outfitted with an arsenal of phones, computers, and tablets, enough to satisfy his most workaholic of guests. It had been Ari who had demanded a suitable office for him in Theo's home, if they'd wanted to lure him away from his princely duties. Ari, who hadn't so much as breathed a hint of his responsibilities to Kristos in the few times they were able to meet here with Kristos on leave. He'd never really given much thought to what his brother did with all those long nights of his. And now he would never know.

He gave Emmaline the codes to dial out of the house and withdrew to the windows, unable to stand so far away as to give her complete privacy. He wanted to know everything about this woman, and he didn't want to turn on the TV to do it. He winced with the thought of her private life unearthed, all due to him, and yet—if he'd had the chance to do it over, he wouldn't have changed anything. It was selfish, but it was true.

Without Emmaline in his life, he'd likely be stuck in an hours-long meeting with his advisors right now, ass-deep in discussions about how he needed to play to the media, hiding his anger, ignoring their insufferable questions about his brother, his family. The men he'd lost in combat. The choices he'd made. Choices he'd suffered for. And if that wasn't enough, the conversation would almost certainly be capped off with a gathering of all the likely suspects who might become a suitable wife. That wouldn't work for anyone.

No, better that he was here, with a mystery woman and a few days left of breathing room. Because unless he was misreading the way Emmaline looked at him when she thought he wasn't watching, it would be an escape with definite benefits.

Thirteen

"I know—yes, of course, I'll call soon. You might want to keep the television off for a few days. Or be ready for the neighbors to look at you funny, if any of them are into celebrity TV."

Emmaline wrapped up her phone conversation with her father, who didn't really seem to be paying much attention. Then again, that wasn't really a surprise. Her mother had had an off day, and whenever that happened, her father seemed to sink a little deeper into his own shame, blaming himself for the distraction that had caused him not to see the oncoming truck that had caused their accident, and blaming himself even more for not being the one who'd suffered a brain injury.

How had she ever justified taking a vacation to Europe in the middle of their recovery? Yes, it had been over a year without so much as a day off, but still. She should have known better, no matter what Fran insisted. Her place was back with her parents, not lolling in some princely chateau in the middle of a country few people had even heard of.

She'd said as much to her father, of course, but to his credit, he hadn't piled on. He seemed distracted, yes, but not as angry as she'd expected. Still, Emmaline couldn't help the guilt that draped her as she spoke at length with the nurse, going over her parents' medications, their upcoming doctor visits, the small wins of the past few days. She'd learned to celebrate every victory, no matter how tiny. It was all she could think of to get through each day.

She completed the call at last and turned again to Kristos. He stood looking out the window to the vast forest beyond. Apparently noticing her attention, he gestured to the vista. "Oûros's border is another hour to the north, and twice that to the east and west. We are not much bigger than your state of Rhode Island, though our roads are a bit less direct. Still, we should be safe here." He glanced at her. "You've texted your friends, I see, not called?"

Em nodded. She didn't feel up to all the questions she knew Fran, Nicki, and especially Lauren would have. Kristos, however, watched her with eyes that seemed too shrewd.

"Is everything well with them?" he pressed. "Are they all right?"

"Yes, they're fine." She shook her head. "This is going to sound stupid. I—well, you heard me with my parents."

His face instantly took on a more somber look. "They're ill, I take it. Your mother has been injured?"

"Both of them—it was an accident, and recovery has been slow and, well, hard, I guess you would say. I left school and have been caring for them for a year."

He lifted his brows. "You weren't able to graduate?"

"Oh no, I graduated. I—it doesn't matter, really. I got a scholarship to study in grad school. But then the accident happened, and I deferred the scholarship and—whatever, that's not the point." She waved off whatever question he was about to ask. "The net result is that I haven't been the one to do anything exciting in my group of friends. Fran has worked overseas and is three breaths from a Masters, Nicki goes off and climbs mountains whenever she gets bored, Lauren learns new languages in between pedicures, and I—don't. So for me to be the one to get swept away on a motorcycle by a European prince, well..." She spread her hands. "It's a story I'd like to keep telling *myself* a little longer, if that makes sense, before I have to tell it to anyone else."

"It makes complete sense." But something had shifted in Kristos's demeanor, and when he walked toward her, Em felt herself grow wary. She knew she shouldn't be so willing to follow this man without asking more questions, making a pros-and-cons list, checking it twice... Yet when he held out his hand, she found herself putting her fingers in his again, ready once again to let him lead.

Kristos tugged her into the hall. "Have you always told yourself stories?" he asked, his words mild, though there seemed to be an undertow to them as dangerous as the one she'd found in the depths of the Aegean Sea.

"Well, sure." Em frowned, trying to regain control of the conversation. It wasn't easy, given that she was walking down an opulent hallway, self-conscious in her sneakers and capris. He didn't need to know about her mom or any of that. *Just keep things light, easy. Explain it all in a very reasonable way.* "I mean, it helps me pass the time, but it also takes me out of wherever I am and into wherever I want to be." She tried to pitch her words more lightly. "Life doesn't get too exciting in Missouri, you know."

He walked past open doorways that led to familiar-looking rooms. "You've lived there your entire life except college?" He didn't wait for her to nod but pushed on. "And what is it you studied that you were so good at that you received a scholarship to graduate school?"

"Oh." Em's cheeks flared, but there wasn't any reason why she shouldn't tell him. Her skill might seem a little weird, but he was a *prince*. That trumped anything she could come up with.

"Violin—violin performance, technically, so that one day I could play in an orchestra."

He blinked at her, and she felt suddenly shy at his admiring gaze. He didn't know that she hadn't played in months. He didn't know that she feared she'd never truly be able to play again. "Then I am sure you are wrong, Emmaline. Your life must be every bit as exciting as your friends' lives."

Before she could contradict him, they reached the edge of the house. Kristos pushed open the doors, treating Em to the view beyond. The villa stretched out over the forest, with a tiled veranda covered by a stucco overhang, and she found herself drawn to the far side. When she looked over the banister, it was her chance to gasp again. A gorgeously landscaped pool surrounded by formal gardens gleamed from the terrace below, before the manicured plots gave way to thick forests all the way around. She couldn't see the Aegean from here, but the forest was almost as imposing, rising in an emerald swell that made it seem like civilization was very, *very* far away.

"It's beautiful."

Kristos didn't hesitate. "It's very pretty, yes. But *you* are beautiful, *koukla mou*. There is a distinct difference."

Em blinked, her gaze swiveling to meet Kristos's. "*Koukla mou?*"

"I think you would translate it as 'doll', or 'sweetheart.'" He grinned.

Yes, he'd totally just flirted with her. She wasn't imagining it. But she had no game whatsoever to flirt back at him.

Fortunately, he didn't seem to mind. "We're going to be here for a few days." Kristos was suddenly right there, his breath warm against her cheek. "I should want to know everything about you in that time, if possible."

"Ah... I can't imagine anything left that's all that interesting. You pretty much know all there is to know about me already."

"Once more, you're wrong." He dropped his head forward to where the line of her tank top lay against her shoulder, and grazed the skin with his lips. "I have never kissed your shoulder, you see. Here already is something new that you might teach me."

Tell him no. Tell him no, Em suggested to herself. Strongly. She was a grown woman who had, up until a short while ago, been pursuing an advanced degree. An American. A guest in his country. There was no way the freaking crown prince of Oûros wouldn't stop if she said *no.*

Only, she found she didn't want to say no.

So that was a problem.

"And your neck," he murmured, moving up the curve of her skin to brush his lips against the pulse throbbing there. "I haven't yet had the chance to get to know your neck. This seems a terrible waste, when time is so short."

She opened her mouth to protest, she really did, but only managed a halfhearted whimper. *Impressive, Em.*

However, it was all the encouragement Kristos needed. He turned Em around, reaching out to tip her chin up with long fingers, his gaze searching hers. "I've never held you at midnight, or in the light of a new day."

"Kristos—"

"Shhh... Don't think for a moment more. Let me taste you instead."

He kissed her then, and it happened all over again—the sense of time stopping, as if all Em needed to do was step into this man's arms and everything around her would cease to be, and there would only be her, and him, and maybe a magic carpet to whisk them off to someplace exotic and strange.

Except, the magic carpet had been replaced with a motorcycle, and her prince wasn't some whimsical boy in silk pants and a turban, but a real, live, hot-blooded man. She didn't know if Kristos was only interested in her because she happened to be the only woman in this chateau under the age of fifty that she'd seen, or because he really wanted her. But surely he wouldn't have brought her here if he didn't at least feel *some* legitimate attraction to her, right?

And what did she want to do about that?

Em jumped as the prince's hands dropped to her waistline, snaking up beneath the tank top to press against her skin. "You're shaking," he murmured. "Are you cold?"

He didn't let her answer but pulled her into his body, surrounding her with his warmth. He deepened the kiss then, and Em arched beneath him, her mind momentarily on hold as everything inside her heated up and demanded more. She felt something strange and liquid spiral within her, like a shivery tremor, but of heat, delicious heat, warming her in places she'd thought had long ago faded into dust. "I'm not cold," she managed when he finally broke away.

Kristos's eyes were intent as he looked down at her. "Then why are you shivering, *koukla mou*?"

"Well, it's not because I'm cold." Her hands firmed on his chest, and she tried to convince herself that she wasn't actually dreaming, that this was happening and wasn't one of her wild fantasies.

No, no. Do not think of the word "fantasies."

But it was already too late. Kristos's eyes narrowed on her, as if he knew the reason behind the blush that crawled up her cheeks. Thank heavens he couldn't read minds, or she'd die of mortification.

"I think I want to know more of these stories you are making up in your head, Emmaline. And as your host, I think it's only polite that I help you create this latest one," he murmured, and when her gaze flew to his, he smiled, slow and certain. "For example, if you're the reluctant princess and I'm the marauding prince, I think it's time we discuss the terms of your abduction."

"Hmmm." She shook her head. "You're going to have to work a lot harder than that if you want to convince me that you're some evil villain bent on stealing my virtue."

He stared at her, his expression turning a shade darker. "I look forward to it."

Fourteen

Hours later, Kristos was still watching Emmaline, this time over the rim of his wineglass, trying to decide how best to play this. There was so much he wanted to experience with her. It was simply a matter of where he should begin.

They'd no sooner emerged from the veranda, heading back to the house, when the housekeeper, Marte, had appeared again. Kristos had been grateful that Emmaline had been walking in front of him and had shielded his body from view—since anyone could see at a glance that he was rock hard.

By the time they'd climbed to the second-floor sleeping quarters—separate suites, of course, to appease the staff's sense of propriety—he'd at least had his body under control. Nevertheless, Emmaline's room was directly across the hallway from his, so he suspected his control would not be lasting long.

And Emmaline wasn't helping matters. She'd begged for a shower the moment they'd reached their rooms, and he'd let her go, recognizing her need for escape even if she didn't. But now he felt an odd anxiety at letting her out of his sight again. Part of that was the sense that she could fly away from him at any moment. And part of it was his own fault for letting the world encroach upon them once more.

But what was he supposed to do? He'd used the time she was showering to return to Theo's guest office, flipping on screens and settling into the virtual mission control that Theo had set up for his older brother. There still had been no arrests in the theft of the Americans' passports, but the damage had been done. The media storm was bigger than he'd imagined, with the girls' parade of photos emblazoned across the screen. Emmaline's revealed a birth name unusually long for an American—Emmaline Aphrodite Grace Andrews—and showed a serious, hollow-eyed girl with her hair pulled back and her expression too grim, even by passport standards. Her friend Nicole Clark, the only young woman he hadn't met yet, seemed to be staring down the camera of the passport agent as if she had a problem with it, while Francesca Simmons and Lauren Grant had apparently mastered the art of official document photos. Both their expressions were composed, if a little coy, their hair perfect, their makeup professional. Lovely women, all four of them, each in her own way.

And three of them were safely in the castle. Which meant he could focus on the one who wasn't.

Speaking of the castle, he'd received more news than he'd wanted to from that quarter. An e-mail from Stefan with the background checks on each of the women attached. Another e-mail from his father demanding his and Emmaline's return to the city. He'd filed the latter, but Stefan's had proven more difficult to ignore.

He'd hovered over the attachments detailing the history of the four women now under the Crown's care, spending the longest time on Emmaline's before he finally closed out of his e-mail without clicking on any of the documents. If she'd been a true threat to his security, Stefan would've already tracked them down—and could have, easily enough, despite Theo's assertions of the complete privacy of his computer setup. He had a feeling Stefan had overturned every rock in their tiny kingdom at one time or another, and Theo's home was an easy guess as a hideaway for Kristos. But, for the moment, his half-cousin seemed content to let Kristos remain hidden. His father had too, which could only mean one thing:

The castle must be besieged.

Kristos hadn't had the stomach to watch the news beyond the quick clips of the girls' information and one breathless reporter asserting that the disappearance of the young American and her friends inside the castle was the harbinger of wedding bells. Everyone was scrambling to find proof of a previous meeting, with the tabloids providing the wildest options, as usual. His parents had issued a warm statement about welcoming the friends of the crown prince into their royal embrace, but saying nothing further. Predictably polite, predictably vague.

And that, in a nutshell, was the life that was waiting for him back in the capital city.

Predictable.

But it wasn't the life before him tonight.

"Did you see any of the media coverage?" His question seemed to recall Emmaline from wherever it was she was so used to going, her gaze jerking swiftly back to him as the sun set over the far western borders of the country.

"I turned it on long enough to see my passport photo. That was enough for me." She grimaced. "But before I could get the remote to work, I caught sight of the limo taking Nicki and the others into the castle. I can't imagine what that must be like for them, especially Nicki. She's not used to being cooped up anywhere. She's training for an adventure triathlon, and the only way she agreed to come on this trip with Lauren was if we stayed at places that allowed her full access to running and climbing routes."

Kristos nodded. No wonder Stefan wasn't bothering him as much as he could be. He probably had his hands full keeping track of an American who would think nothing of scaling the palace walls. "What of your other friends—Francesca and Lauren? How distraught will this make them?"

"Distraught?" Emmaline's laugh was short but filled with affection. "Lauren doesn't do distraught. It's not in her vocabulary. And Frannie—well, she's a counselor-in-training and life coach working on her master's degree in counseling. Even if she wanted to curl up and die inside, she's trained not to show it."

"A counselor?" Kristos wouldn't have guessed that about the woman. "That must be rewarding work."

Emmaline hesitated a moment, swirling the wine in her glass. "It can be. She worked for a few years with returning military vets. Her coursework focused on PTSD treatment. But she burned out on that, I think. It's hard, the way she sinks into her surroundings, almost like a chameleon, until whoever she's treating thinks she's part of the landscape. That's when they talk, she says. When they think only the floors and walls can hear them."

"And you? What about your studies? How long until you can join an orchestra?"

"First I'd have to audition." Em took another sip of her wine. "An orchestra is a long way off for me."

"You're too modest, I suspect." Kristos watched her closely, trying to pierce her underlying melancholy. "You received a scholarship, did you not? To graduate school?"

"Well, yes. Back when I played all the time I—I wasn't bad, I suppose." Her smile was more genuine now as she shook her head. "I received a scholarship to get into undergrad too. But jobs for musicians are really, really rare." She looked like she might say more, but her gaze returned to the forested vista, her mind shifting and tumbling through thoughts he could only guess at.

"So why the violin? Of all the instruments you could have chosen, why did you pick that?"

Emmaline snorted. "If I'd been smart, I should have held out for the tuba. But I had a mother who knew every myth, fairy tale, and medieval romance ever written, and she was *convinced* I should play the violin. She had a thing about..." She shook her head, a blush flaring along her cheeks. "It doesn't matter. Fortunately, I turned out to be okay at the violin, and so it was fairly easy to get a spot in various high school level orchestras—without ever having to go to band camp." Her expression turned a little wistful. "I have a lot of hours of practice under my belt."

"Your hands," he said, nodding. "The fingers are calloused. I'd wondered why."

"Oh! Yeah." She didn't seem surprised that he'd noticed, but simply lifted her left hand, her thumb running over her fingertips. "I don't think Mom had that in mind when she was channeling her fairy-tale princesses, or the fact that I'd actually have to train my neck muscles to hold the violin. But I seemed to take to it naturally."

"You still play, of course."

"Hmm?" She blinked back at him as if he'd startled her once again, her gaze snapping into focus on his. "No. Not really, not anymore. Life has a way of reminding you what's important." Emmaline lifted her wineglass again and drained it, returning her gaze to the forest. The sun was beginning to dip down over the horizon, lending an almost ethereal air to the evening. "I have to thank you, though. You couldn't have picked a more beautiful place to help me forget, for a little while longer, the world I've left behind."

And why did she want to forget it? The odd phrasing of her

words caught at Kristos, but no more so than the perfect curve of her cheek as she sat in half profile to him. In her borrowed clothes, she could be any one of Theo's acquaintances that he'd encountered over the years—women of means, of great beauty, and some with fiery intellect too. He didn't think he'd ever encountered a musician among them, however, and he thought of Emmaline's abrupt dismissal of the idea that she still played. How could someone who'd dedicated her entire life to music suddenly turn her back on it? It didn't make sense. She seemed like a woman out of place, not quite sure where she belonged.

He had a few suggestions of where she might try. In his experience, there were only a few things that could stave off the march of time. They all involved a woman.

And right now, they most definitely involved *this* woman.

Fifteen

E m almost didn't realize that Kristos had stepped up to her, holding out his hand. "The gardens are beautiful in the daytime, but I've always enjoyed them more at night. Would you walk with me?"

"At night?" She frowned at him as she stood. "But how can you see?" She drew in a sharp breath as Kristos stopped in front of a panel, punching a few buttons. Instantly, a cascade of fairy lights winked on over the space, leading in a path down to the manicured gardens. "Oh!" she exclaimed. "You're totally losing your status as marauding prince, you know."

He laughed. "Not at all. I've stolen your privacy from you, which is a very grave offense. The least I can do is burn a little of my friend's electricity to take you on a walk."

They stepped together down the long stairway and onto the grassy path, and Em knew her shiver had nothing to do with the cool breeze that was now skirting along the carefully trimmed topiary bushes and ruffling the flowers. She was walking through a magical garden with a *prince*, for heaven's sake. The only way she wouldn't be shivering was if she were dead.

"When was the last time you were here?" she asked, pleased that her voice sounded steady. Normal, even.

Kristos considered the question. "Six months ago. I could have—perhaps should have—gone home with my unexpected leave, but I was in no rush to return to the palace. My father and his advisors were pretty clear on me needing to do my royal duty the moment I walked through the doors, so it seemed advisable to avoid the capital city until the last possible minute."

"Which was this morning?"

"Yesterday morning, actually. After I made it through one day unscathed, I actually was starting to feel a little hopeful that I still had some time left with my men." He shook his head. "I should have known something was wrong by the mere fact that Cyril didn't show up that first day. I wouldn't put it past him to have created those maneuvers specifically so he could trap me on the beach. I should have seen that coming."

"So being the crown prince is that awful?"

"Not awful, no." His smile was rueful. "But it does mean I have to take on the responsibility of running the country instead of merely defending it. From what I've seen, running a country involves a lot of pointless meetings and being polite to foreigners while figuring out how to one-up them at the same time. It means a lot of travel, speeches, and dancing, none of which I'm good at." Kristos's teeth flashed in the artificial light. "And it means I can't kiss a pretty girl on a beach without it becoming national news. So I'm not very much a fan so far."

Em's brows lifted. She used to be told she was pretty all the time. Still, "college guy pretty" and "prince pretty" had to be on two different scales. And at this point in her life, as weathered as she felt from her day-to-day caretaking chores and constant worry, any nod of appreciation was, well, appreciated.

"But now you've gotten away from all of that for a little while, it looks like." She held up a hand at his glance, forestalling his response. He had to understand that she knew the score here. "I know it's only for a couple of days, until things die down and you go back to your world and I go back to mine."

Kristos's words were unexpectedly cautionary. "It might be more than a couple of days."

"That's not the point." She walked ahead a few steps, trailing her fingers along the blossoms that looked lush and velvety under the tiny white lights. "Kristos—I'm walking in a gorgeous garden on a private estate with a man named *Kristos*. It's a memory I won't ever have to give up. If I've learned nothing else in the past few years, it's that you sometimes don't get to choose how things go in this world. You sometimes get handed something you didn't plan for, aren't prepared for, something you really don't like. So good memories are worth celebrating."

She felt the urge to cry, suddenly, and she stamped down that feeling as ruthlessly as she pushed away her nerves, her tension—even her sense of propriety. She was alone with a prince, and he'd already kissed her! If she didn't at least manage a serious make-out session with the man while she was here, then she had only herself to blame.

She forced herself to look at Kristos. He hadn't followed her down the pathway but was now staring at her, apparently shocked by her words. Well, she probably deserved that. She struggled to try to explain herself better. "And not all surprises are bad, either. I mean sometimes, like right now, you get handed something you never could have expected, something you didn't plan for either, aren't really prepared for—but that you *do* really like. And those times, it makes sense to make the most of the opportunity, you know? To take it and live it to the fullest, because God only knows when you'll get the chance to live like this again."

"Emmaline." Kristos's tone was fierce, and she took an involuntary step backward as he strode the few steps to reach her and just that quickly, pulled her into his arms. He smelled of warm sunshine despite the darkness drawing down, and when he bent to kiss her, she lifted herself on her toes as well. The moment their lips touched, Kristos tightened his hold. His strength seemed to lock in place, and her own desperate need leaped higher as well, her heart beginning to race, a shiver rolling down her spine.

He broke away from her, but only to begin the slow trail of kisses up her jawline until he reached her ear. He took the soft lobe into his mouth, and she willed herself to stand perfectly still, though her knees wanted to buckle and her fingers yearned to twist into his shirt, to pull him to her and give herself over to him completely.

Down girl, she implored herself. For all her talk of wanting to live life to the fullest, she didn't want to be some kind of crazed American who threw herself at his—

At that moment, Kristos breathed a soft, warm whisper of breath against her ear, murmuring something in Greek or Oûrois or *whatever, who cares*, and Em swayed against him, unable to keep herself upright without his help. His chuckle reverberated through her.

"As tempting as it would be to continue this here, I am almost certain Theo has cameras throughout the grounds," he whispered, this time in English. "No, no." He pulled away, shaking his head as she stiffened. "Once again, you have done nothing wrong. But I couldn't keep looking at you and hearing your words without touching you." His gaze was an invitation, warm and sure. "I don't think I will tire of touching you for a very long time."

He turned, and instead of taking her hand in his, he brought his hand to her shoulder, pulling her close to him, so their bodies pressed against each other. And as they strolled back toward the chateau, Kristos's hand slid down the thin material of her dress until his palm rested against the small of her back, the act so unconsciously possessive that once again Em felt out of her element. Her brain scrambled to make some sense of what was happening. Were they—there was no way they *weren't* going to have sex, right? She wasn't reading all these signs wrong? It'd been way too long, granted, but surely she wasn't screwing this up? Because that really *would* be a tragedy.

Kristos paused at the garden entrance long enough to turn out the fairy lights, and the gloom that plunged around them seemed to urge them toward the beautiful white chateau. It gleamed from a sweep of security lights that winked on and off as they passed, and then they were at the wide veranda. Dimly, through her haze of desire, Em noticed that the table had been cleared away. Her gaze only swung forward, though, when Kristos went stock-still, his entire body at attention. She blinked and realized he was staring at a man who stood half-hidden in the shadows, watching them. A man she recognized.

Kristos's next words were once again in his native tongue, but there was no mistaking the sharp, guttural slap of his curse.

Sixteen

"Who died?" Kristos demanded, scowling at Dimitri Korba. "Because someone had better be dead for you to be here."

"You didn't check in, and you have no security detail in this place." His bodyguard's goofy grin had turned warm for the benefit of Emmaline as he switched to English. "I didn't mean to startle you," he said. "I have been sent to ensure your safety."

"Safety? Has there been any trouble at the castle?" Emmaline went still beside Kristos, all her heat seeming to roll off her like a discarded coat. *Dammit.* He was used to women responding to him with eagerness, with excitement and anticipation. And some could even handle the moment where they saw what his military life had done to him, their image of a perfect prince altered forever. But with Emmaline, it was different. She'd held on to him not with the need of a desperate woman or even a simply aroused female willing and ready to share his bed. No. Her need had been more fundamental, more basic, and it called to him on a level that seemed as crucial as life itself.

He'd sensed her skittishness too—her desire to push things

further, but also her uncertainty about what she could do or say that wouldn't be inappropriate. He had no problem putting her at ease on that score as well. In fact, there was no end to the things he was happy to show her—but now, over two hundred pounds of muscle and attitude stood in his way, and he suspected that everything about his plans for the evening had suddenly become a lot more difficult.

"No trouble, I have been assured." Dimitri's gaze took in both of them. "I haven't been on-site since your friends were safely delivered, and the attention at the castle seems contained for the moment—though, admittedly, the prospect of a wedding announcement has turned things up a notch or six. They have begun external patrols of the walls and surrounding villas, to root out the paparazzi looking for a shot inside. The women have been asked to remain indoors for the time being, but they are in danger of nothing more than an errant photograph at this point. Cyril is keeping watch, and every member of the ONSF in the city has been pressed into guard duty, though more for show than with any expectation of a need for force. After all." He waggled his brows. "We have a prince and his bride-to-be to protect. If we didn't put up a good front, people would begin to suspect all was not as it seemed at the castle."

"Uh-huh. And how did *you* escape?"

Dimitri's expression turned even more gleeful. "By not being there when the limo arrived. Stefan radioed me that you'd gone rogue, and there were only so many chateaux you would be likely to choose, given where you had the fruit truck dump you off. Neatly played, that. There's been no indication that you were seen."

Kristos nodded. "And the driver of the truck?"

"Shot."

As Dimitri had clearly intended, Em gasped and drew back sharply, giving Dimitri a reason to wave his hands at her. "Kidding, kidding," he said, his laughter echoing around the veranda. "He was well paid to keep quiet, and since he is the only one who knew where he dropped you, if that information were to reach the press, there would be little doubt as to how it got there. He knows that as well, so he has additional incentive to keep his mouth shut."

"And now what?" Kristos motioned them all forward, his arm still anchoring Emmaline to him as they entered a large sitting room, its windows opened to allow the soft breezes to filter in through the curtains. A fire had been laid in the hearth of the central fireplace, which took the chill off the breeze, and soft lights beckoned. "You can't imagine I'm in any danger up here."

Dimitri looked around, then strode to the center of the room, where more wine was laid out along with the thick, sugary pastries of Oûros. Demigods had several advantages over ordinary humans, and one was their preternatural ability to stay in shape no matter what they ate or drank. Dimitri helped himself to a large glass of wine, then offered the bottle to Kristos before returning it to the table.

"For myself? No, I do not think there's any danger here," Dimitri said, continuing to speak in English. "For the king and Cyril, I will be more cautionary in my reports. Otherwise they'd probably drag me back there to terrify the photographers."

Kristos narrowed his eyes. "You're not going to tell him where we are."

"Not precisely, no. Though you could be discovered up here easily enough. The country, it is not so large as that."

"Except no one is looking for us."

Dimitri stretched his hand, the wine sloshing in his glass but not quite reaching the rim. Another advantage of being a demigod. "All the more reason to have a bodyguard you trust on hand versus the large security detail the king would doubtless insist upon, to protect both you and your beloved Princess Aphrodite."

He waggled his brows again at Emmaline, and she laughed, the sound winging through Kristos. "Well, I thank you most kindly," she said, bowing solemnly at Dimitri before turning to Kristos. Her eyes asked the question that she didn't want to speak aloud, he knew. Should she stay or go? Propriety dictated that he send her to her room, allow her to rest. Propriety dictated that he spend time with his brother's good friend and his own teammate and catch up on the business of the ONSF, since Dimitri was now an officer and Kristos had effectively been removed from duty—or was about to be.

But propriety would keep him from that which he wanted most in this world, on this night, which was to kiss the woman whose touch electrified him, whose every move drew his eye and set his body humming with need.

He focused his stare on Dimitri. "You know you're killing me here, right?" he asked in their own language.

Dimitri was no fool. His eyes brightened with understanding and mirth. "It's what I do best." He switched to English again. "I plan to do a thorough search of the grounds, since I have our new gear to test anyway. We have evidence of rogue naiads in the area we need to track down."

Though Emmaline giggled as she was meant to, not realizing that Dimitri was being fully truthful, his words caught Kristos's attention. Updated models of ONSF vision gear had been requisitioned months ago. Of course, it *would* finally come in right as he was taken out of active duty. Still, he nodded, content with his end of this night's bargain. "Let me know what you learn."

"Of course, Your Highness." Dimitri managed to say the words without a trace of sarcasm, but Kristos narrowed his eyes anyway. It would take some time to get used to hearing that honorific from his fellow soldiers. Maybe the rest of his life. But Dimitri didn't seem to notice his uneasiness. He gave Emmaline another short bow, also perfectly respectable, then turned before she became nervous enough to bow back. He strode out the front door, whistling like a man who knew a secret.

"Have you been friends long?" Emmaline asked, looking after him. Her relaxed manner had him glancing at her sharply. She lifted a hand to her mouth to smother a yawn.

You've got to be joking. She had every reason to be exhausted, of course, but Kristos hadn't expected fatigue to catch up with her so quickly. He'd missed his window of opportunity. Maybe Dimitri had already figured out the same thing and that was the reason for his good mood. *Ass.*

"Yes," he said, not willing to ruin the moment further by mentioning that it was Ari and Dimitri who had been friends first. "He's trustworthy, though his timing could be improved." He nodded to Emmaline, forcing the regret and disappointment out of his voice. "You should get some sleep. I'll check in with the media and see if we're having our first child tomorrow or anything."

The relief that jumped in her eyes confirmed his suspicion that there was more going on here than simple exhaustion. So did the speed with which she turned toward the stairs. Before Dimitri had interrupted them, she had seemed more than happy to throw caution to the wind. Now, her mind was whispering for her to be careful, and he had only himself to blame. He'd let those embers grow cool.

She had every right to be nervous, in truth. They'd known each other for barely twelve hours. But still.

Kristos sighed and headed for Theo's office. If Dimitri found any of the rogue naiads rumored to be assembling on this side of the gates, he'd need Kristos's help to interrogate them. The mischievous minor goddesses of lakes and streams knew everything that happened in the interior of the kingdom, though they were notoriously shy about sharing their knowledge with humans. Still, maybe they'd heard something new from the oceanids, their sisters in the sea, about Ari's lost plane.

If so—and it was a big if—at least the night wouldn't be a total waste.

Seventeen

What a total waste of a night, Em thought bitterly as she climbed the stairs. Would Princess Emmaline Aphrodite Grace have chosen that moment to yawn, completely turning off the first guy who'd been interested in her in forever? *No.* No, she most certainly would not. Especially when the good princess hadn't had sex in over two years.

Dammit.

Em stomped onto the second floor landing. She couldn't deny that she'd felt a momentary surge of relief when Kristos had given her the out—at least before embarrassment at her own relief had flooded through her. It *had* been a long time. What if she somehow did the wrong thing? Heck, what if they had weird sex traditions in Oûros that she knew nothing about?

She giggled a little, despite her irritation. The floors above this one seemed deserted. Where did all the staff live? Surely not above them. Maybe not in the main house at all, but in some sort of secondary building on the estate. They'd want their own privacy, though given how opulent this place was down to the ornate door handles, she had no doubt that their living quarters were far more extravagant than the simple ranch home she shared with her parents back in Missouri.

Her parents. For the first time since she'd left on her European vacation, Em thought of them without a lurch of anxiety. Instead, the only thing making her nervous was apparently Prince Hottie Adonis Guy. In front of whom she'd just *yawned.*

Turning down the corridor, Em saw the twin doors near the end of the hallway, one marking hers, the other Kristos's. Though she'd gratefully showered earlier today, she didn't think he'd even *been* to his room yet, and curiosity thrummed through her. Was it a mirror image of her own? Or had he given her the better room out of some misplaced chivalry?

Or, even more intriguingly, was his room some sort of palatial bedchamber fit for, well, a prince?

Em's eyes widened as she regarded the closed door. Kristos had seemed pretty determined to go to Theo's guest office, and she suspected he, like most men, would get wrapped up pretty quickly in streaming video and Internet. So she would have time, definitely, to take a little peek.

Another thought struck her. *Does Kristos have a girlfriend he needs to contact?* Surely not. He would never have kissed Emmaline, not once but *three* times, swept her off on a motorcycle, and dropped her in the center of a hidden villa if he'd had a girlfriend.

And yet, how could he not? Even among the other Oûrois soldiers she'd seen, most of whom were impossibly hotter than the guys back home, he looked like a supermodel. Tall, dark, lean, and dangerous. And those golden eyes...

Em chewed her lip, pausing in front of her door before looking back over her shoulder. What would it harm to take a look?

She stepped across the hall and turned the handle on Kristos's door. It moved easily in her hand, and she pushed the door open, grateful that moonlight poured in through the open windows, blanketing the room with a soft glow. His room *was* similar to hers—same tile floors, same enormous, plush bed, same *en suite* bathroom. It didn't feel like he'd been there yet, as she'd suspected. The drawers were untouched, the bathroom door was standing open at a precise angle. The whole place had that staged look that hers had also had when she'd entered it earlier that day.

The bed, of course, was untouched.

She considered it now, draped in its pool of moonlight, its coverlet light enough that the soft breeze sent it rippling, almost inviting her to climb up onto its high, plush pillows. Now that her vision was becoming accustomed to the gloom, she peered toward the window and crossed the cool tiles to push aside the light curtains.

It was all so beautiful. The view was almost identical to hers, though her room looked over the gardens and pool while his showed a more unremitting view of forest—and maybe a gleam of a lake or something in the distance?

Actually...were there more lights than reasonable around that lake, leaping and twirling? It must be a trick of the stars.

She focused on the far glimmers of light, leaning against the window frame as she let her mind wander, the events of the day finally catching up to her. When she'd woken up this morning, she'd expected her day would have little more excitement than nursing Lauren back to health after her run-in with the *tsipouro*. Now here she was on the other end of the country, hiding out from the paparazzi with, well, a prince.

She allowed herself a long sigh. Princess Emmaline Aphrodite Grace gazed out over her vast and beautiful kingdom, the enchanted realm of Oûros, and thought about the pressing news of the day. There would be a royal wedding soon, everyone said, and the idea should gladden her heart, lift her spirits and—

"I'm pretty sure this is my room."

The words would have shot her straight out through the window pane, except firm hands were suddenly on her hips, anchoring her in place as a very large, very masculine body fitted itself up against hers. Kristos's heady, spicy scent swirled around her as he bent to nuzzle her neck, drawing his mouth up against Em's ear in a move that practically made her eyes cross. "You want to tell me what you're doing here?"

"I thought you had to...work or something." Em tried to convince herself to move out of his embrace, but he slipped his hands around her further, drawing his fingers along the silky material of her dress, moving up, up, until he captured her breasts in his palms. Her knees seemed to give up the will to live at that point, and she sagged against him, managing little more than a gasp.

"There was nothing to see on any of the monitors. But you haven't answered the question," Kristos murmured, then bent deeper to kiss her shoulder, his fingers beginning to knead her breasts in a sensual rhythm. "Why are you here?"

She turned, not even remotely trying to escape, and as if he realized that, Kristos let her move, his mouth claiming hers as she lifted her face toward him. Apparently, that was all the additional information he required. He pulled her almost roughly against him, heat and desire evident in every line of his body. Em pressed back, her hands lifting to his beautiful face as he kissed her, unable to believe that *she* was here, that *they* were here, and that *this*—

Kristos didn't let her get her bearings any further. He walked her backward across the tiled floor, kissing her brows, her cheeks, her lips, her chin, as if he couldn't get enough of a taste of her without roaming over her skin. His left hand stretched around her, cupping her backside, and heat pooled inside Em's belly with urgent force, her heart rate jumping, her brain unable to focus on any one sensation except the backs of her legs hitting the bed.

"This would be a very good time for you to suggest that we stop, *koukla mou*," Kristos rasped as he lifted his head from hers, his eyes looking slightly dazed. "If you do, I swear I will let you go and not continue—"

"I don't want you to stop," Em blurted, shocked at the need in her own voice. She had no idea if that answer startled Kristos, but he responded with a growl of his own, lifting her and settling her back on the bed, laying her out flat while he pressed the entire length of his body over hers, both of them sinking into the plush mattress.

Fire exploded inside her, her urgency so intense it was almost a panic. Kristos moved quickly, his hands shifting down the length of her dress until they found the hem, then pressing the sleek material up her thighs to her waist. He lifted off her just enough to pull the dress farther, whisking it over her outstretched arms and then capturing her wrists in his grip as he stared down at her, drinking in her body with his eyes.

In that moment, even through the haze of her own desire, Em died a thousand deaths under Kristos's gaze, her overactive brain going completely rogue in a litany of neuroses. *Am I too thin? Too flabby?* She'd never had a hard body like Nicki's, or Lauren's sleek, languid grace. She too often forgot to eat and get out into the daylight, and now her skin was tinged pink from sun exposure despite trying to remember the sunblock at every turn. She squirmed, embarrassment flooding her, and Kristos's gaze lifted to meet hers. Something almost tender warred with the heat she found there.

"You are beautiful, *koukla mou*." He leaned down to kiss her, his lips soft with promise. "But you are still overdressed."

Eighteen

Kristos fought to keep his own desire checked as he rolled off Emmaline long enough to pull his shirt over his head.

Then her gasp shot through him, burning off his need with a cold jolt of reality. He froze, unable to speak for a moment. *Ah, no.*

She was clearly shocked at the picture he'd just boldly presented her. Of course she would be shocked. Probably even horrified. Why had he not *warned* her? How could he have forgotten?

"My God, Kristos." Emmaline had scrambled off the bed, and he felt her cool hands on his back, where the worst of the scarring caught the moonlight. But her voice didn't hold the revulsion or even the fear he'd heard in so many women's voices. It didn't hold the prurient excitement he'd heard either, or the weird fascination at so much damage on skin that had been expected to be perfect. "How could you have endured so much pain?"

His voice was still stuck in his throat as she turned him around to see his chest, her breath catching again as she pressed her hand to his right abdomen. The scars here were neater, but there were more of them. She placed her hands over them like a benediction, leaning forward to sear his chest with the brush of her lips. "How long ago?"

"Two years." His words were spoken in a strange rasp, and he closed his eyes against the rush of emotion he never expected to stop feeling. He could still see the images vividly, the battle against the minions of Typhon that had taken too many of his own men. The orders he had approved when he should have withdrawn. They'd held their position in the blazing hot trench, sand and smoke clogging the air, but the price had been high. Too high. He'd learned more in that one afternoon than in ten years of training drills. Learned enough to know the cost of guessing wrong. Learned enough to know he would spend the rest of his life at war, honoring the lives of those who had trusted him even to their deaths.

Now he turned his gaze down to Emmaline, catching up her hands against his chest. "I should have warned you," he gritted out. "I didn't mean to shock you."

Her gaze met his, but he couldn't read the emotion in her eyes. She lifted one brow. "These are nothing. You haven't seen the nasty scrape on my ankle from my new sandals. I'm pretty sure you'll faint."

Before he could respond, she leaned up and touched her lips to his, silencing any further apology. "But I think I need to see the rest of you naked now," she murmured, and her hands were at his trousers, unhooking them and sliding them down his legs. She sank down along with them, her mouth trailing over the long, brutal slash that marred his right thigh, the thick ridge of scarring on his calf. "You don't do such a good job of staying out of trouble, do you?" She rocked back on her heels, looking up at him. Now her eyes did speak with clear emotion. There was understanding there. And certainty. "And I do get it. There are some things you can't give up. Not even to be prince."

"No." Something raw shifted in Kristos. He reached for her, pulling her up against him even as he stepped out of his trousers. He laid her back on the bed, following her down into its softness. This was something else he didn't plan on giving up either. Not anytime soon. Emmaline was so impossibly perfect, so delicate beneath his hands that he thought he might break her, but he knew better in the short time he'd had her in his arms. Her fire seemed to emanate from a place deep within her, a fire completely at odds with her sweet nature and gentle temperament.

A fire he wanted to watch burn a little higher, a little stronger.

He reached down and unhooked Emmaline's bra, watching the flare of heat that wasn't entirely desire flush her cheeks. After all she'd seen of him, how could she be embarrassed? Her small, soft body was absolutely flawless, her breasts fitting into his hands as he covered her mouth again, kissing her so she didn't see him closing his eyes as he reveled in the pure physical sensation of her skin against his. Her legs fell apart as he shifted, her lips softening on a groan, and he could feel her body react to the press of him into the vee of her thighs. Despite the fact that he was still wearing his boxer briefs, there was no chance she could miss that he was as hard as a pole. That more than anything should tell her that she had nothing to be embarrassed about.

Just then, he felt her cool fingers on the waistband of his boxers, and sucked in a deep breath as she snagged the edge, pulling them partway down. "Emmaline," he warned raggedly, though what he was warning her about, he couldn't say. When her fingers brushed against his shaft, he shuddered, dropping to his side on the overstuffed bed.

Her cheeks were still flushed red, and he frowned. "Have I made you uncomfortable?"

"Oh, *God*, no. Not even remotely." Still, she pressed her lips together as if to keep herself from saying anything more. When he simply watched her, however, letting the moment play out, it was as if the need to speak grew unbearable for her, as if silence in this moment was simply not something she could endure. "Sorry—I... Sorry." She flopped her other hand helplessly. "This is so stupid. I'm not a virgin or anything, but—"

His brows shot up. Of all the things she could have said, that was not one he expected. But really, what did he know of her? "There would be no shame in that."

"No. Really, I'm not. It's just that it's, um—it's been a while. And I don't know why I'm so freaking *awkward*."

Kristos blinked at her, unable to stop the laugh from rumbling in his chest, even knowing that it drove the flames of embarrassment higher in her cheeks. "Then I'll have to do my best to put you at ease."

Without hesitating, he leaned forward and kissed her mouth. Softly, sensually. Her lips parted beneath his, and she sighed against him, relaxing a little bit. He fought down the surge of triumph. Emmaline Andrews wasn't a conquest to be won. She was a puzzle to be opened, bit by subtle bit. Starting now.

He dropped down to her neck, nuzzling the hollow of her collarbone, relishing the way Emmaline's deep, ragged sigh seemed ripped out of her, one of her hands on his shoulder, the other fisted in the soft sheets. She whimpered but didn't tense when he moved over the gentle curve of her breast, taking it into his mouth and drifting his tongue over it once, twice. The force of her beating heart sounded thunderously loud in his ears, and her heat rose around him, her breath catching sharply as his left hand closed around her right breast, rolling the nipple gently between his fingers.

He lifted his head to look at her again. She was no longer

watching him with wide-eyed anxiety. Instead, her lids had dropped to half-mast, and her mouth was slightly open. "Better?" he asked, and she managed a smile, one that faltered as he shifted his body farther down hers.

Once again, the embarrassment flared in Emmaline's cheeks, but Kristos didn't give her time to process his actions. He dipped down to nuzzle her softly curved belly, easing over her smooth skin.

Everywhere he touched seemed supersensitized, and he forestalled a chuckle as she jumped when he pressed his lips hard against her hipbone. The top edge of her panties lay perilously close to his mouth, and Emmaline's breathing had gone shallow.

Good. Her response fired through him, and he drew his tongue along that silken border. She shifted beneath him, but she didn't ask him to stop. Didn't drop her hand on his shoulder or his head. Still, when he replaced his mouth with his fingers, she almost visibly relaxed beneath his body, her head falling back and her muscles loosening.

He trailed his fingers lightly along, not tugging, not pulling, but stroking down to where the material was already damp. He kissed the top of Emmaline's thigh, pressing his fingers against her heat, and her half sigh turned into a moan, her body angling back, her thighs moving as if she was desperate to sink into the moment and no longer think, no longer process.

He heartily approved of that idea.

"Kristos," she murmured, the words almost a groan. "I want you inside me."

She didn't have to ask him twice. He slipped off her panties with a quick, decisive movement, rolling atop her to cover her nakedness. She sighed beneath the weight of his body, her body shifting naturally to accommodate him, to take him in. But he couldn't do that—not yet anyway.

"A moment, *koukla mou*," he growled, moving up her body and away until he could fumble at the bedside table, where he'd tossed his pants. Beside and beneath him, Emmaline leaned forward, and Kristos's jaw tightened as her lips touched the head of his shaft. Years of military training was the only thing that kept him locked in place as she tentatively pressed her lips against him, taking him into her mouth. When she practically purred, her shoulders dropping, he knew this, at least, was not something she was nervous about. A fact that was not helping him maintain his control, frankly. He snagged the condom, tearing the package open as he withdrew his shaft from her mouth.

She blinked up at him, clearly expecting him to let her play for a while longer. But he was too close for that, barely holding it together as he sheathed himself. Then he reached for her, the desire to bury himself inside her suddenly stronger than he would have thought possible. "Now where were we?" he murmured. "Still feeling awkward?"

Her answering laugh as she stretched beneath him all the response he needed. Tonight was for exploration of the simplest kind.

There would be time to play later.

He'd make sure of it.

Nineteen

E m felt the clash of excitement and desire as Kristos's weight sank again onto her body. Her nerves had settled down at last, and as she wrapped her arms around him, feeling the sinewy muscles that corded his back and dipped down to his narrow waist, she finally, fully relaxed.

He clearly realized that as well. He nudged against her, and she looked up to meet his gaze. "Don't look so worried. I'm fine, ah..."

"Worry is no longer my chief concern, *koukla mou.*"

Then he was easing into her, inch by careful inch, as she shifted beneath him, her body adjusting naturally to take him more deeply. It felt impossibly tight and impossibly amazing at the same time.

Lord, she'd forgotten exactly how good this felt. Not just the pressure of Kristos's shaft swelling inside her, but the entire tactile experience of their bodies tangled together. The weight of his legs on hers, his arms caging her body, biceps flexed, forearms braced. The intensity of a face wrapped in tight concentration, eyes tracking her every expression, her every sigh. Her hands flattened on Kristos's skin, and she felt his warmth and vitality filling her up—and realized for the first time in she didn't remember how long that *Dammit, I really like sex.*

Kristos quirked a smile. "I'm glad to hear it."

Em's eyes refocused. She hadn't realized she was speaking out loud, but she didn't have time to explain as Kristos leaned down and reclaimed her mouth, kissing her deeply as she drank him in. With each thrust, he seemed to be shattering through the months and even years of solitude that had built up a barrier between herself and her emotions, her sensations, and—

"Ohhh, that's really good," she whispered.

"Please, you need to stop sounding so surprised."

"Mmm." Em lifted her legs and wrapped her ankles around Kristos's hips, the action causing him to hiss.

"Emmaline," he gritted out, but she felt a new pressure, an unexpected sensation against her body where Kristos's body connected with hers. She didn't know if it was his position, braced as he was above her, the way he was shaped, how he was moving—she didn't know, but it had the effect of a flint strike. Her eyes popped wide, and she locked her feet together more tightly, her breath hitching in her throat.

Kristos may have asked her a question. She didn't know. She couldn't think. She sank more deeply into the sensations he was creating inside her and allowed them to take over her whole being, knowing her face was relaxing, her back curving, her breathing deeper, fuller, as she sought to meet Kristos stroke for stroke. Her hands now gripped his upper arms, her nails digging into him as she reached up further. She was close, so close! *So impossibly, unbelievably close and—*

She gasped harshly, the sound a virtual cry as she felt the orgasm rip through her more strongly than any release she'd ever had before—it happened so fast! So differently! She bucked up against Kristos, her body riding the tide of pleasure, and then he shattered too, his body going rigid as his own cry burst from his mouth. He surged forward, grabbing Em up in his arms and rolling with her on the bed until they were a tangle of sheets and limbs, and suddenly she was falling—off him, off the bed, and he lurched for her, barely in time to break her fall as she slid down a mountain of pillows and covers and smacked hard onto the cold tile floor.

"Ouch."

Kristos lifted his head then, the moonlight catching his face, his eyes, his wide and triumphant smile. He grabbed her face with both hands and kissed her thoroughly once more, then bounded out of the bed, moving across the tiles in long strides toward the bathroom. As she heard the water splashing in the sink, Em dragged herself up to her feet, wrapping herself in the rich cotton sheets and half crawling, half tumbling back onto the bed. She was suddenly and quite unexpectedly...exhausted. Stretching luxuriously in the bed, she listened to the running water. Her gaze caught the curtains fluttering in the breeze, and she heard the sounds of nighttime beyond the window pane. She felt the lull of sleep calling her as the bed dipped and the presence of warm, vital man surrounded her once more.

"I have already worn you out." Even Kristos's voice was soothing, nudging her toward dreamland as he fit himself against her body, his long fingers smoothing the hair out of her eyes.

"I'm sorry," Em managed, and his laughter rumbled over her.

"Do not apologize to me because I am too much man for you to handle. It happens."

And for the first time in longer than she could remember, Em drifted off to sleep with the sound of her own laughter in her ears.

Twenty

Kristos stared down at Emmaline, more content than he knew he had any right to be. He was used to sleeping whenever he could. But tonight, he was far happier to watch this beautiful and ridiculously neurotic woman relax into the bliss of slumber, her brow no longer furrowed in its slight frown, her eyes no longer watchful or concerned.

She really was lovely, though not in a way he would typically have noticed beyond a second or third glance. Without the flush of embarrassment darkening her cheeks, she looked almost like one of the porcelain figurines his mother kept bringing back from her travels, with pale cheeks and shoulder-length dark hair, her lashes a dusky fringe against her skin. He couldn't see her soft brown eyes now, but he'd already lost himself in them enough to never forget them. A musician who had set aside her music to care for her parents, completely willing and ready to sacrifice for the greater good of her family.

His lips twisted. If he didn't know better, he would think his mother had somehow maneuvered their run-in deliberately, to give Kristos a taste of how a child should properly embrace his or her filial duty.

But Emmaline hadn't completely defected to the good side. He leaned down and dropped a kiss on her shoulder, the pressure of his mouth teasing a smile from her lips that he was certain she didn't think he was observing. Much as he knew that she'd had no idea that he'd tuned in to the video screens downstairs to survey the grounds...but had ended up seeing something entirely unexpected.

He'd watched Dimitri weave in and out of the shadows for only a moment before the movement on a side monitor distracted him, a shifting figure in the upper-floor hallway of the mansion had caught his gaze. He'd watched, transfixed, as Emmaline had paused before her own room, then had looked curiously toward his. She'd seemed to have an argument with herself, and then, with a quick glance over her shoulder, she'd stepped to his door and ventured inside his room, not even closing the door fully behind her.

He'd abandoned his post immediately, kicking off his loafers and taking advantage of the still-open door to sneak up on Emmaline as she'd gazed out the window.

What had prompted her to sneak into his room? It wasn't like she had to pick a lock—nothing in this chateau was locked, as far as he knew. But she'd clearly been seeking *something* here. And that something hadn't been him, since he'd been downstairs. She'd been surprised when he'd come upon her so quickly, but he could tell immediately that she'd also been lost in one of her daydreams. Being pulled out of her own imagination was probably a very commonplace feeling for her.

Still, Emmaline's response to him had been clear enough. She'd wanted to be with him. And he'd been happy to oblige. He looked out the large bedroom windows and couldn't see anything but the inky shadows of the forest far beyond these chateau walls. This room looked out over the southern expanse of Oûros, the forest that stretched eventually as far as the ocean.

It was so peaceful here, in Theo's idyll in the mountains. He hadn't been willing to break that peace, not even when he'd checked his e-mail. His parents had sent him three separate messages, and Cyril had flooded his phone with texts. Only Stefan had been quiet, as he'd said he would be, unless the need was great.

It hadn't been, apparently.

He allowed a small sigh to whisper over Emmaline's shoulder, but she didn't stir. Based on what he'd seen of the television coverage, the story had nearly peaked by early evening. The international media community was a vulture, but it was also a creature of needs. It fed off any carrion thrust in front of it. But if there was no new meat to tear apart, the bird would be forced to fly on and seek its stories elsewhere.

Kristos was sure everyone at the castle was doing their level best to bury any interest in an ongoing story too. Nevertheless, there was no denying the fact that the Accession Ball for his much-vaunted status as crown prince was going to happen later this week. Putting it off would simply feed the rumor mill that there was more occurring in the castle than they'd presented, and that was a nightmare nobody wanted to endure.

But he'd have at least one more day to himself with Emmaline. And considering how much he'd been able to accomplish in the first fifteen hours of their acquaintance, the prospect of at least another thirty-six was definitely good news.

There was still far too much he wanted to know about Emmaline Andrews—enigmatic American, former musician, current caregiver, bedder of terrible lovers before him—and he was determined to get the answers.

"Emmaline," he murmured, leaning down over her.

"Mm?" she didn't so much as respond coherently as force herself back to consciousness out of an innate need to ensure everyone was okay, taken care of, he knew. It was one of her most immediately obvious attributes—not one he necessarily liked, but as much a part of her as were her hair and eyes.

He briefly weighed what he wanted to ask of her and found the questions coming to mind were not at all useful. So he settled on something simple. "What would you like to do tomorrow, *koukla mou?*" he asked.

She answered so quietly, he had to lean forward to hear her words, and then it took him a moment to process what she was saying. "The lake."

He frowned at her. "The lake?"

She made a halfhearted gesture to the window, then snuggled more deeply into the sheets, leaving him so curious that he kissed her again on the shoulder, then moved out of the bed to stand at the window where he'd found her. A scan of the far horizon identified the gleam of water, and he nodded. The lake. She meant Estral Falls.

Of course they could go there.

A sudden chirring of night creatures took his gaze back down to the forest beneath him, and he squinted in the darkness. Dimitri must still be down there, and Kristos leaned out the window to scan the walls and tiled rooftops of the chateau. Theo had not been too concerned with securing his house from on-foot attacks, which meant Kristos could easily escape.

With only a second's hesitation, Kristos moved to the chest of drawers, pulling them open to remove pants and a shirt that he always kept here. His running shoes were in the closet. It took him only a few minutes more to return to the window, stepping on top of the wide sill, steadying himself for a moment. Behind him, Emmaline breathed in a rhythmic cadence. She wouldn't be waking any time soon. And if he could get the jump on Dimitri...

The drop to the tiled rooftop of the next tier of the chateau was short, and Kristos was already running as his feet connected with the hard surface. If Dimitri was anywhere close, he would definitely have heard the noise. But would he make the connection that it was Kristos dropping on him from above? Kristos didn't think so.

Scaling the walls was short work, and he dropped easily into the narrow grassy space between the house and the forest. He stepped into the shadows, going completely still, waiting for his heart rate to slow so he could hear the sounds of forest around him.

Dimitri was definitely not aware of him—or at least, not entirely certain. A soft curse sounded to his right, at some distance, and Kristos took off through the trees. Dimitri had the advantage of night-vision goggles, but Kristos had spent many hours in this forest. He would still be the one with the upper—

A figure stepped out of the trees immediately in front of him, eyes glowing eerily red. Clearly acting on instinct, Dimitri ducked, then plowed into Kristos's chest, sending him flying. They rolled together, and Kristos took a hard elbow to the temple before delivering a roundhouse crack that took his larger attacker off his heels.

The man's curse as he connected with a tree trunk was *very* satisfying. "Since when did you think you could beat me in a fair fight, you big ox?"

"I wasn't trying to fight you." Dimitri blew out a hard breath, doubled over. "If I was trying to fight you, you'd be dead. I heard you lumbering over the rooftops like some sort of vagrant, and my duty is to protect you, even from yourself."

Kristos was on his feet now, his hands loose, his stance wide. "I don't need protecting."

"Yes, you do," Dimitri said. He stood and rubbed a hand over his face, pulling off his goggles. "Here." He handed the set to Kristos, laughing as Kristos grabbed the prize and immediately put it to his face. Through the filtered image, he saw Dimitri staring back at him, his gaze unexpectedly chagrined.

"Ari didn't want to be crown prince either, you know. You two are not so different from each other."

That stopped Kristos. He fixed his stare on Dimitri, then pulled the goggles off. Some moonlight filtered through the trees —enough for him to see his brother's best friend. "He talked to you about it?"

Dimitri shrugged. "Enough. He wanted to find a way to serve in the military with you, despite being the heir apparent. He wanted to put an end to the round of ceremonial ribbon cuttings and foreign travel that did nothing more than remind the world that Oûros existed, when it should be known for something more than its newest prince." He looked away into the forest. "Part of me thinks he knew what he was doing when he flew off in that untested plane. Part of me knows he would never have done that to his family."

"Or to you."

Dimitri snorted. "Me, he would screw over in a heartbeat. And now I've been saddled with Frederick. I never thought I'd see the day when I'd wish to be stuck with you on a mission. He's an idiot."

"Yeah, well, infrared mark his gear. You'll always know where to find him when the trouble starts."

"Ah." Dimitri's worried expression turned into a wide grin. "That makes it official. You'll make an excellent king one day."

Twenty-One

Emmaline woke with a start, not sure for a moment where she was. White, gauzy curtains fluttered in the morning breeze, and sunlight spilled brightly over dark tiles. Her body felt strange, rested and languorous, the kind of feeling she usually only had when...

Her eyes shot wide as the sound of water pouring from a shower finally penetrated her brain. She was in Kristos's room, and they'd—they'd actually—

Holy crap! She'd just met the guy yesterday morning!

Emmaline sat up, her hands going to her face. Her borrowed dress was now neatly folded over the chair, and she frowned down at herself, checking beneath the sheet.

Nope. No clothes.

And Kristos was in the shower. What was she supposed to do here? All her careful planning deserted her, and she felt an unparalleled desire to make a list. Of something. She couldn't just throw on her dress and slut-walk out of the room. That would make their next meeting almost unbearable. Plus, if she encountered a housekeeper or maid or someone like that, she would pretty much self-immolate on the spot. Which would cause a stain, if nothing else.

She might get up and brazenly waltz into Kristos's shower, only she wouldn't really know what to do once she got there. As beautiful as Oûros accommodations were, they were tiny, built to a European scale. Both the hotel shower and the one in her guest bedroom here had been about the size of a coffin and just as inviting.

Or she could maybe go all '40s bombshell and loll back against the pillows? Except most of those were on the floor, it looked like. Maybe she should just fake going back to sleep?

The sound of a buzzing phone made her jerk her head to the right. Kristos's phone. Not the one that he'd given her either. Was there news from the castle?

And had she really just had a thought that involved the word "castle"?

Emmaline had gathered enough sheets around her for dignity when the shower shut off. It was way too late for her to try a loll, but she attempted nonchalant, turning toward the door of the bathroom, as—

Jesus, Mary, and Joseph.

Kristos paused in the doorway, wiping his face and chest with a snowy-white towel before tossing it back into the bathroom. That left only a towel wrapped around his hips, a very *loosely* wrapped towel, slung very *low* around his hips, and baring the most incredible expanse of rugged, battle-scarred male torso she'd ever seen in her life. The ridges of his abs alone were worth a study all on their own, and—

"Good morning." Kristos's words brought her gaze up with a snap. He looked more than a little amused as he strode over to her, putting his big hands on her shoulders and squeezing her gently as he leaned down to kiss her on the forehead. Then he was off again, turning away to pick up his still-buzzing phone. "I hope I didn't wake you, or that this thing didn't."

"I was awake." Em broke off as he held up a finger.

"I'm sorry, I must take this one, of all of them." He tucked the phone against his ear, rummaging through his dresser drawers. Emmaline heard the word *"mana"* and that more than anything else had her out of the bed and diving for her dress while Kristos's back was turned. She didn't know much Oûrois, but in Greek, even she knew that "mana" meant "mom."

She suddenly felt like she was seventeen again, hiding out in her boyfriend's basement while he convinced his mom he was playing video games. What was she doing in a prince's bed?

Scratch that. Nobody could fault her for that. But why had she *stayed*?

She scooped up her underwear and bra and waved to Kristos, pointing at the door. He frowned at her, but she didn't give him a chance to argue. She was not going to have him cut short a conversation with his *mother*, for God's sake, to talk to the girl still hanging out in his bedroom.

Fortunately, there were no maids scurrying through the hall, and Em hurried across the small space and into her room, closing the door behind her as she glanced around. The room looked...completely unused.

What would the housekeeper think? Em moved immediately to the bed and pulled out the sheets, making it look reasonably rumpled, then dropped her underclothes on it. She entered the bathroom and considered the tiny rain-shower-style stall, but turned resolutely away to stare at her face. Lovely. She hadn't had much makeup on, and most of that had worn off, but she still looked bedraggled with her mussed hair and tired eyes. She turned on the faucets and scrubbed at her face, praying that the water would calm her overheated skin.

"Emmal—"

"What!" She whirled, half screaming the word, and staggered against the sink, embarrassment flaring anew as Kristos stepped back with a laugh.

He held out the phone. "Your friend Lauren is on the phone and wants to be sure I haven't molested you," he said, his eyes alight with humor. "I decided this was a question better answered by you."

Oh no. Em shook her head furiously, but Kristos stepped farther into the room, holding the phone out to her. He shook it, and she scowled, grabbing the phone from him before turning back toward the sink.

Of course, the sink was topped with a broad mirror, so she was treated to another view of Kristos's extraordinary shirtless upper body, his grin now threatening to split his face in two.

"Lauren! Hi!" Em said, glaring at Kristos's reflection.

Lauren didn't hesitate. "Are you okay? You can say you have a headache if he's done anything to you."

Em blinked. "No! No, no. It's been wonderful here." She shooed Kristos away, but instead he stepped forward, crowding into her. "We're staying at a friend's chateau or whatever and, I guess, waiting for the story to die down."

"Well, it's dying from lack of oxygen, I'll give these guys that. There hasn't been so much as a royal dust bunny allowed out into daylight since we got here, and we might as well be in quarantine for all the direct sunlight we've seen. Even the party planners for this big Accession Ball thing later this week have all had to come to the castle, which apparently is upsetting the locals because they were looking forward to the return of the royal family to the streets. Store owners are starting to take potshots at the paparazzi."

"That's good, right?" Em stiffened as Kristos lifted a lazy right hand and drew it along her cheek, his own gaze riveted on the mirror. She swallowed any reaction and struggled to keep her voice steady. "Have they given any indication when we might come back?"

"The queen's pretty ticked off that you're not here now, actually. From what I overheard with her just now when she and Special K were talking, I think you'll be back tomorrow. That feels about right. The ball and everything is on Friday, which of course we've been invited to, so you've got to have time to get ready for that."

Special K? Em's gaze connected with Kristos, and she got the reference. That more than anything helped take her mind off the fact that Kristos was leaning forward now to drop a kiss on the crown of her head, both of his thick arms bracketing her in place against the sink.

"And are we still going to be here for the ball?"

"Well...the royal family of Oûros is outfitting us in *designer gowns*—which they will then ship back home for us. So you better believe we're still going to be here," Lauren said with a chuckle. "But—um, Prince Charming isn't anywhere close, is he?"

Em's gaze connected with Kristos's in the glass, and she suddenly understood his deeply focused attention. "I can get him?"

His narrowing eyes told her that he noted her non-answer.

"Yeah, no," Lauren said. "You might want to let him know that Mommykins has six or seven brides-to-be picked out for his review the moment he gets back. It's totally *The Bachelor: Royals Edition* down here, and I swear to God, it wouldn't surprise me if there'll be a rose ceremony before the week is out. Probably would be good for him to be prepared."

Em's brows lifted as Kristos closed his eyes and shook his head. He grimaced, then pulled away from her and left the bathroom. "I'll tell him. Are the others okay?"

"Nicki's about to lose her mind, and Frannie's good as long

as she's by a pool with access to her magazines. They've rigged up this inner courtyard so you're outdoors enough to get a tan, yet sheltered from aerial view at the same time. Pretty cool. Nicki got to use the training facilities here, but she's still ready to climb the walls. Literally."

"And you?"

"Well, the queen's been *most* forthcoming about how to run a castle. You never know when that might come in handy."

Em was still laughing when they disconnected, and she exited the bathroom to find Kristos staring out the window.

"Thanks for letting me use your phone." He took it from her and pocketed it, still looking out over the forest. "You—were you expecting your mother to call?"

"I'd hoped to avoid it. I'm sure she thinks the story of the ball will further take the attention off you and your friends, and I am glad for that, of course."

"But it doesn't take you out of the spotlight."

"That it definitely does not. The actions of the crown prince are always the most interesting for the first few years after he takes up his royal duties, though. I remember my brother saying that."

She hesitated, realizing that they'd never actually spoken about Ari Andris. And what exactly would she say? *Sorry that your brother died?* She'd known this man for all of one day. And yet...

Before she could lose her nerve, Emmaline reached out and touched Kristos's arm. "I'm sorry, Kristos. All this must remind you of losing him."

He covered her hand with his and squeezed it, as if she were the one who needed comfort, not him. "Every day. And it'll get worse before it gets better, as Cyril is fond of saying." He turned and regarded her, his expression serious again. "We could leave today, if that would be better for you. There's no real reason we can't sneak our way into the castle this afternoon instead of tomorrow. Would you like that?"

Startled, Em searched his gaze, hoping he wasn't trying to get rid of her. But when she answered, her response had far less to do with accommodating the needs of a reluctant prince struggling to begin his official life than with her own desperate need to store up every precious memory she could. "Well, let me think. Up here in the mountains, I have you all to myself," she teased. "Why would I go and change that? They can have you for the rest of their lives, right? I can certainly have you today."

His answering laugh made her feel like she'd scored some sort of victory. At least until the gleam in his eyes turned speculative, and his words came out in an accented drawl. "And how would you like to have me, exactly?"

Em couldn't fight the blush, but Kristos was already stepping close to her, lifting his hands to her cheeks and leaning down to drop a lingering kiss on her lips. He tasted like mint and cinnamon, and Em's mind flashed back to how she'd felt in his arms...and in his bed.

"Because, I confess," Kristos continued. "I have some ideas."

Twenty-Two

It was another three hours before Kristos could begin to put his plans for Emmaline into action, though. A soft knock on her door and a lilting voice had interrupted them even as he was considering trying out the bed in *her* room, the maid letting them know that breakfast was waiting for them both on the veranda. After Emmaline had convinced him she didn't need any help dressing herself, he'd met her downstairs a few minutes later, unsurprised to see Dimitri already there, helping himself to the spread of fruits, meat, cheese, and pastries.

Emmaline had been entranced by everything the staff had put in front of her, her enjoyment so pure it made him ache. What was her life really like back in Missouri? Besides the terrible lovers she'd endured?

That thought made him happy, and she turned to him now, her death grip on the roll bar of the ATV relaxing only slightly as they straightened out of a turn and headed deeper into the forest. "Why are you laughing?"

"Because you need to let go of that bar before you hurt yourself. You want to hold on to something, hold on to me."

"I could give her other options that are far more worthwhile." Dimitri shouted this from the backseat, where he'd insisted that he ride as he accompanied them both to Estral Falls. Kristos hadn't informed Emmaline of their destination, and her genuine curiosity told him she had no idea she'd been the impetus behind their impromptu journey. She also, he was learning quickly, had absolutely no sense of direction.

Dimitri entertained her with stories about the local wildlife, and Kristos concentrated on driving the narrow and occasionally blocked "road" that led through Theo's property and then through the national park. Estral Falls was technically on private property, but their trek through the park could be picked up by careful watchers, and that was perhaps one leak too many. Tomorrow morning they would have to bid good-bye to this place or risk Theo's home becoming the center of a media blitz.

When they finally cleared the last stretch of trees and entered the valley of the falls, Emmaline looked up—then stared. Unexpectedly, tears seemed to shine in her eyes, and she looked away sharply, swallowing hard.

Dimitri's startled look at Kristos in the rearview mirror was followed by a roll of the bodyguard's eyes. "This is good!" Dimitri called out, banging the roll bars and causing Emmaline to jump. The sudden downshifting of the vehicle seemed to help her compose herself, though, and she frowned as Kristos slowed the vehicle, allowing Dimitri to jump out easily.

"What are you doing?"

"Dimitri has equipment to test," Kristos said, enjoying the play of emotions on Emmaline's face as she realized the two of them would be continuing alone. "He wanted a more remote location, and we've got it."

"It's certainly that." Still, she settled back in her seat and seemed to relax again. As the light ricocheted off the glassy lake below, she leaned forward. "I think—I think I saw this last night.

From your room. Only there were a lot of dancing lights around it. Is it illuminated at night?"

"Illuminated?" Kristos met Dimitri's gaze again. "Not... usually."

"Or at least, it wasn't the last time we were here" Dimitri grinned. "An excellent opportunity to test the equipment, in any event." He peeled out of the ATV and banged the back fender in a sharp salute, then took off through the forest.

"He'll be okay out here?" Emmaline asked as Kristos put the ATV in gear again and rolled on.

"Dimitri has traveled every inch of Oûros and most of the ocean surrounding her for...a really long time," Kristos said. This wasn't an especially good time to explain how long-lived demigods could choose to be. "He'll be more than okay."

He drove on, pointing out various landmarks until they reached the edge of the lake, a natural rocky outcropping that framed the crystal waters perfectly. "This place has a rich tradition with our family, especially since it is one of the few nonpublic treasures of Oûros that we don't own."

"Someone owns this? It's not a national park?"

"No, despite long generations of lobbying. But in return, it remains pristine and cared for, and that has value too."

"It's stunning." Emmaline's awed voice made him unaccountably pleased, as if he'd given her a present she'd never expected.

"We have only a few hours before Dimitri finishes his work, then he'll be back to demand lunch and bore you with more of his stories," Kristos said. "So here." He reached into the back and picked up a small cloth bag. "Change." He tossed it to her.

She frowned, opening the bag. "You can't be serious."

"I know you're a good swimmer, or you wouldn't have held up so well in the open water," he said. "And I promise you, away from the falls, the water is warm, and there are no unexpected currents to worry about. The falls that feed this place empty into a river at the far end of the pool, but the opening there is narrow, and you won't even notice the water moving in that direction. You'll be safe." He shrugged. "Or safe enough."

Emmaline narrowed her eyes. "Well, do me the courtesy of turning around or something. God only knows what size bathing suit you put in here."

Kristos looked on approvingly as she pulled out the two-piece suit—vastly different from the functional red tank suit she'd worn at the beach.

"Really? Strings?"

"One size fits most," he offered. But per her instructions, he turned away and pulled off his own shirt, aware from the sounds behind him that she'd stopped to watch him do so. He unbuckled his pants, and she started scurrying again, only to stop once more when he removed both his pants and briefs and strode naked toward the water. He didn't stifle his grin as he stepped up on the rocks. "It's deep enough to dive here, but be careful of the bottom. It can be rocky."

Whatever response she gave was lost as he plunged into the crystal-clear pool. By the time he surfaced, Emmaline was at the water's edge, looking dubiously over the side. "No matter how I hit the water, this thing is going to come flying off me," she grumbled, tugging on the hem of the suit. It looked, as he'd expected, absolutely perfect on her. But it would look much better off.

"I'll watch for it."

"I bet."

Surprising him, she took a few steps back from the pool, then raced forward, hurtling over him and curling her body into a ball such that she landed with a tremendous splash. The burst of water had him turning away, and by the time he spun back around, she was stroking hard and sure across the water, toward the falls.

He propelled his body forward to swim after her. The sun on his back, water sluicing around him—it was as if he had been granted another unexpected reprieve. Whenever he thought of Emmaline in the years to come, he would always think of her as this: a final reprieve between the life he'd been born to live, and the life he was forced to take on.

Twenty-Three

Emmaline surfaced in front of the crashing sheet of water. Estral Falls was a pretty straightforward waterfall, a torrent spilling over sheer, high cliffs.

As she regarded the watery wall, Kristos barreled into her and answered her question about what lay beyond the foaming falls. They burst through the cascading water into a narrow, tranquil pool beneath filtered sunlight, framed by cliff walls. Kristos turned with her in his arms, his head cocked as he peered up into the shadows. Did she hear a faint sound of giggling?

"What are you looking for? Is there anyone else here?"

He shook his head. "Not for a very long time. But rumor has it that this was once a favorite location of the naiads, when they wanted a break from Olympus."

"Naiads!" Emmaline peered upwards, as if she could see one of the slender water nymphs dancing in the filtered sunlight. "Are they friendly?"

"They are—but shy. We don't like to disturb them, unless it's really important."

She shot him a look, wondering if he was making fun of her,

but Kristos's expression remained open and curious as he studied the rock wall.

"It's been a while since I've come here," he finally said, glancing back to her as his treading stopped. "Don't kick hard—the rock juts out to form a ledge, and it will damn near break your feet if you aren't careful."

Em braced her hands on his arms as she tried touching down. She could reach the bottom, but not easily. "I'm not quite tall enough," she spluttered, coming up for breath.

He grinned. "I guess I'll have to hold you, then."

Before she could say anything else, he dipped his head toward her. At first, he kissed her lightly, almost as a friend, then his arms tightened and he pulled her close. With the buoyancy of the water, Em lifted her legs easily and locked them around Kristos—remembering too late that he wasn't wearing swim trunks. His dark golden eyes flashed as she pressed up against him.

"You're still overdressed. This is becoming an unfortunate trend."

"It's your fault for choosing such sturdy swimwear for me." Em circled her arms around his shoulders and leaned back from him. "I totally thought it would—hey!"

Kristos's right hand returned to her side, his left smoothly drawing the remains of her swimsuit bottom out from between her legs. "Another benefit of the string bikini," he murmured as he tossed the suit toward the falls. "Easy access."

He shifted back against the smooth cavern wall then, in an act so unself-conscious she wondered, fleetingly, how many women he'd brought up here over the years. She didn't kid herself into thinking she was the only one. Prince Kristos might have been the younger brother of the royal pair of heirs, but he was fierce and hot-blooded, and his body—*God, his body*. He'd been so worried about her reaction to his brutal scars, but how could anyone not be impressed by the evidence of his strength, his intensity, his dedication to his country? He was a walking dream come true.

And she was in his arms.

"Do I want to know what you are thinking?" Kristos's gaze was hard upon her again, and Em tilted her head back.

"Maybe I was wondering what was taking you so long," she said, laughing as his eyes widened in surprise. "Marauding prince, visiting maiden, magical lake, disappearing swimsuit..."

"It definitely seems like a situation to be taken advantage of."

They both seemed to shift at the same time, and then the hard length of Kristos's shaft nudged up against her, exactly where he needed to be, and her body was more than ready for him despite the strangeness of the water all around. As time seemed almost to suspend in place, he slipped in and out of her body slowly, adjusting perfectly when she sighed and angled herself to take more of him inside. Still, with another shift he seemed to shudder, and he clamped his hands on her hips, closing his eyes and tightening his jaw with such focus and concentration that it took her a moment to realize why.

No condom.

She closed her eyes as well so he wouldn't see her surprise—or the completely non-PC sense of triumph that surged through her. They weren't using protection. And *she* was always the careful one, with all those dotted i's and crossed t's. She chose her boyfriends with equal care, and what they lost in the excitement department, they made up for in the safety zone.

But Princess Emmaline Aphrodite Grace didn't have to worry about things like safety. Not with a vaunted prince of the realm.

"Are you worried, Emmaline?" Kristos murmured. "I won't let things get that far."

"Oh, really?" she teased, though hearing him speak her name in his heavily accented voice made any ideas of safety completely unappealing.

"Really. But you, on the other hand, should feel free to go as far as you'd like." He shifted her weight to one side and slipped a hand between them, chuckling as she tensed.

"You don't like to be touched?" As he spoke, he pressed his fingers against her sex, just above the point where their bodies met. At the unexpected pressure, her body constricted around him, heightening the sensation and causing her to suck in a shaky grasp.

"I like—yes. I like to be touched, God—stop that."

He chuckled. "I've always been very proud of my understanding of English, but you lost me there." He drifted his fingers over her thighs and back to the center of her, brushing her clit and moving on despite her sharp intake of breath. As he continued the slow underwater exploration of her body, he swelled within her, his hips thrusting smoothly and rhythmically, carrying her higher on a tide of need. When he returned a third time, he didn't stray.

Em bent up to him as he pressed his fingers home, his shaft seeming to thicken further, and the delicious pressure building within her suddenly became too full—too great. Too much to manage with the strange buoyancy of the water and his fingers *right there*, the sensation of him surrounding her body, becoming one with her in every sense of the word. She shattered in his arms and he held her, his legs braced, his arms locked, his jaw working. His rough gasp of urgency made her feel like the most powerful woman in the world as she clenched around his shaft, the crash of water streaming all around them.

"Emmaline!" Kristos managed, and her head snapped up again, her dazed eyes finding his. Instantly, she realized he was shaking—his body practically vibrating against hers.

"What's wrong?" She immediately tensed up, and his hands gripped her so hard, she suspected they'd leave a bruise. "What did I—did I do something wrong? Did I hurt you?"

"Move...very slowly. Backward."

Awareness flared through her. "So I *do* have some effect on you."

"Some," Kristos gritted out. "More than you will want if you are not very, very careful."

Em considered that. The tiniest, most perverse corner of her mind urged her to be even wilder, more dangerous than she had been already, but she instantly rejected the thought. She slid backward until she felt Kristos's shaft slip free of her body, but when he turned away from her to sag against the cliff wall, panting like he'd just completed a marathon, she wasn't about to let him recover so easily.

Taking advantage of his heaving lungs, his shivering distraction, Em moved behind Kristos, then curled her hand around the hard planes of his hips. Before he could shift, her questing hand found his shaft. When she wrapped her fingers around it, he straightened, as if suddenly realizing he was trapped.

"Emmaline." His voice was harsh.

"What—you don't like to be touched?" She threw his own words back at him as she drew her palm along his shaft, but as Kristos sighed in tight frustration, she wanted—needed more. She needed him inside her, whatever way she could get him. Em looked beyond him to the fall of water.

"Kristos? Would you do me a favor?"

His laughter sounded wrung out. "Anything."

"Close your eyes?"

Frowning as she turned him, he nevertheless closed his eyes and allowed her to move him away from their ledge, splashing deeper into the shimmering pool as they neared the curtain of the falls once more. One of the large stones had been worn to a slant under the torrent, and as mist billowed up all around them, she treaded water, pushing Kristos forward. "Open your eyes now."

He did, his hands bracing on the rock as water cascaded down, his gaze confused as it locked on hers. "What are you doing?" he demanded. But when she moved his body up against the rock, farther out of the water, he understood her intentions, and he grinned. "This is *me* granting *you* a favor?"

"I like it when you grant me favors."

Power pounded through her with the same force of the water crashing around them. Kristos moaned in a guttural sound of pleasure as she positioned herself in front of him, pressing close, lifting herself out of the water to take his shaft into her mouth. It was still thick and heavy, and she thrilled to the realization that *she* had done this to him, that without a doubt he *wanted* her, at least for now—even if only for now.

Because now was enough, she decided. Now was more than enough.

Em slipped Kristos's shaft into her mouth, then completely withdrew, freeing him to press her lips to the inside of his thigh. She watched his muscles spasm beneath his skin, saw the clenching of his fist, but to his credit, Kristos neither stopped her nor urged her on. He let her explore his body as he'd explored hers, as if he could wait the rest of the day for her to finish him.

Twenty-Four

If she didn't put her mouth back over his cock soon, he was going to explode.

Kristos tightened his jaw and fought to keep from swearing as Emmaline traced kisses he could barely feel over his thighs—and then his eyes almost crossed as she laved his sac with her tongue, the pressure of her hand coming up to carry its weight as she shifted higher again. Her feet must have gained purchase somewhere, because as she fitted her mouth once more over his cock, she lifted her right hand as well, her fingers encircling the base of his shaft in a tight hold.

That about did it. He'd already been wound up by plunging into Emmaline without protection, the feel of her body filled with his better than he could have imagined. And now, what she was doing to him...

Emmaline seemed to sense it too. She began to move in a sensual rhythm, taking him so deeply into her mouth that her lips touched her fingers, then moving back and forward again, back and forward, until the blood pounding in Kristos's head matched the thudding of his heart.

This sure as hell wasn't the first time a woman had placed

her mouth on him, and yet he felt like he might as well be a frantic teenager the need built in him so quickly. Then again, a few short minutes earlier, he'd watched her break in front of him with a kind of transported ecstasy that he'd never seen before. It was as if she'd allowed herself to think of nothing but the sensations she was feeling, sensations he had caused—had felt as he'd filled her to the brink, her body as tight around him as her mouth was now. A mouth that was hot and wet and perfect and—

He convulsed with a ragged cry, Emmaline and his need and desire all fusing together for an impossibly long moment of crystal clarity. It was quite possibly the best orgasm of his life, or of anyone's lifetimes, anywhere. Dizziness swamped him, his sight flaring with pinpricks of light, his heart pounding in his ears. He felt like he'd died and gone to heaven.

Hell, maybe he *was* dead.

Either way, he wasn't going to be found lying dead on this goddamned rock. With the last of his strength, he pushed Emmaline off his body and slid, almost boneless, into the crystal pool.

After a long moment of blissful weightlessness, a soft giggle somehow reached his ears through the fog. Kristos pawed the empty water, reaching for Emmaline, knowing she would be exactly where she most needed to be. On his second swipe, his arm encountered her shoulders, and he pulled her to him, still refusing to open his eyes.

"Are you treading water in your sleep?" she asked in a mock whisper. "Do they teach you that in your military?"

He opened one eye. They were both moving in the water almost lazily, the combined strength of their legs keeping them afloat. "Our military training is very specific. Anything that allows us to come in contact with beautiful women, we consider to be a tactical advantage."

"I'll bet you do."

She looked so impossibly perfect that he was tempted to show her a few more of his training maneuvers, only his body felt like it had been shot full of some kind of drug. If he'd had to walk right now instead of merely float, he didn't think he could have managed it.

Instead, he drifted, reveling in the feel of Emmaline as she sighed and snuggled close. He'd met this woman only a day before. In another day's time, he would return her to her friends. In two, he would see her—probably for the last time—at a ball where he was supposed to play host to the daughters of allies and family friends who actually thought they wanted to marry him.

It was all completely insane. But for now, he didn't have to worry about any of it.

"Kristos."

He looked down at Emmaline, his heart shifting oddly at the frank admiration in her eyes as she gazed at him. "What is it, *koukla mou*?"

"Why do you love it so much, specifically? The work you do in the military?"

He could deflect the question, he knew. There was no reason for her to know, none for her to pry, and her natural reticence would flare up immediately if he showed the slightest irritation. But he found that he wanted to share something more with this woman, some piece of himself that was his alone to give. He tightened his hold on her, turning them both in the water.

"My entire existence is made possible because of Oûros. Because of all who have come before me and guarded—and kept our country safe. I owe my life, the lives of every one of my family and friends, to people I will never meet. Serving in the military, pledging my life to ensure the safety of my country, it's the only thing I've ever wanted to do, to honor those who've fought before me. The thing I was meant to do."

"You've suffered a lot because of it, though."

"I've not suffered anything." His arms firmed around her body, but she didn't try to break away, didn't try to shut him down, even though the conversation was perhaps not what she expected. "The scars on my back were the exit wounds of gunshots I took on a day where a third of my unit died fighting the army of our enemies. My soldiers and their families were the ones who suffered. I lived. My leg was clipped by shrapnel in another firefight, but I walked away from that battle too. Others didn't. Still others remain in harm's way even now, while I come home to a castle filled with *photographers*." He didn't fight the snarl in his tone as he said the last word. "To smile and dance and bow. I have no purpose here. I will never have a purpose here."

"So why are they asking you to do it? Isn't there anyone else who could serve as prince? A cousin or—"

"Frederick." Kristos grimaced, imagining Cyril having to train the crown cousin in matters of diplomacy. Then again, how did it make more sense to allow Frederick to rise within the military ranks, where he could cause real damage versus just upsetting some minor diplomat visiting on holiday. Still, even as Kristos imagined that possibility, he saw again the weariness of his father, the almost manic cheer of his mother. They believed Kristos's role was as a figurehead. *How do I know they aren't right?*

"Frederick, then." Emmaline leaned up and kissed Kristos firmly, her bright manner instantly pulling him out of his gloom. "He's probably a handsomer Prince Charming anyway."

Kristos barked his laughter as Emmaline darted away from him. They splashed once more through the wall of water and angled back toward the ATV, Emmaline's voice so filled with joy that he didn't wait for her to order him out of the water to reclaim her clothes. Their bags were suspiciously close to the water's edge, and he shook his head as he pulled on his shorts, not bothering to look for Dimitri. The guard was many things, but subtle wasn't one of them. His reasons for coming on this adventure had nothing to do with testing equipment, Kristos knew, and everything to do with not letting another prince out of his sight. Even if the prospect of finding a few stray naiads was enticing, Kristos doubted that Dimitri would leave him and Emmaline alone for long.

How long had Dimitri stayed up, sleepless, in the days and weeks following the disappearance of Ari? How much had he blamed himself for not anticipating that the crown prince of Oûros would take off in a plane filled with experimental gadgetry, not willing to wait for his bodyguard to return to escort him?

It had been a long, hard year for Dimitri, and one devoid of happiness. Kristos was not about to make things difficult for him now.

Well, not any more difficult than the man deserved on general principles.

He returned to the edge of the water, setting down the bag and tossing Emmaline's shift to the rock. "It will dry fast if you want to dress in the water."

"Such a gentleman." Emmaline snagged the shift and pulled it over her head as she scrambled out of the water, giving Kristos only the briefest of glimpses of her bikini-less hips as she did. She finished dressing as he lay back on the rock. "What will you do when your neighbor accuses you of littering his property with partial bathing suits?"

Kristos shrugged. "He's used to it."

They sat there talking a good half an hour more, a surprise to Kristos, since he damned well knew that Dimitri was near.

Still, he would take it. By the time the bodyguard did finally arrive, coincidentally just as Emmaline was pulling out food for their lunch, the sun was high in the sky. It was another gorgeous summer day, so typical of June in Oûros, and Emmaline seemed to have come alive—as if the water of the Estral Falls had worked their magic on her, finally drawing her out. Then again, how was he to know that this was not her natural way? Perhaps her nerves and embarrassment were a shield until she felt comfortable, but once she let her guard down, she was laughter and sunshine and music.

Even now, she was looking at Dimitri as if he was some kind of superhero. "You're the actual captain of the guard *and* a bodyguard? How do you do both?"

"Poorly," Kristos put in as Dimitri waved him off.

"He is jealous. The Crown sees fit to put me where they have the greatest need. I am currently stationed in the capital city and have had to slow my pace to keep this one out of trouble for the past year. Now that he is moving into his royal status, I will be able to focus on my own men."

Kristos snorted. "You'll be able to focus on my useless cousin, you mean. So don't get too comfortable."

They stayed longer than they intended in the beautiful sunlit park, though Dimitri's eyes continually scanned the horizon. Still, no one disturbed them. It looked like the place hadn't been visited in years, though Kristos knew that wasn't true—he'd come here himself recently, after all. But their mood grew increasingly more somber as they drove back through the heavy forests, and he felt an uneasiness creep over him that was only partly due to Dimitri's vigilance.

Something didn't feel right suddenly. Something was coming up on him too fast.

Emmaline seemed to notice it too. She chattered brightly for half the way home, demanding to know the history of Oûros, its greatest accomplishments, and the prowess of its military. She stared wide-eyed when he explained that some of the people in the mountains never ventured down to the sea, as if defining the borders of their tiny kingdom would somehow shatter their understanding of their place in it. She nodded sympathetically when he talked about the brain drain of universities calling Oûros's best and brightest students abroad—some of them only to return many years later as tourists to their own birthplace. She made him see Oûros through the eyes of a newcomer, which made him love it all the more.

But even she fell quiet as they broke out of the forest to the more well-used track that led onto Theo's land. Evening had fallen on the mountains, and the night pressed close, but the sounds of the darkening forest were lost to them as the ATV ground its way along. Then the trees cleared for a moment, and Emmaline turned her gaze to the chateau.

Her eyes flew wide. Behind him, Dimitri cursed.

"They've lit it up like a signal flare."

Without saying anything further, Kristos angled back into the forest, killing the engine as they stared at Theo's home. A helicopter with its call letters slashed across it in English and Oûrois circled the area, shining a light down on the beautiful mountain home.

"I don't suppose that's the ONSF coming to check in on us?" Emmaline's hand was tight on the roll bar of the ATV, though they'd stopped moving.

"Those call letters are from the main network in Oûros." Kristos scowled at Dimitri. "Who leaked?"

"Maybe no one. The story was dying, but it's such a good one, it might deserve an extra shot at coming back to life. Imagine the coup if a reporter found the missing prince and Princess Aphrodite after all." He slid Kristos a wry glance. "We do have a habit of misplacing those two."

A second helicopter lifted over the horizon, and they all reflexively ducked. But the pair suddenly banked and angled away to the northwest. "A sweep, then, nothing more," Dimitri said, satisfied. "They're probably hitting every chateau ever associated with the royal family. But though they have left, we can't be certain it's for good. They've doubtless left a drone or two behind."

"Drones?" Emmaline gaped at him. "In the air? To spy on us?"

"It's not so surprising. A sweep with a reporter makes sense because you can report on the spot if you find something. But leave a drone behind to record images, and you can keep eyes on a location for a lot longer."

"But how is that legal?" she asked, aghast. "This is private property."

Kristos tightened his jaw. "The laws haven't kept up with technology," he said. "Theo owns the ground, not the sky above it. He's a private citizen, not government." He passed a hand over his face. "But if you are right, Dimitri, then what? We make a run for it?"

Dimitri pulled the blankets aside, revealing two additional containers snugged into the ATV. "We have enough gas to get us wherever we need to go. But the best location is Melios, two clicks down the mountain. I'll call ahead. Think you can get us there in the dark?"

Kristos popped the center console of the vehicle, hauling out Dimitri's night-vision goggles. "You weren't the only one who came prepared."

Twenty-Five

E m dug her fingers into her seat harness, trying not to grab for the roll bar every time Kristos swerved from one patch of utter darkness to the next. Dimitri, behind them, was working an app on his satellite phone that seemed to be some sort of a special-edition compass, warning not only of directional changes but of major topographical features, which Kristos recited back to him as he saw them come up. They were crashing down the far side of the mountain without the benefit of roads, but her dread had less to do with fearing they'd end up dead in a ditch, and more with returning to the real world.

It wasn't fair. She wasn't ready yet.

She turned her head resolutely away from Kristos and stared into the utter blackness, unsure of how much detail he could pick up with his otherworldly night goggles. She knew she should be happy to be reunited with her friends, but today had been so extraordinary because it had actually seemed *normal*. Just three people enjoying a day at the lake.

The fact that the lake had been the private property of a multimillionaire, and her picnic mates had been a prince and his bodyguard, was beside the point. Kristos and Dimitri had talked about their shared battles, the work they were doing with the new recruits, their plans for upgrading the military's training and technology. He'd come alive with his friend, and she'd never seen someone so unselfconsciously passionate about his work. She'd reveled in his excitement, and thought she would never tire of his stories—his sudden, bright laughter, his thoughtful silences. By the time they'd left the falls, she'd felt more relaxed than she had in years. Since her parents' accident, surely. Probably quite a while before.

She rubbed her thumbs over her fingers, which, as Kristos had noted, were still callused despite her now only occasional play. She'd spent most of her early life bent over her bow, letting the music take her to places she'd one day expected to follow with her feet. The endless practices had seemed worthwhile, however, because she could see her own improvement. There was always more that she could learn, more music yet to discover. Then high school had merged into college, and, almost before she realized it, that had ended too. When she'd been faced with the idea of competing for a professional orchestra, her music had quieted within her. So she had opted for university instead, and only a few short months later, the call about her parents had turned everything upside down.

She'd never looked back, but she'd stopped really looking forward too. She'd stopped performing, she'd stopped practicing. In many ways, she'd stopped dreaming.

And now she was being rushed back into the reality of her life before she could fully process what had happened between her and Kristos these last two days.

Nothing has happened between you, she reminded herself. You were two people who took advantage of an impromptu vacation from your lives. Enjoy it for what it is, then suck it up. Like you always do.

And yet, what if she *didn't* have to suck it up this time? What if she could find some way to make this fairy tale real?

Impossible. She knew it was impossible, and the heaviness of her heart was just something else she was going to have to get used to.

Even the best pieces of music came to an end, after all.

"Am I scaring you?" Kristos's voice shouted over the grind of the ATV, and she turned back to him, peering into his weirdly distorted face with its gleaming red eyes.

"Only by how you look."

Dimitri snorted as he leaned forward. "He gets that a lot. Watch out, Kristos—water."

Kristos whooped as the ATV lumbered across a small stream, but the forest was already beginning to thin, and within another few short minutes, they were rolling into the village. Their ATV was covered with mud, they *all* were covered with mud, yet the few people out on the streets didn't give them a second glance.

"Two streets up, gas station," Dimitri reported. "The car is waiting there."

"You can't expect me to get into any self-respecting car like this," Em protested, wiping a muddy hand down her spattered sundress. "I'll destroy it."

Kristos sighed. "Well, if you must go naked..."

Dimitri barked a laugh as she punched Kristos's shoulder, and they drove the last hundred yards to the gas station. The car waiting for them was a beat-up SUV, but clean enough, and Dimitri handed blankets all around. "I'll drive. You get in the back." He spoke briefly in the fluid language of Oûrois, and the man who apparently owned the car nodded, pocketing money and turning away. Obligingly, Kristos held out a hand and helped Em up into the vehicle. "Hunker down. The trip into the city is only about ninety minutes from here, and Dimitri's already checked in. The castle is expecting us."

"The castle," Em said dully. "Great."

"Shhh." Kristos shifted beside her and opened his arms. "You're shivering again."

"I am?"

His teeth flashed in the streetlights that began slipping across their windows. "I'm almost certain. Let me hold you."

She thought a moment about preserving her dignity, but... *The hell with that.* As Dimitri gunned the engine, she more than ever had the impression that they were closing the door on their fairy tale, and if she could spend another hour in Kristos's arms, creating memories to carry her through her long gray days, why wouldn't she?

She turned and settled against him, and he draped his own blanket around her. "You seem very sad, *koukla mou*," he murmured into her hair. His voice was light, prodding, and she sighed, forcing her darker thoughts away. "Are you not happy to see your friends again?"

"It's only been a day—a little over a day." *C'mon, Em.* What was she, fourteen? She needed to grow up. "I'm mainly not impressed with the idea of seeing anyone while I'm dressed like a drowned rat."

"Hmm. That concern is understandable. Dimitri—"

The two of them spoke in rapid Oûrois, clearly in an argument. "Dimitri thinks you worry too much," he said in an aside as Dimitri railed on, and dropped a kiss on her forehead before arguing some more.

"Dimitri doesn't have to face an inquisition by three curious women."

Kristos's arms tightened on her, and after another few sharp interchanges, he spoke again. "You'll stay in the royal apartments tonight. No one but my parents will know we've returned."

Em was glad he couldn't see her face. *Oh, like that's a reprieve?* Instead of being presented to her friends at her worst, she'd get to meet his *parents?*

Kristos chuckled as if reading her mind. "And *they* will not be informed until we've arrived through the military barracks. It is unorthodox, and the barracks are probably being watched, but that's why we have Dimitri. Once in the barracks, there are showers, and we'll have fresh clothing for you. I trust that will make you more comfortable?"

Tension seemed to sluice out of her. "Much." What was it about a hot shower that somehow made everything better?

"Excellent." Kristos seemed almost excessively pleased with the situation. Did he find her reluctance to meet his parents funny? And why was Dimitri so annoyed? Surely both men could understand her not wanting to show up covered in mud as her first impression on a monarch.

But Kristos's arms were tight around her, his lips at her ear, and he spoke to her in his language from time to time as they watched the lights go by. He could have been reciting the ingredients to his favorite sandwich, but Em didn't care. It seemed as if, wrapped in blankets, hurtling along the darkened highway, they were in their last, brief time out of time.

At one point, she reached for his hands, and they interlaced fingers. She truly felt like she *was* fourteen again, riding with a hundred other kids to one of dozens of orchestra competitions, staring out the window and wondering what the world would hold for her whenever the lumbering yellow bus reached its final destination. Even way back then, she'd been a daydreamer, clasping her own hands together tightly, imagining what could be.

Only now she was clasping Kristos's hands. His fingers were

warm and rough and vital, and she fought to sear the impression of them into her memory. There would be so much she needed to remember from these short days. Perhaps the room they put her in tonight would have paper and pen—something. She didn't want to forget any of it.

At length, they slowed, and Em looked up, squinting through the tinted windows as the streetlights seemed to multiply exponentially. Dimitri's voice was clipped once more, professional. "We're coming up on it now—no one move, not even when we're through the gates. This isn't exactly a standard military vehicle. Anyone with half a brain will know something is going on."

Kristos snorted. "And it would have been so much better to approach the castle proper in this truck."

"It would have made sense to enter the delivery section, yes. That's where the staff report—not through the barracks, which are currently of extreme interest to the media."

"No showers there."

"Oh God, I'm sorry." Em tried to struggle upright, but Kristos held her in place. "I didn't think about that. I don't have to shower."

"Every choice is calculated risk," Kristos said. "You'll get used to it."

Still, Em held her breath as they rolled to a near stop at the gate, the metal barricade already sliding open as if to let someone else pass. Sure enough, an enormous military truck rumbled out of the opening as they approached, its muffler sounding in desperate need of repair.

"*That* is your plan?" Kristos asked, his head turning slightly from their huddled position. Em could see the media vans on either side of the street, but strangely there was no one in sight to watch their approach. "To deafen them into submission?"

"We punctured the mufflers and started sending trucks out

an hour ago," Dimitri said, his eyes focused on the narrow approach. He barely avoided clipping one, then slipped into the gate before a second one lumbered past. "After the first four, the paparazzi started sheltering in their vehicles. By the seventh, they stayed there. We are now on the tenth." His teeth flashed in the rearview mirror. "And we are running out of mufflers."

"You'll keep it up?" Kristos's voice betrayed his amusement.

"For another half hour. But so far, so good. We're in safely, and perhaps unnoticed. Only time will tell."

They moved quickly across the courtyard and into a large garage, then Dimitri cut the engine. Men filed out as they entered—not in a rush, but clearly under orders to depart the area. Em didn't have a chance to marvel at their evacuation, though, as Dimitri hopped out of the vehicle and opened her door, reaching for her. Kristos shed his blanket though she still clutched hers around her, and marched with them into the deserted corridor. No guard stood watch here, and after a dozen steps, they halted in front of a room marked with a small placard in Oûrois.

"I'll watch over her," Kristos said, and Dimitri rolled his eyes.

"I'm sure you will."

"Really, I'm good now," Em said, pushing through the door. She hadn't moved three feet into the room, however, before she understood the new problem.

It was a shower room, all right, but she'd clearly entered on the boys' side of the barracks. Stark metal showerheads hung down from the ceiling at even intervals—and nothing else.

"Umm—"

"More efficient this way." Kristos's voice floated out to her as he flipped on a switch. Water drizzled, then pounded down from one of the nearest showerheads. "I needed to shower too."

Twenty-Six

Kristos gave thanks for every hard turn of the ATV and the unusually prolific rainy season as Emmaline gave up the last shred of her dignity and shucked out of her muddy sundress and marginally cleaner underwear, dashing forward to stand under the rush of steaming water. He would never be able to shower in this room again without the image of her, naked and laughing, reaching up to untangle the snarl of her hair. He grabbed a thick bar of soap from the dispenser and strode over to her, his own clothes left behind in a puddle at the entryway.

Dimitri would deposit fresh clothes inside the door, but the bodyguard's warning had not been made lightly. It would not take long for word of their arrival to reach Kristos's parents. If he didn't want to explain why he was holding a naked woman in his arms in the ONSF royal barracks showers, they needed to move quickly.

Fortunately, speed would not be an issue for him.

Pushing Emmaline's hands away from her head, he stepped into the pounding spray himself and held up the soap to the water, squeezing it as it softened to pour over her hair. When she was coated with suds, he dropped the bar into her hands, working his fingers through her hair as she moaned beneath him, the sound bringing him to full and almost painful readiness in the space of a heartbeat.

"All that and you do hair too?"

"The work of a prince is never done." He fanned her hair out around her, working the knots for only a moment more before he could no longer resist the woman beneath that rich mane. He drew his hands along Emmaline's shoulders. "You got too much sun today."

"I hadn't noticed—oh." She stiffened against him as his hands circled around her and cupped her breasts, their tips peaked. She was facing the wall, and she reached out blindly for support, her hand firming against the cold tile as she pressed back into him, her ass rounding up against his groin.

He couldn't stop the growl from rumbling in his throat. "Emmaline—"

"Calculated risk, right?" She turned to glance at him over her shoulder. "How much time do we have?"

"Enough to do this." Kristos shifted her forward, sliding into her in a movement that was already becoming as essential to him as breath. Beneath him, Emmaline groaned again, one of her hands leaving the wall to cover his as it kneaded her breast.

"Yes," she hissed beneath the sound of the pounding spray. "Oh God, yes."

She didn't need to explain anything more. Kristos pressed into her, hearing her sigh of surprise, of pleasure, her hands now both returning to the tiles, giving her leverage to thrust back toward him, as if she wanted to forcibly take as much pleasure as she could from this moment, his body, his touch.

And he wanted to give it to her.

Kristos's hands locked on either side of Emmaline's hips,

steadying her as he gave himself over to the pound of the water, the thrum of desire, her own half-articulate gasps of pleasure. She was speaking English, he was sure of it, but he could no longer understand her words as he drove into her with greater intensity. There was only the water and Emmaline and his racing need, the swell of it building inside him, heavier and thicker, until all he wanted to do was spill inside Emmaline and fill her to the brink, to own every inch of her, to claim her as his own.

At the last second, however, he pulled out and exploded into the downpour of water, both of them gasping in the deluge, lungs heaving. Before he could think rationally, Kristos reached out and grabbed Emmaline tightly to him, crushing her lips to his as if she could give him her very life's breath. For her part, she clung to him every bit as fiercely, because she knew—*of course she knows*—that everything would be different now, that the two people they were when they'd walked into this room would be replaced by the two people who walked out, their priorities straight, their understanding clear.

But for this moment, none of that mattered.

"Emmaline," he whispered over and over again, kissing her face, her brows, her lips, her cheeks. He held her tightly enough to bruise her, he feared, but she gripped him just as hard, her fingers digging into his back, her intensity equally desperate.

It was she who pulled away first, however. "They—they're waiting for us," she said, and he nodded, pulling her quickly away from the sheeting water as he turned off the flow at the wall faucet. The room seemed instantly too cold without the shower surrounding them, and Em giggled as they dashed over the tile, reaching the pile of towels first, stacked neatly inside the door.

She held up the rich, thick white cotton. "These don't look like military grade."

"Dimitri is ever resourceful." The clothes were equally well chosen. Familiar pants and shirt for him, and a knee-length tunic dress for Emmaline—one that could fit any woman roughly her size, with slip-on sandals to match.

"Seriously, the man has a gift. I'll even forgive him for not including new underwear."

"He values his life too much."

Emmaline laughed, hurriedly towel-drying her hair after she slipped into the shift, then finger-combing it into place as he dressed. He looked up to find her surveying herself critically in the mirror. "Not exactly the way I envisioned meeting the queen."

"And the king too."

"Not helping." She scowled, but to him, she had never looked lovelier, her eyes bright, her damp hair curling around her shoulders.

"Come—Dimitri is probably grinding his teeth to dust. We might as well get the introduction finished, so you can rest. If you're sure you don't want to return to your friends yet?"

She chewed her lip, glancing away from his reflection in the mirror as she worked the last of the water out of her hair. "Do they know I'm here?"

"Not at all."

"Then no," she decided. "They know that I'm safe. They're not worrying about me. Another night won't change that. Unless..." She frowned at him. "Oh, Kristos, I didn't think. Of course it's an imposition to your housekeeping staff to put me up in separate rooms. I don't at all want that. I'm sorry, I can—"

Kristos cut her off with a raised hand. "It is no imposition. In fact, I suspect my mother will insist upon it." He lifted his brows at her. "Just remember, she can be a ruthless interrogator. The only way to get her off a subject is to bring up her charity work—or clothes. Neither of which will work tonight, I suspect."

A knock sounded on the doorway, and Kristos reached for her. "Are you ready?"

The emotions that played over her face told him that she clearly was not, though she nodded quickly. "Of course." She put her hand in his, and they stepped out of the doorway to where an equally tidied Dimitri stood, his expression carefully polite as he raked his gaze over them.

Two palace guards in dress uniform stood behind him.

"Your Highness," he said, gesturing with all pomp for Kristos to precede him. He glanced down at their joined hands. "Unless you want more questions than you can possibly want to answer, you may want to let her walk behind you with me." He glanced meaningfully down the hall, and Kristos sighed. Cameras. Theo wasn't the only one with a penchant for spying on his own household.

He turned and lifted Emmaline's hand to his lips, but she removed her fingers from his grasp almost before his mouth touched the knuckles.

"It's perfectly all right," she said, only a shade too cheerfully. "I won't have to curtsy or anything, will I?"

Dimitri laughed. "Only if you'd like. Most American women shake hands."

They moved down the corridor, and Kristos felt the loss of Emmaline's touch like a physical ache. He shook himself. *She* was reacting with grace and dignity to their changed situation. He should as well.

But he couldn't keep his hands from closing into fists as he walked, no matter who was watching.

It took less time than he would have imagined to traverse the distance to the reception hall, the second of two that the castle boasted and by far the smaller one. Dimitri stopped and turned, glancing down to Emmaline. "They're very excited to see you both," he said, and she nodded in gratitude at his bolstering words.

But as his eyes lifted to connect with Kristos's gaze, his look was plain.

The time for freedom is over.

Twenty-Seven

E m almost swallowed her tongue as she walked into the sumptuously decorated room and took in the two figures standing at the far end, both of them dressed not in gown and crown, as she'd expected, but like well-appointed business professionals.

King Jasen and his wife, Catherine, were an absolutely stunning couple, their regal stature augmented by exotic good looks and thick, dark hair. The only concession to their true station was the queen's delicate tiara. Em tried not to fixate on it, instead clasping her hands demurely—what she hoped was demurely—in front of her and attempting not to stumble.

"Relax. They'll think I ravished you if you don't ease up," Kristos said, startling her, and she blinked at him as he strode the final steps forward to greet his parents.

"Mother, Father, I'm honored to present Miss Emmaline Andrews. She's been gracious enough to endure the results of our first meeting for these past few days, and I'm sure very glad to be back to normal." He turned to her, his expression wry. "Well, almost back to normal."

"Miss Andrews." King Jasen spoke first, and his deep, resonant voice drew Em's attention. His gaze was kind but remote, a diplomat used to maneuvering through shifting waters. "Please accept our apologies for your introduction to Oûros. Normally, our media are not quite so enthusiastic. But we have awaited the accession of a crown prince for a good while now, and the story was ready to happen."

"Of course, Your Majesty." He had bowed to her, so Em inclined her head in a way that she hoped wasn't stupid. Was that what she was supposed to do? She wasn't going to stick her hand out, no matter what Dimitri said.

"Emmaline." Unlike her husband, Kristos's mother held both of her hands out in clear welcome, stepping toward Em with a warmth that didn't quite mask the shrewdness of her gaze. Acting on instinct, Em lifted her hands as well and found herself enveloped in the elegant embrace of the queen of Oûros. "Kristos has been selfish to keep you all to himself, but I've enjoyed meeting your other friends so much."

Em winced. She could count on Lauren and Fran to hold their own, but how had Nicki behaved? Not well, she expected. "Thank you for hosting them. We would have had a far more difficult time of it on our own."

"The media can do so much good, but they can also be exhausting." Queen Catherine tightened her hands on Em's before withdrawing. "And you've seen them on some of their less well-behaved days, I'm afraid. But your adventure took you —where?"

"Theo's." Kristos's words were placating. "We were perfectly safe, and to make sure of it, Dimitri was with us."

"I'm not sure I would necessarily classify him as safe, but very well. And why didn't you see fit to inform us as to your whereabouts?"

Em tensed. Kristos was correct. She got the feeling that his mother enjoyed asking these sorts of questions with the same passion that a bulldog pursued a bone, but Kristos met her head-on. "We suspected that our communications might be compromised. And though we were careful, we might well have been right. Tonight's change of plans was precipitated by media helicopters making a sweep of the area. Theo might return home to find that he has a drone or two hovering, waiting for someone interesting to appear."

King Jasen shifted. "Did they see you?"

"We don't think so. Our entry into the castle an hour ago was a bit more problematic, but even that appeared not to draw attention."

"Such a charming introduction to our own home as well." His mother sniffed. "Stefan would have told us if anything had shown up in the local chatter, but we will leave you two to that discussion. Emmaline looks like she's about to drop on her feet. Come along, dear."

Em nodded and turned to Kristos, surprised when he stopped her by reaching for her hand once more. He brought her hand to his lips and kissed it perfunctorily, but the look in his eye was anything but dismissive. "Good night, Emmaline," he said, inflecting her name with the weight of a foreign word. "Try not to let my mother railroad you."

King Jasen might have humphed, but Catherine swept forward, drawing Em with her. "Oh, enough. Go read your reports or whatever it is you two do when you act like you have the cares of the world on your shoulders. Emmaline and I will see you in the morning."

She turned and led Emmaline through a side door in the room, and they stepped into a long tiled hallway, centered by a thick Persian rug. "I had rugs installed in every hallway in the palace when I first came here," Catherine confided, walking briskly. "I have to be careful that no one creeps up on me unawares, but by the reverse token, I learn ever so much more than I would otherwise, simply by lurking at doors."

At Em's surprised look, she laughed. "The men of the Andris family have many worthwhile qualities, don't get me wrong. But one of their most irritating quirks—of which they are all guilty, including Jasen's father, Jasen, *and* his sons—is their belief that women cannot think of anything more complicated than running a household and overseeing charitable works. Never realizing that those are two very different and valuable jobs in and of themselves, but not jobs that are best served by keeping me in a vacuum. Ah, here we are."

She turned and ushered Em into a room not dissimilar to the one she'd had at the hotel, only far more opulent. Rich red tile gleamed underfoot, brilliantly white furniture fairly glowed in the warm light of faux candle sconces and the very real flames of the gas fire, and she could see the corner of an enormous bed through the far door of the bedroom, a door that stood open and inviting. Sleep clawed at the back of Em's eyes, which surprised her. She hadn't thought she'd want to let this day end.

"I would very much like for you to chat more with me as soon as you've gotten some rest," Catherine was saying, recalling her attention again. "Kristos might have warned you that I am inquisitive by nature, but I assure you I don't mean to pry in the manner of the media hounds." She shrugged elegantly. "On a need-to-know basis, I simply always need to know. It's the only way I can survive such an exasperating household."

Em shook her head. "I'm afraid I don't have very much to tell you about myself. I only met your son yesterday, and quite by accident, as I'm sure you've already been told. I confess I didn't know much about your country at all before Lauren suggested we all take this trip."

"Lauren, yes." Catherine hesitated. "I promised I wouldn't tire you more, but would you like to share a brief drink? I admit I'm not eager to go back to my rooms while Jasen is reading Kristos his rights over whisking you away." Without waiting for Em to answer, she moved over to where several bottles of wine stood on a thick-topped shelf that rested against the wall, the glasses lined up beside them like eager soldiers. She selected a bottle that stood at the center of the collection and poured a clear liquid into two small glasses resting in a bowl of ice, then offered one of those glasses to Em.

Em took it, then followed Catherine to the plush white chairs. She sniffed the clear liquid and wrinkled her nose. "That's strong!"

"*Tsipouro*," Catherine said, settling into her chair. "Definitely an acquired taste, though in this country, you acquire it around the age of five." She raised her glass to Em. "To your safe homecoming."

"Thank you." Em watched Catherine take a measured drink, and matched her as best she could, though her sip was much less assured. She eyed the glass curiously. "This is what Lauren was drinking the other night when she tried to hold her own against a local in some kind of ill-advised contest."

"She told me that story." Catherine's smile was approving. "There's not much that holds her back from doing what she sets out to do, it seems."

"Ha! Definitely not." Anticipating the queen's next question, she continued. "We met in college, freshman year, all of us in the honors wing of the women's dorm. Nicki was in journalism, Frannie was studying...you know, I don't remember what she started out in. But she switched to psychology midway through our first year. And Lauren was business. She always thought she'd go into law, but she switched majors after she realized that the law students weren't all that much fun. Or at least that's what she told us."

"And yourself?" Catherine's brows lifted at the obvious detail missing from Em's story. "What did you study?"

Em tightened her lips. Why was admitting her field of study to these people so difficult? Then again, why should they be any different from anyone else she'd ever met, who seemed to consider the study of music about as useful as the study of migratory dodo birds? "It almost seems silly now that I've graduated, and that's all so far away. But I studied musical performance. Specifically the violin, though I've also played the harp and viola. Not the cello, though it is beautiful. I never had the right reach."

She was beginning to babble, and she eyed her drink thoughtfully. She should probably set the glass down, but it felt right in her hand, round and full, perfectly weighted. It was easier to keep holding it than to set it anywhere anyhow. The small coffee table was not well positioned for that use.

In any event, Catherine was continuing. "Violin! But that's lovely. Do you still play?"

And at that moment, Em was glad for her drink. She rolled the glass in her hand, watching the clear liquid slide almost to the rim, then back again. "Only for my own entertainment these days," she said. She could hear the note of regret in her voice, and she firmed her resolve. "My parents were involved in an accident about a year ago. It was quite severe. My father is finally recovering, his injuries healing, but my mother suffered some brain damage as a result of the collision. It's reversible, they say, but her recovery has been slow. Her mind...is not what it was, and with my father not recovering as fast as he should either, it's been an adjustment." She waved the glass expressively, hoping the rest spoke for itself.

Catherine nodded. "You quit your music to go help them."

"I gave up my scholarship, yes." At the flicker of surprise on Catherine's face, she rushed on, feeling the need to explain.

"Graduate studies. I'd earned a scholarship for advanced musical studies at another university and had accepted when I received the call about my parents." She found herself staring at the glass again, the *tsipouro* forming patterns against the backdrop of her memories.

"That must have been very hard."

"Oh, it wasn't really," she said, her voice seeming to echo in her own ears. "They're my parents, and I love them. My father blamed himself for the accident—still blames himself—and my mother is lost in her daydreams for a good portion of the time. She's happy there, and I believe they're helping her recover as well. She's simply doing it in her own time and way." Em's smile seemed to lose its form on her face, and she forced it to remain steady. "She was the brains of the family, my father always said. It's been difficult on him."

"Difficult on you too, I would suspect."

Em shook her head again. "I have the easy part. My father won't forgive himself for a slip anyone could have made. My mother is trying to find a path she's forgotten existed. That trumps missing out on a few years of music."

"You don't play for them?"

She blew out a long breath. "My father feels a lot of guilt. Hearing me play reminds him of my mother. She thought the violin was the perfect instrument for a prin—" Em caught herself in time, trying to redirect. "Well, what I mean is, she teaches literature at the college level—including a lot of mythology—only she fell in love with fairy tales when she was a little girl. So she became a bit of a scholar on fairy tales and would spin the most amazing stories when I was young, about princes and violins and kingdoms full of music. Most of them, I understand now, were simply her means of convincing me to practice." She lifted a hand to encompass the whole palace. "She would have loved this place, really and truly. When she was young, she traveled Europe and visited any castle she could find. She said she even named me the way a princess should be named."

The queen's brow furrowed. "Emmaline?"

"Not that part, but she considered Aphrodite the princess of the gods, and she was a tremendous fan of Princess Grace, and she decided that Emmaline might one day be a good name for a prin—well." Em stopped herself just in time. *Really? Can I please not embarrass myself any more for one day?* "She always did love a good fairy tale."

"She sounds like a wonderful person." Catherine's tone was warm, her words almost too understanding. "Your father too. His pain at his wife's injury is understandable. Men always blame themselves, even when they've no right to do so."

Em nodded but didn't trust herself to say more. As if sensing her sudden awkwardness, Catherine stood. "I have kept you awake long enough. If you need anything, don't hesitate to ask."

"Of course." Em stood as well, then a sudden thought struck her. "Do you have notepaper I could use? A pen, anything like that?"

Catherine nodded. "Yes, certainly. In the drawer. There are envelopes too, and postcards if you prefer to write something shorter."

"Oh, it's not a letter." Em shook her head, too distracted to explain, despite Catherine's surprised glance.

When the queen of Oûros finally took her leave, however, Em found her pursuit of notepaper and pen still delayed. The thick, creamy stationery was exactly where Catherine had said it would be, but it lay next to a DVD of "Oûros, Jewel of the Aegean."

"You have got to be joking." Em lifted the video out of the drawer like it was some kind of buried treasure, blinking at the images of the castle she herself was staying in, a picture of Jasen and Catherine standing in formal attire in front of a crowd, another of Kristos rigidly at attention in full military dress.

She practically ran to the large flat-screen TV that dominated the sitting room, sliding the DVD in the slot on its side. Clicking on the remote, she took an involuntary step back as already-familiar images filled the screen. The royal residences of Oûros, the king and queen, the tragic death but honored life of Aristotle, and finally, Kristos.

Em's breath caught, and she sat down hard on the couch as Kristos filled the screen. His rich voice spoke in the lush accent of Oûrois, but that was the only soft thing about his presentation. Though the captions that ran at the bottom of the screen were full of hopeful rhetoric, and though everyone around him was smiling gamely at the media assembled before the podium, Kristos might as well be announcing some horrible catastrophe. He looked nothing like the man she'd held in her arms just hours ago, laughing and splashing through the water. His bearing was excruciatingly formal, even more than his military uniform required. His jaw was tight, his eyes flinty and hollow. All of his bright passion was gone, replaced with a surly intensity that seemed almost foreign on his handsome face.

She checked the date stamp as a caption flared at the bottom of the image, and even that seemed impossible. It was only a few months ago! How had he changed so much in such a short time? And who was the real Kristos?

Em curled up on the couch with the images still flashing in front of her. She muted the sound, then traded the remote for a pen and the first piece of stationery. One thing was certain, she wasn't going to sleep tonight anytime soon.

Twenty-Eight

He was never going to get to sleep.

Kristos stared bleary-eyed as his father slid another stack of papers in front of him. "Tomorrow you will be expected to read these and sign them, Kristos," Jasen said sternly. "Ari never took the time to look through them either, and you need to know what it is you're agreeing to."

"What am I *not* agreeing to?" Kristos shoved the papers away. "We've been through three hours of this, and it is everything I expected, which is that my entire life will be now dedicated to the state of Oûros, end of story. So why don't we cut to the chase and discuss what that *doesn't* actually include? Once I become crown prince—and king, though if you die anytime soon, I will hunt you down in the afterlife and kill you again myself—in what areas of my life *specifically* will I still have control?"

Jasen looked as though he were about to snap back at him, then settled back in his chair, contemplative. "I've never considered the matter from that perspective," he said, sounding surprised. "I came to the throne at about your age. But I too had a younger brother, though in that case, no one was hoping he would take the throne."

"Like father, like son." Kristos grimaced, thinking of Frederick. He'd met Frederick's father, of course, and Jasen was right. The apple didn't fall far from the tree. Frederick was only twenty, so they needed to cut him a break, but a more rebellious soldier he'd never met. And a rebellious soldier usually ended up getting other soldiers killed.

Jasen nodded. "It was a shock to my system as well, though I'd been groomed for it since my teen years. All the paperwork, the travel, the endless sessions of the Council. And, of course, the social duties of the role."

"Of course." Kristos twisted his lips. "We can't forget that."

Jasen watched him. "I was fortunate in that I had already met your mother at several events prior to the Accession Ball. It was something of a foregone conclusion that we would marry, though my own mother did her level best to put other women out there in front of me—the best and brightest of Oûros, Greece, and half a dozen other countries as well."

"Half a dozen!" Kristos looked at him, aghast. "You can't be serious."

"I wasn't. She was." Jasen shrugged. "She had a conviction that we needed a new perspective in the royal halls. New blood. To ease her acceptance of my choice in brides, my father created an external counselor role with access to the king and queen, a role that became the EU counselor in the mid-nineties." He shrugged, looking weary but satisfied. "There is always more than one solution to a problem."

"So you already knew you were going to choose Mother. What if you hadn't? What will happen on Friday if I don't make some sort of formal declaration—which is the stupidest, most insane thing I've ever heard of, by the way. Are we going to sacrifice a bull on the steps of the palace as well?"

His father ignored his sharp tone. "If you don't make a declaration, then the media and a good portion of the population of Oûros will set up a Wedding Watch, not dissimilar, I'm sorry to say, to Rome's convocation of cardinals as they prepare to announce a new pope."

"Please tell me you're joking."

"Only slightly. You'll not be barricaded behind closed doors, and the nation won't hold its collective breath until white smoke wafts above the palace, but everywhere you go, everything you do, it will be the very first question. And not just for you but for the women who have been singled out as your primary candidates."

Kristos rolled his eyes. "Do the English princes go through this? I don't seem to recall this level of frenzy."

"The blood of the English does not run as hot as that of the Oûrois. And their king—or queen—doesn't rule the country directly. Your succession plan is arguably a bit more of interest here."

Kristos wanted to argue that point but couldn't. Instead, he poked at the pages in front of him. None of this made any sense. He simply shouldn't be here.

"You never answered the question. Out of all my personal rights that I'm signing away tomorrow, what do I keep? I've already had to bar the guards from stationing themselves outside the bathroom for fear I'll fall into the tub and drown."

"And they listened to you, which is an important distinction. You have the right to mandate your own level of personal security within the castle. You do not have the right to mandate it outside of it, and you will not be allowed to put yourself at unnecessary risk."

"Like Ari and his plane."

His father nodded once. "Had he already acceded to the crown, that plane would never have left the ground. You are allowed to choose your wife, as long as she's approved by the ministers, which is generally a formality."

"How reassuring."

"You're allowed to raise your children as you see fit, and in the event that you do not have a son, your firstborn daughter will be elevated to crown princess when the time comes. Should you have no children, the line reverts to any siblings, offspring of those siblings, then—"

He trailed off, and Kristos finished for him. "Frederick."

"I'm afraid so."

Kristos rubbed a hand over his face. "Anything else?"

"The money of the royal household is yours to spend as you wish, once you become king, but your royal holdings are immediately your own to manage. You can pursue any line of work or hobby you wish outside of your royal duties, provided it does not run counter to those duties. So, no—you cannot rejoin the military, Kristos. Not and run the country as well. Your patriotism is lauded, but the country could not weather another death in the family." He sighed. "Neither could your mother, I suspect."

But the military is where I belong.

Kristos stared down at the stacks of paperwork, not trusting himself to speak for a moment. His entire life, his parents had worked hard not to judge him by the decisions, abilities, or actions of his brother. Where Ari had excelled in school, Kristos had gone after every sport with unstinting gusto. Where Ari had been fascinated with tinkering with technology, Kristos had only been interested in what that technology allowed him to do. He didn't need to build the plane, he'd often told his brother. He simply needed to fly it.

But now it seemed Kristos's entire world was being circumscribed by one fatal act of a man who wasn't even around to explain it. And the most preposterous things being asked of him were clearly the ones of greatest importance to his family and to his people. It was ridiculous—but perhaps no more ridiculous than the idea of a ruling monarchy in the twenty-first century. Or protecting the world against the return of the ancient gods, though they had mercifully seemed content to remain behind their gates these past fifteen hundred years, for the most part. You had to take the good with the bad, he supposed.

And yet.

It was almost dawn by the time he finally made it to his rooms. His bed was turned down but empty. He couldn't see Emmaline, couldn't hear her laughter. When the sun came up, she would be awakened to rejoin her friends, and the wheels of their respective lives would churn on, taking them ever farther apart from each other. Even though he would see her in a few short days at the Accession Ball, she would be surrounded by her friends, her world, her life. Gone from him.

He didn't want to let her go, though. Not that quickly. Not quite yet.

He moved to the door of his room. He'd dismissed his guards, but that didn't mean the palace wouldn't be crawling with the men and women assigned to protect the royal family. Still, his father's words had been clear. Within this very, very narrow scope, Kristos had ultimate freedom.

He planned on exercising that freedom one last time. Tonight.

He opened the door, and a familiar figure lounged across the hallway, leaning against the wall.

"I so knew this was going to happen." Dimitri grinned.

Twenty-Nine

E m rolled over in her opulent bed, unable to sleep, though she desperately wanted to let the smothering tide of darkness take her away. She'd recorded on palace stationery everything she could remember of the events of the past two days—from her first—literal—run-in with Kristos, to his arms around her on the beach, the flight to the chateau, and the beautiful Estral Falls. She'd absolutely omitted any mention of being in his bedroom and what had happened at the falls and in the showers here at the castle, of course. With her luck, she'd leave those pages behind, and they'd end up on the front page of whatever passed for Oûros's *Star Magazine*.

She turned again, then lifted her head, peering into the gloom. Had she heard her door open? She was ragged with lack of sleep, and there had been two guards outside her door when the queen had left her. She'd heard her giving them instructions in Oûrois, but she still didn't know enough to interpret any of the words. Hopefully Catherine hadn't ordered them to come in and kill her, because honestly, she was too tired to care at this point.

The bedchamber the queen had granted her was

extraordinary in every way—other than it was a fully interior room, which meant no windows. She supposed that was typical of a lot of the rooms in a building this big. There was only so much real estate you could mete out, but nevertheless, it gave the entire room the feeling of being a strange sort of cocoon. She wouldn't want to stay here for long. Then again, perhaps that was why it was used for visiting dignitaries. Anything to hasten tedious guests along their way.

She let her eyes drift shut again, sleep finally starting to pull her under with its tempting touch. It seemed to stroll up to her on cat's paws, soft, stealthy, and so, so sweet—

"Emmaline."

Em's gasping scream was cut short by a warm, heavy hand pressed over her mouth, and her eyes snapped open only to have her vision filled with Kristos's face. "Please don't scream," he whispered, trying for stern and failing miserably. "You'll ruin my reputation."

He lifted his hand away, and Em scooted up against the headboard with its overflow of pillows, staring at him, unsure whether to laugh or cry or throw herself at him. "What are you doing here?" she hissed, looking from him to the door. She *had* heard someone enter. "Weren't there guards outside?"

"Apparently, being a prince has its privileges." Still, Kristos hesitated, looking impossibly gorgeous as he stood at her bedside, with his white shirt open at the neck, his fine trousers creased and rumpled. Her wide-eyed perusal of him brought a frown to his face. "I've startled you too much. I'll go. I'm sorry."

"Please don't." Em felt her cheeks flame, but she pushed the blankets down and shifted farther over in the bed, her invitation for Kristos to join her clear. "Can you stay long?"

"Not long," he said. But he was already shucking his shirt, throwing it to the chair beside the bed. His pants and briefs followed immediately after, the action so swift it had Em blinking. Her own nightgown was barely there—a fine white cotton tank-top-style sheath embroidered at the neck and sleeves that she'd found folded neatly on the bed with a note about how it was handcrafted in Oûros. Now it seemed scarcely any barrier at all to the man climbing into her bed, his body making the mattress dip, his hands reaching for her.

"I thought I wouldn't see you again—like this," Em said, surprised at how her voice wobbled.

"I know." Kristos pulled her close to him, brushing his lips against hers. "I decided I couldn't stand the idea of that, and technically, tomorrow is not yet here." He tightened his hold briefly. "Besides, there is still one nagging concern that I cannot put aside."

"A concern." Em managed to keep her hold on semi-coherency as Kristos's head dipped into the curve of her neck. He followed the trail of her pulse down to where it throbbed at the base of her throat, then lingered there, breathing her in as his hands slid beneath her shift and along her body until they closed over her breasts. She sucked in a deep breath as she arched beneath him, and he growled in response before drop-ping to nuzzle her breasts through the thin fabric with his mouth, his tongue. The touch of him with the barrier between them seemed almost more erotic than if she'd been naked, and heat flooded through her, the ache in her core almost a living thing. "Kristos," she gasped.

He shifted down to place a kiss on her belly, and his fingers curled around the edge of her panties. Em groaned as his touch trailed down to cup her intimately, his fingers exploring the soft dampness.

"That is becoming my favorite sound," he said, and his breath against her sensitive skin mesmerized her as he leaned down to kiss the base of her belly, the inside of her thigh. "There is nothing about you I do not wish to know, Emmaline, nothing I do not wish to taste or touch. My concern is over everything I may have missed."

"Oh," Em breathed out shallowly, her heart pounding, as Kristos pulled her panties down her legs and spread her legs farther to allow him to position himself more completely. She felt exposed, vulnerable, but when he kissed her again on the inside of her knee, she also couldn't stop her body from arching up, subconsciously trying to guide him to where she most needed him to be. "Oh dear God." Em jolted as she felt the slow slide of Kristos's tongue, the sensation at once foreign and somehow taboo and so, *so*—

"Good?" Kristos breathed against her, turning her inside out with his mouth, his tongue, seeming to know exactly when she was about to break and deliberately shifting away before she could reach her release, then moving back to torment her before she could regain her breath. Every time he did so, her need surged higher, her climax closer, and she found herself lost in a sea of sensation that she'd always suspected was possible but had never allowed herself to try. When Kristos murmured something in Oûrois against her, she cried out, only to bring her fist to her mouth, stifling her own cries.

"The walls are thick," he said, or she suspected he said it. She couldn't think, could barely breathe as he pressed forward again, and this time it was not only his tongue but the sensation of pressure inside her that caught her up short, his fingers dipping into her in such a shockingly intimate intrusion that the combination of sensations seemed to crystallize in one long, impossible moment—then sent her catapulting over the edge again faster and harder than she would ever have thought possible.

"Kristos!" She hissed as her body fairly vibrated off the bed, and then he was sliding up her body, pausing only long enough to sheathe himself with a condom before his mouth was on her shoulder, her neck, at her ear, whispering more unfamiliar words, the pressure of his shaft inside her sending her into another rat-a-tat-ing stream of mini orgasms as he filled her completely. She breathed in deeply, reveling in the feel of him, and he loomed above her, timing his strokes in perfect counterpoint to her body's clenching reaction. She moaned, almost dazed, until she was pulled into the steady rhythm of his thrusts, her body moving unconsciously, her hands gripping his forearms, and a heady, bone-deep relaxation swept over her, unlike anything she'd ever felt before.

Thirty

The intense look of satisfaction on Emmaline's face was *definitely* not helping Kristos to control himself. He stared down at her, cataloging her every change of expression, her slightest reaction, reveling in how changeable her face, her eyes, even her lips were.

"You're beautiful," he said to her in Oûrois. Though she couldn't know the content of the words, she sensed their meaning, and her cheeks flushed with the lightest rush of pink. She stared up at him and shifted her body, lifting her legs to take him inside her more deeply.

"You feel—really, really amazing," she said, her lids drifting closed as she concentrated on him. "I think you've maybe ruined me for any other man."

Good. Though he suspected her comment was somewhat in jest, Kristos's response was immediate and visceral. He was glad he wasn't holding her, as his hands clenched into fists and twisted in the sheets, but he drove into her with yet more force, causing her to sink back into the pillows, her head thrown back. She was clearly savoring this experience as much as he was.

"Emmaline," he murmured and she opened her eyes again.

Her gaze found his almost drunkenly, her expression loose and unfocused, more swept up in emotion than any woman he'd ever seen. Was this how she looked when she played music? He wondered suddenly. Transported to some other place?

"Look at me," he commanded, and her gaze firmed on him. "I want to watch you while you come again." Right along with him, he knew, as Emmaline flushed scarlet at his stark demand.

"I'm not anywhere—oh—" Her eyes widened in surprise as he pressed up and into her, his knowledge of her body becoming more detailed with their every interaction. They moved together in a rhythm that was already familiar and welcome, and he filled her in such a way that her already-triggered nerve endings responded with swift and sudden force. Her mouth tightened as her fingers clamped on his arms more fiercely, her eyes wild as she convulsed against him as he let himself go as well, the thundering tide of their shared release pounding over and through him, sweeping him away into one of Em's fantasies—if only for a brief, perfect moment.

He collapsed on top of her and rolled off, ridding himself of the condom as he stood. He strode to the bathroom and discarded the thing, then was back at Emmaline's side before she'd scrambled to a fully seated position. He knelt upon the bed, not trusting himself to recline again, as exhaustion and the powerful urge to *stay* with this woman threatened to finally catch up with him.

She understood immediately, her eyes shifting to the clock. "You have to go," she said, but there were no tears in her voice at least. That would be more than he could manage at this moment.

He caught her face in his hands, kissing her brows, her cheeks, and finally her lips. "I have to go. I would not wish to cause you any distress, and there will be much distress if you are not safely alone and under the care of the guards when my mother sends staff to check on you. Which will be any moment now, unless I miss my guess."

She clasped his forearms and sighed, though her smile never wavered. "I will see you again, though, won't I? There's that dance you have in a few days?"

The Accession Ball. He nodded, trying not to scowl. "You'll see me then. And at meals, I suspect, though I have no idea what my schedule will be until I complete all the paperwork that's on my desk."

That did make her brows lift. "Paperwork? It takes paperwork to become a crown prince? I thought your dad would, I don't know, lay the tip of a sword on your shoulders and pronounce you the future king of Oûros."

He grimaced. "Sadly, it is not so easy anymore. The kingdom needs its assurances, and those are bound by contracts that stretch back for generations."

She nodded, the softness of her gaze washing through him. Then her face took on a serious, thin-lipped severity. "I assume you have a noncompete clause, right?" she said sternly. "I mean, if you ever quit being prince here, we can't have you going to a competing kingdom to become *their* prince."

Despite himself, Kristos laughed, feeling another knot of tension unravel within him at Emmaline's answering grin. "I haven't checked that requirement specifically, but given all the places I'm supposed to sign, it would not surprise me."

"And an NDA too, right?" she continued in her light tone, obviously trying to cheer him up. Surprisingly enough, it was working. "To make sure you won't give out state secrets while you're out fraternizing with the international elite." She tilted her head, her face a mask of mock seriousness. "You haven't told *me* any state secrets, have you? Other than the way to trespass out of Theo's property?"

Kristos glowered at her in his own attempt at severity. "That is knowledge you'll need to take to your grave, I'm afraid. You'll also need to keep our shower in the soldiers' barracks under tight silence," he ordered. "If the men find out that their private domain was breached by a female, we'll never be able to maintain control."

"Noted. And as far as this little visit... It never happened."

"I see you are beginning to understand the complexities of being prince." Still, even as they shared a last, quiet laugh, Kristos knew the truth.

No, Emmaline, there you are wrong. This definitely happened. And I wouldn't change it for the world.

With a final kiss, he rolled away from her. "Stay," he ordered when she would have stood. "I would rather think of you this way, and if you slip out of that bed, it would become my number one priority to get you back into it, with me included."

She shook her head as if he'd made another joke. He let her believe that as he dressed, turning back only for the briefest kiss before heading for the door.

A kiss that turned out to be not so brief.

He knew he would regret it if he lingered, but for this last, precious moment, he was content with the sensation of her body welcoming his once more, her arms wrapping around him, pulling him close. The sensation of being entirely surrounded by her grace, her caring, her unique ability to give herself completely to every moment, to make him feel like he was the center of her being.

The way she was becoming the center of his.

"Yes," she whispered brokenly though he'd said nothing more, and he brought his mouth to hers a final time, tasting hello and good-bye and a lifetime in between, all in a single kiss.

Once again, Dimitri was waiting for him outside, touching his earpiece and giving orders as the two of them walked up the long corridor. As Kristos strode ahead of him, Dimitri looked back. He nodded, watching the returning guards for a short moment before glancing to Kristos. They continued in silence until they turned the corner, but he could feel the bodyguard's assessing gaze on him.

"A long day ahead of you," Dimitri finally said, and Kristos glanced to him, grateful that his friend also had his focus where it needed to be. On the future.

"When do you return to the field?"

"Not soon enough. Your mother has insisted that we keep a full contingent of men at the castle until the ball, then, assuming the Americans leave without issue and the media lie low, I can escape to see what destruction has occurred in my absence."

"You'll keep me posted? I know you can manage it very well on your own—"

"But I also know how strange it is to not be in the middle of it. I will keep you posted, Kristos. You are, first and foremost, a soldier. You always were. Even if you dress a lot nicer now."

Kristos smiled as he was meant to do, but his mind was already moving ahead to the events of the coming days. The ball was not merely a mating ritual for the royal family, as much as it felt like it. It also marked the first official gathering presided over not only by the king, but also the crown prince. Dignitaries of nearby nation states would be in attendance, along with any representatives foreign governments saw fit to include. Security would be tight, but it was a good exercise for what lay in store for him moving forward.

After that, Dimitri would return to the field, Emmaline and her friends would be released to continue the rest of their European vacation...and he would be alone, no matter what his matchmaking mother had planned for him.

Even he had his limits.

Thirty-One

"Em!" Nicki, predictably, saw her first, and for about the fiftieth time, Em silently thanked Queen Catherine's foresight in not dumping her back into the middle of her friends before she'd had her morning coffee. She'd felt a bit like she was being returned to life from an alien planet. But now, seeing them around the pool, it was all suddenly right.

Nicki bounded up and hugged her hard, swinging her around immediately to tug her toward the others, who were also on their feet.

"You're alive!" Lauren came forward next, adding her hugs, then Frannie. "You have to tell us everything, you know that, right? Everything completely. Did you take notes? Tell me you took notes."

"I took notes." Laughing, Em squinted up at the large, sloping ceiling of the inner courtyard. "You can actually get sun this way?"

"Solar panels," Frannie confirmed. "The latest in sunbathing technology, allowing you to get your sun on without any prying eyes taking photos. It's pretty much a miracle."

"Look! There are the most incredible fruit and chocolate

pastry things ever made by man," Nicki said, tugging her to the low table. "And they even made a sort of blended power drink that I swear to God tastes better than anything I've ever had in the States."

"Don't get her started on the benefits versus downsides of castle living," Lauren said, retaking her own seat, though she watched Em with keen eyes. "She's been the biggest nuisance of us all."

"Yeah, well, I'm warming up to it." Nicki shrugged. "They have a complete training facility in the base of this place, which they finally let me use. I think the guards got tired of running after me down the hallways."

"But where were *you*?" Fran turned back to Em. "We weren't exactly worried, what with announcements almost on the hour provided by your security detail, but they wouldn't give us any specifics."

Security detail? That had to be Dimitri, but neither he nor Kristos had seemed to be slipping off to give regular reports. "Kristos drove us to a friend's chateau north of the city. It was amazing. I'm sure we can find it online, but you would have loved it, Lauren. Mountain views all around, and even a water-fall off in the distance."

"No beach, no interest," Lauren said, waving her fingers in a "give me more" gesture. "So you stayed there until when—this morning?"

"We moved overnight," Em said. More or less true. She snagged a glass and poured some of the brilliantly colored orange juice. "One of the media helicopters found us out, I think, and the royal family didn't want to take the risk of us being caught again."

"Yeah, that's been a nightmare," Nicki said. "Lauren here might be used to it, but every picture they posted of me made me look like an overbaked cream puff. We've been on the phone round the clock with parents and friends, letting them know we're not in jail or whatever. It's been crazy."

"I called Dad," Em said, then frowned. She'd called on the first night, yes, but there'd been no time to reconnect with him after they'd returned from Estral Falls. And once they'd hit the castle, she'd hardly been able to catch her breath. But still, she should have called them again. A good daughter would have called them.

Guilt returned with a vengeance, weighing down on her like a lead blanket. "I should call again, though. What time is it there?"

"Middle of the night," Lauren supplied. "I wouldn't call now. I texted the nurses, though—they said they're both fine. Neither of them is really worried, and of course, your mom was happy once she understood you were with a prince. Even your dad seems like he's in a lighter mood."

That news should have made Em feel better, but it didn't. Her mom would have enjoyed her stories, even if she couldn't fully understand them. Em should have called from her room after the queen had left. But then she'd been caught up with the video and her writing—and then Kristos—and she'd been so, so tired.

She would call them today. And be home soon enough. And then she'd send her decline letter to Northwestern, and everything would be settled.

Squaring her shoulders against the still-faint pang in her heart at this almost-definitely certain decision, she nodded to Lauren. "What has this detour done to the schedule? Weren't we supposed to be in France by now?"

"Cannes's beach isn't as nice as this castle." Lauren's wave took in the gracious pool area. "And remember, we've got a ticket to the Accession Ball tomorrow. Really, I couldn't have scripted a better vacation for us—even if it does mean that Nicki's going to have to wear a dress."

"I'll have you know that my shoulders *rock* in a dress," Nicki said, picking up another piece of fruit. "I'm probably going to make the entire royal family faint in admiration tomorrow night."

"Since when would that be a surprise?" Frannie had settled back into her lounge chair. "We've got our fittings in an hour, though, so you may want to lay off the juice."

Em raised her brows. "Fittings?"

"Right?" Nicki grinned broadly. "I didn't think you got fittings for anything but a wedding gown anymore. But they'll have the jewelry we're borrowing there too."

They talked on, Em filling them in on the flight to the chateau with Kristos, the idyllic home in the mountains. When Nicki asked how far she'd gotten with the crown prince, she shook her head. "About as far as you'd imagine." She laughed.

"I don't know, I can imagine pretty far," Frannie said, her dark eyes curious over the rims of her sunglasses.

"Well, not far enough to cause an international incident. How about that?"

"More's the pity." Lauren's gentle expression softened her rebuke. "It would have made the perfect fairy tale, right?"

"Oh, like that's what I would want to go back and tell my mom." The sun beat down on them as they talked, lulling her into a quiet relaxation. Eventually Nicki took to the pool once more, creating a mesmerizing image as she moved strong and sure through the water.

Inexorably, Em's mind drifted back over the morning—the night—the last few impossible days. And then her thoughts shifted further, to crisp-edged words on thick cream stationery with a university crest, inviting her to step back into a world she'd thought was lost to her. A world of music and study and performance. She let her heart open enough, bit by bit, until the ache of all she was saying good-bye to filled her up completely. A few tears leaked out beneath her sunglasses, but only a few. Her music had gotten her here, she whispered silently to that same heart. It would always be a part of her life, even without the grand swell of an orchestra, the rustle of all the long concert gowns, the quiet, excited plinks and plunks and thrums and ahhs of a group of performers preparing to hold an audience transfixed.

But was that all she was saying good-bye to, now? Unbidden, images of Kristos filled her mind. Kristos, his parents whom she'd just met, the castle, Theo's, the falls, the beach. Not really hers to hold on to, and yet it all had become so vital, so real. She'd only just begun to experience life again—was she truly going to let that all go so quickly?

The pain crested a little higher, and she rode it, letting it stretch through her entire body and sing its quiet song. *It would be okay. It would all be okay.*

At length, the long, sleepless night caught up with Em, and even pain could not hold its sway within her. Eventually, she let her mind drift...and drift.

Seemingly moments later, she was startled awake by Nicki standing over her. "Yo, Em. You gotta get rolling. We've got to go to this fitting thing, but you haven't picked out your dress yet. So you've been called on the carpet by Her Majesty, the queen." She said the last with dramatic affectation, and Em squinted at her, trying to get her bearings as she pulled her sunglasses from her face.

"The queen? Why?"

"She helped us pick out all our gowns," Frannie said, already standing and refilling her tote bag. "She's got an incredible eye for it, I'll give her that. But I couldn't help thinking it was all merely a front for her to give me the third degree. So watch out for that."

Definitely sounded like the queen she'd met. "Good to know." Em stood, nodding at the two staff members who now stood beside the pool. "Are these our, um, handlers?"

"One for you, one for us, I suspect," Lauren said. "They don't let us go anywhere in the castle without a shadow. Nicki's impromptu fifty-yard dashes have not gone over well, as you may imagine."

"And none of you have been seen by anyone wielding a camera?"

"Not so much as a hint of it." They walked around the pool, the water reflecting the cloudless blue of the sky visible through the angled solar panels. "I checked the news streams this morning too, and other than run-up talk for the Accession Ball, that story, she is dead. There was an awesome blog speculating that we'd all been killed by the royal family, but that's about the only thing that's still out there. They've made an official announcement that we'll be attending the ball, but it's pretty clear that it's out of politeness. Which just adds to their royal cred, I think."

"Talk about my fifteen minutes of fame." Frannie sniffed. "I don't think we even got fifteen seconds."

"Yeah, whatever," Nicki said. "At least your passports weren't immortalized with a picture that made you look like a chubby escaped convict."

They parted ways at the edge of the pool, and Em felt a pang of uneasiness as she watched them go. Couldn't the queen have brought in additional gowns or whatever while the girls were getting their fittings?

When she was led to an unfamiliar part of the castle, she tensed up even more. Her escort opened the doors to a bright, airy space, with a high glass dome and a forest of verdant plants and flowers spilling out everywhere. Except for the foliage, it looked like a miniature model of the grand ballroom in the Visitors' Palace, and she stopped, momentarily amazed by this lush splendor in the middle of the castle.

"Miss Andrews! I'm in the center of the solarium. Thank you so much for joining me here." The queen's voice rolled out over the small space, and Em stepped forward, trying to hide her grimace. As if she'd been given a choice.

Still, why were they meeting here? There didn't seem to be racks of clothing anywhere close, and when she cleared the last leafy bower, she frowned, trying to make sense of what she saw.

A short man in a fastidious suit was turning the knobs on one of three violins that sat on the table before the queen, all of them polished to a high sheen. Em's gaze went from them to the clearly delighted monarch. "Violins?" she asked weakly.

"I know it's an imposition, and that you haven't played professionally in quite some time. But—I was hoping you could play something for me? I haven't had an excuse to visit the solarium in an age, and it was meant to be filled with music. It would mean so much."

Em, of course, was already shaking her head. "It doesn't work like that. I haven't practiced in weeks—months, actually, not in any real way. The last composition I played was for seven-year-olds."

"But would you mind terribly?" The queen glanced with meaning to the older man. "Solon here is a local music store owner, and being called to the castle caused him so much excitement. I told him you might play one of his violins, and he nearly fainted with joy."

It was true. The short older man turned to her with bright eyes, bowing and saying something in his native language that of course she didn't understand. Em immediately felt obligated to at least admire the instruments, and she drifted forward, her gaze falling on the nearest violin.

It was beautiful. Carved in long, clean lines, it practically begged to be played. When she touched it, the man burst out in excited chatter until the queen waved him to be quiet, laughing. "Carpathian spruce, he wants you to know. Very fine, very clear tones. He would be most honored for you to try it."

"It's been so long…" Still, the violin seemed to call to her, and she picked up the gorgeous instrument. Adjusting the chin rest slightly for her preference, she fit it under her chin. Solon, the music store owner, pressed a long, delicate bow into her hand, and she tried a few draws across the strings, the lovely tone submerging her further into the spell of the music. She glanced again at Catherine, who gave her an encouraging nod. Expelling a nervous breath, she immediately thought of her audition piece.

Her heart seized up. *No, no and no.* She couldn't play that, she would ruin it, ruin this moment, ruin everything. That world was gone to her, she dare not even try it.

Beside her, the small music store owner watched her with worried eyes, his joy turning to concern, then even to dread. *No!* She could not ruin this.

Em shook her head slightly, readjusted her chin. Then she bent into "The Lark Ascending." It had always been her favorite.

Thirty-Two

K ristos stamped down the hallway, muttering ever more creative curses as he went. First, his father had him meeting with some of the most prestigious men of the National Council, for the pomp and circumstance of him signing the final papers to render the Crown his upon the death of the king. That alone would put anyone in a foul mood. To make matters worse, however, he'd no sooner finished the first round of that nonsense when his mother had summoned him peremptorily to attend her in the solarium, of all places. He was forcibly reminded of his original reasons for joining the ONSF's ranks at the earliest possible moment when he'd been only seventeen. His parents were a colossal pain in the ass.

He whirled around the corner, already forming in his mind the most polite but firm dismissal he could, when he was brought up short by the unfamiliar sound of music flowing from the open doors of the solarium. A violin—no two violins, were playing in point and counterpoint, a composition he didn't know but was instantly charmed by.

The staff and guards clearly were too, as a small collection of them stood just outside his destination, too polite to intrude but clearly transfixed by the music that came from within. It took Kristos only a moment to realize what his mother had done, and he quickened his pace, striding past the staff and into the verdant gardens of the solarium.

He slowed only as he came around the corner of a small flowering bush and saw Emmaline. She was dressed simply, in a tank tunic and long skirt, but she might as well have been in the formal gown of a concert soloist given the elegant extension of her neck, the graceful arc of her arm as she drew the bow across a gleaming violin. A short man in a suit played next to her, but while Emmaline's eyes were closed, his were fixed on her, her movements, her angles, playing an underpinning of riffs and rolls as if to extend the reach of Emmaline's violin.

With the music filling the solarium, Kristos didn't glance at his mother, though he knew she was sitting beyond Emmaline. Instead, he focused on Emmaline's face, her transported expression telling him that she was no longer in this space, in this castle, but somewhere riding the whispers of her own daydreams, in a place where there was only light and music, where stories always turned out the way they should. He swallowed hard and stood his ground, not trusting himself to go closer, lest he break the spell that Emmaline wove around them.

After another several measures, Emmaline's eyes fluttered open, her attention going to Catherine as she seemed to recall herself to the current place and time. She turned to her fellow violinist, her smile filled with sweetness, and for once, it wasn't she who blushed but the much older man, as together they drew the song to a close, the melody seeming to drift up, up, up until it finally winked out.

"Oh! That was lovely!" His mother clasped her hands together and stood, her manner almost overly bright. "And look who has joined us in time to hear it as well."

Emmaline, frowning, turned his way and nearly dropped

her violin in surprise. "Kri—Prince Kristos!" she stammered, the expressions chasing over her face an unexpected balm.

"That was beautiful," he said, bowing to Em. He turned to his mother. "I am sorry to interrupt you both, but I was told you needed me?"

Her smile was guileless. "Well, I did, the hour ago that I sent for you. But I know you are busy."

"Hour? The message was only just delivered."

"Mm. Then I have your father to blame, it appears, and not you."

Kristos closed his eyes. That, he could believe. His father might love his bride as much today as the day they'd married, but that didn't mean he always bowed to her demands until he was ready. "My apologies."

"Think nothing of it," his mother said, less perturbed by far than she usually was when she was made to wait. "But now that you're here, I do have a request for you. Something that's a bit delicate."

Her gaze shifted to Emmaline, who seemed to take its meaning immediately.

"I'll explore the gardens," she said. She offered her violin to the man in the suit, who pushed it back into her hands, his voice eager, his words a flurry.

"Accept it, please, or he'll be heartbroken," his mother said as Emmaline's eyes widened. "We'll repay him, I promise."

"I—" Emmaline swallowed but graciously held the violin close, as if it were a precious child. She bowed to the old man. "How do I tell him the violin is lovely?"

"*Absolutely beautiful.*" Kristos's translation drew Emmaline's gaze, and whatever she saw in his eyes did cause a blush to flare in her cheeks. She transferred her attention to the violin maker, however, and repeated the words with her soft voice, trying to not destroy the words with her accent. The older man bowed to her again, and then a second time, but before he could burst into more chatter, the queen redirected the man's attention, thanking him for his time and advising him that an aide would be waiting to guide him out of the castle. The violin seller devolved into a series of statements about his heartfelt thanks. After watching him for a moment, Emmaline turned into the gardens as if she really did plan to explore their very depths—depths that extended only about twenty feet.

"Kristos."

He glanced back at his mother, suddenly wondering if she'd set him up to catch him by surprise with Emmaline's playing. He certainly wouldn't put it past the woman. She'd been benignly manipulative his entire life, getting what she wanted with soft words when no amount of brute force would have succeeded...but getting what she wanted all the same.

His mother was no longer looking at him, however. She leaned down at her feet and picked up a large folder, gesturing for him to sit. "I won't keep you, especially not with Emmaline here as well, but I didn't know when I'd get the chance to speak with you prior to tomorrow's events. Your father was quite insistent that you would not have time for social planning in the scant thirty-six hours he had to prepare you for your meetings with the Council." She shook her head. "Why we can wait a solid year to move forward with your accession and then have to do everything in a rush is simply beyond me, but the influx of media has heightened everyone's tensions. I rather suspect he thinks he can leverage it to let drop some of our recent foreign policy decisions he wants publicized, but I can tell you for a fact that this particular media contingent is interested only in the newest and undeniably attractive royal prince—and whom he might wed."

Kristos stared at his mother, trying to process everything she'd just managed to say in one breath. He wasn't even sure she was looking for an answer, but she used his momentary lapse in focus to open the folder on the table between them. At first glance, he knew this was not where he wanted to be.

"I don't have time for this."

"Nonsense. Sit down and go through it with me. You need to be aware of who will be presented to you tomorrow night. No one expects you to make any sort of choice—other than your father, the Council, and most of Oûros—but you should know at least enough to be polite to these girls. They are from the finest families in Oûros and of our allies."

"Allies." Kristos frowned, even as he dutifully took a seat opposite her. "How could you possibly have assembled anyone to come in this quickly, Mother? I was informed my time was up only two days ago. Surely this ball hasn't been on some sort of national calendar."

"The expectation that it was going to happen this week or next has been on the minds of the interested parties for several months now, Kristos. You're worth clearing a schedule for. You need to be aware of that. Now look. Irina is probably the best-looking of the bunch, so you'll notice her straight away." She tapped the folder, drawing his attention down to a classically beautiful Greek woman with large eyes and full lips. The dossier had several photos of her, as well as a listing of her education, extracurricular activities, and charitable work.

"I can't believe you're making me look at this."

"Very well, another choice is Maria. I've always liked her family." The first set of pages was replaced with a second and the image of a woman Kristos vaguely remembered.

"This is barbaric."

"Well, get used to it," his mother snapped, her veneer of civilized calm thinning as she glared at him with unexpected irritation. "All these young women are entertaining hopes of catching your eye tomorrow night. Like it or not, they are being held up for your consideration, and you can treat them with scorn and dismissal, or you can treat them with kindness and grace. The former may be your natural inclination, but it is certainly not becoming of the behavior of a prince."

Kristos scowled at her. "I don't see the reason for this stupid tradition at all. It's outdated and ridiculous."

"One could easily say the same for the idea of a single family serving as the governing power for a modern nation-state," Catherine shot back, echoing aloud the words he'd already thought to himself countless times. "Or the idea of defending Earth against a wholesale return of the gods. You cannot pick and choose the traditions that suit you best at any given time. Whether you are the president of the United States, the prime minister of England, or the grand sultan of Turkey, there are certain expectations and affectations that come along with the position. And how you perform and treat others within the context of those expectations will have a profound effect, whether or not you want it to. So I would ask you to sit here and review the guest list with an eye toward treating these young women the way a future king would, and not mock them for being trapped in the same system in which you, quite gratefully, I should hope, find yourself at the top."

"Your Highness?"

The queen's tirade was cut short as Emmaline emerged from beneath an orange tree. She spoke with bright cheerfulness, as if she hadn't just interrupted a family spat. "I was hoping I could call my parents while you continued your discussion. I'm happy to return here after that, if you would like?"

"That is an excellent idea." Catherine removed a cell phone from the table and hit a few buttons. Almost immediately, an aide appeared at the far edge of the solarium, and she spoke to her in quick Oûrois, then turned back to Emmaline. "She'll bring you to wherever I find myself, depending on how far

Kristos and I progress." She beamed as Emmaline departed, while Kristos managed only a polite nod, grateful beyond measure that Emmaline neither understood his country's language—nor the farce that was about to be enacted.

Once Emmaline had passed through the solarium doors, his mother returned her gaze to him. "I've memorized it," he said tersely, indicating the papers in front of them. "Show me the next."

Instead, she leaned back, a frown marring her brow. "Kristos, your preference for military life is no secret. If you should truly wish to return to that world, it would be a sacrifice for us, but one we could make."

He blinked at her. "What are you talking about? I've just spent the last twelve hours being drilled on my responsibilities to the Crown."

"Responsibilities, yes. Obligations, in fact. But you need to *want* to be king as well."

He stiffened. "That may be asking too much."

"You seem so eager to return to the military, even though you would give up so much—"

He leaned forward. "I would gladly do so. You know that."

"—perhaps more than you even realize," his mother continued inexorably. "The chance for family, actual love... those are in short supply for a man who dedicates himself to battle as a way of life."

"Love!" Kristos sensed the danger here, but he couldn't root it out. "My love for my country is enough." He gestured to the folder, the pictures. "These women here—they don't know me. They won't miss me."

"And Emmaline?"

The question was asked so softly, he wasn't sure he'd heard it. He found his gaze shifting to where Emmaline had just stood, framed by the overhang of the orange tree, her manner soft and gentle, her eyes almost transparent with her emotion. She wasn't one of the options before him on the table; she couldn't be. His mother knew that more than anyone. "She would never be accepted by the ministers." He gave her a small, grim smile. "Only the gods themselves could make her my queen."

"Oh, well. *That* would never happen." His mother's manner shifted so quickly, Kristos jerked back, startled. She leaned forward to shift the papers, not looking at him. "It was just theoretical, a question of what it would take for you to be happy. Perhaps you'll only find that vaunted state in the military, but that's not a choice you can make in any event until after the Accession Ball. For now, you must play a different part." She glanced up, and offered him another page. "A part the country needs no less than another man at arms, regardless of how skilled that man might be."

He gaped at her. "So you would *not* condone me returning to the military?"

His mother shrugged. "I would condone anything that would make you happy, Kristos, as long as it's for the good of the country as well. And today, what's good for the country is for you to at least consider a life *commanding* Oûros's forces, not serving in them. So come, then." She shook the page in her hand when he didn't take it immediately. "Consider this different future for a bit longer. A leader must understand what he's giving up, before he can choose what he wants to take on."

Thirty-Three

The aide stood at the doorway, at a far enough distance that Em didn't feel crowded, though she did wonder if her voice echoed as loudly as she thought it did in the expansive office. Her hands shook as she waited for the line to connect, as if she'd done something wrong and was calling to report her failings to her parents. What was wrong with her? She was twenty-three years old and on vacation for the first time in a year. Her parents were fine, her parents were—

"Hello?"

Her father's gruff voice made her heart lodge in her throat. "Dad!"

"Emmaline? Are you okay? What happened to you? Are you safe?"

The rush of words was so unlike her father that Em wasted another precious moment trying to swallow the lump in her throat. When he said her name again, more urgently, she forced the words out.

"Yes! Yes, I'm fine, I'm safe. I'm sorry I haven't called sooner, but we've been on lockdown and—"

"Don't talk to me about lockdown," her father grumped, his

sudden return to his taciturn self serving to calm her nerves. "After those idiots talked to your mother this morning, I've told everyone to leave us the hell alone."

Em frowned. "Idiots?"

"Oh, some fools calling her, trying to find out more about you. I think it was Channel 2. You know how lousy their news is. Wouldn't be surprised if they quoted the *National Enquirer* as their confidential source."

"She—Mom didn't say anything, did she? Was she upset?"

"Nah, I don't think so. I got to her quick enough. And *that* pissed me off, tell you the truth. If I'd known I could move that fast without that damned walker slowing me down, I would've thrown the fool thing away months ago."

Em pursed her lips into a smile that somehow seemed her only barrier to tears. They'd been quietly urging her father to take more control of his exercise plan, to get out and walk, but he'd not been up to doing much more than stare at Mom, as if he could will her brain to mend more quickly than it was. And her mother *was* improving, she was. She could speak now, though her words were still slurred, and she could eat on her own. She could also walk, though she got so dizzy that walking any distance made her ill.

But she still wasn't anywhere near recovered. She just wasn't fully present anymore, not the way she used to be. Not the way Em had always known her. And that was the hardest part for her father as well. "Well, I'm glad you're getting around better as well. Is the nurse still okay? You don't need me?"

"Of course I need you. I'll never stop needing you," her father snapped, and Em blinked, a strange, sharp reaction welling up inside her. She flashed to the image she'd just seen in the solarium, Kristos and his mother. Did Kristos's mom need him the way her father needed her? What would the queen do to ensure her son's safety?

Her father drew her attention back. "The nurse is fine, brainiac pain in the ass is what she is, and, yes, I *know you're listening*." Her father pitched his voice to be heard by whoever else was in the room with him. "Knows more than any one girl should except your mother, or at least how, how she—"

"You be nice to the nurse," Em said quickly, her words smoothing over the catch in her father's voice. "She probably knows more about how you're recovering than *you* do, and you'd do well to take notes. I'll be home all too soon, and then you'll be back to your regular physical therapists."

"Well, at least they're less pushy." He paused. "When are you coming home, Em? Your mother misses you."

She hesitated, hearing the transparent need in her father's voice as guilt stabbed at her. Now wasn't the time to be thinking about daydreams of Kristos, no matter how he'd looked at her, or how she'd felt when she'd seen him in the solarium just now. Or on the video. Or at Estral Falls. How could she think of doing anything but head back home? The piece she'd just played was an old favorite, not her audition piece. She hadn't mastered that in longer than she could remember. Besides, her music wasn't more important than her parents. Her fantasies about Kristos weren't either. "Is she awake now?"

"Nah. She tried walking a little while ago. Wore her out."

Em closed her eyes. Her mother used to walk all the time before the accident, long treks through the wooded trails near their home. It was her way to unwind, to think, to give her brain permission to walk around too, she always said. "I'm glad she was up, though. The doctors said—"

"I know what the doctors said. When are you back? Monday?"

"A week from Monday." Em said the words a little more firmly than she intended and immediately felt bad. "As long as there's no emergency?"

"No, no, don't mind us." Her father's disappointment sharpened his voice, and Em winced, knowing what was coming next. "You keep jet-setting with your friends. Just don't forget where you came from, okay? We need you back here."

She hung up the phone, feeling more unsettled than she had before. What had she expected her father to say? *Go ahead, enjoy your friends, we're holding down the fort?* That wasn't fair of her to expect. He'd given up the main caregiving role to her easily when she'd offered, preferring to shuttle with his walker between his work at the local library, then home.

That library was saving him now, more so than anything she could do. It was how he and her mother had met, all those years ago: a mutual love of books. Em had no idea how he was with his patrons, but at home he'd only recently begun to reengage, and if he was moving without his walker, finally, then he *was* improving. Even if he wasn't ready to admit it.

Truth be told, it was exhausting to think about going home—which certainly wouldn't be winning her any Daughter of the Year awards.

"Miss Andrews?"

The aide's soft words prompted her out of her distraction. "Yes. I'm sorry."

"The queen has moved to a sitting room. She is most insistent that you come as soon as you are ready."

Em couldn't see any reason to forestall the talk, but when she walked into the charmingly decorated room, she was still surprised. The queen was there, of course, but so were three women of indeterminate years, all of whom were glaring at her.

Involuntarily, she took a step back—only to be urged forward by the aide.

"I'm afraid we don't have the luxury of time like we did with your friends," Catherine said, waving her to join her in the center of the room. A small wooden bench, only a few inches high, stood there. The queen took her hand and pulled her up on it. "We're going to have to find a dress that fits based on your measurements."

"My—oh, I'm a size—"

"American sizes don't exactly equate here, dear." Catherine's words were overly polite, and Em shut up. "It's easier for them to know your various measurements and find something that might work. Not as posh, I'm afraid, as the dressing gala your friends enjoyed yesterday, but I've quite underestimated everything that needs to get done in the next day."

"Of course, I completely understand." Em turned this way and that, the women completely willing to press her thin clothing against her legs and waist and bust to get more accurate measurements. "Really, I hate to be a bother at all."

"I'm sure," Catherine said mildly, and Em glanced down at her. The queen really did look a bit harried, but at Em's attention, she gave her another approving nod. "Don't you worry about me, dear. All of this is rather more emotional than I expected, I suppose."

Em tilted her head, suspecting immediately what really bothered the queen. When the women finally withdrew, she stepped down from her small bench and took the extra step toward Catherine, stopping uncertainly so that she didn't commit some new transgression against the royal family. "You miss your oldest son, and your youngest son is here, yet he doesn't seem to be happy," she said quietly. "Of course it's emotional."

"Well. I should make a note not to attempt any negotiations anytime soon, if I'm as easy to read as that." Still, the queen didn't deny her guess. "Aristotle had done all the work in advance of this event, you know. He had met with the families, helped shorten the list of eligible girls." Catherine continued on blithely, and thank heavens she wasn't looking at Em so she couldn't see her react to the idea of Kristos getting paired off so blatantly. *Eligible girls? Is that really a thing?*

Of course it was a thing. Kristos was a prince, for heaven's sake. *You don't think Kate Middleton wasn't thoroughly vetted before William was allowed to pursue his relationship with her?* There were the women that a young prince could be friends with, and the women that he could marry. And those lists most definitely did not always overlap.

But Catherine was continuing. "Kristos would rather face an enemy soldier than a social event, but he's a good man, and he will come around. It's just—well, it doesn't seem as if any of us are quite ready yet."

"But you have to be," Em guessed again.

The queen's glance shifted to her, and she nodded. "We have to be. And not only because of the media. Kristos taking up his position will add strength to the front Oûros can present in every aspect of government—the military, industry, reform—all of it. Dallying any more than a year would be perceived as weakness. And we all have a job to do."

Em nodded in understanding, but with each of the queen's words, she felt worse. Kristos did have a job to do: to take up his work as prince and help do whatever needed to be done to stabilize the country and keep the populace happy. And Em had her job to do too. One on a much smaller scale, maybe, but still her job. She needed to continue to help her father and mother, and officially decline her last chance at a scholarship. And she needed to let Kristos go. As hard as that idea was starting to be.

Still, maybe she could—*would* find some way to continue her music, at least. The stolen moments today with the violin had affected her more than she'd thought they would. She shouldn't give up everything, right? Her father and mother had been broken, but they were coming back. Maybe she could find a way back as well. Maybe giving up one path to her dream didn't mean giving up the dream itself. Not completely. Not forever. Or maybe…

"Em, are you listening?"

She blinked back at Catherine, feeling the blush rise in her cheeks. "I'm sorry. Your words struck a chord," she said. "We do have our jobs to do, but while I'm here, surely I can help you. Is there anything at all I and my friends could do?"

The queen's smile was radiant. And ever so slightly dangerous, Em thought.

"I'm so glad you asked."

Thirty-Four

Kristos schooled his features to be pleasant. Engaged. Interested even, though the next item on his packed itinerary promised to be anything but tolerable. While the Accession Ball tomorrow was apparently his first official social duty, there were an entire series of *unofficial* social requirements running up to that. His life was becoming more and more like one of those reality TV shows both Americans and the Brits were so fond of.

For this evening's event, the two generations of power—current and future—were enjoying a small gathering, one which was traditionally held at the house of the Minister of the Council, but which instead was being hosted at the castle to avoid the media who were still circling the walls, earnestly trying to sniff out their next story.

Not that the change in plans hadn't fostered its own fluttering on the part of the news agencies. Speculation was running rampant about secret doings going on at the castle, and as much as the Crown disavowed any of it, the Americans were inevitably brought up.

Though he'd still refused to read the dossiers on the women,

Kristos watched every telecast with interest, intrigued to learn such a fractured view of Emmaline's friends—particularly Lauren, who had quite captured the entertainment world's talking heads as she was the daughter of a wealthy financier in New York, and had an MBA under her belt as well...but no apparent plans to do anything with it.

Thinking of the relish with which the anchors had related Lauren's somewhat checkered past, Kristos shook his head. His own rebellion, if you could call it that, had taken him into Oûros's *military*, for God's sake, not into every nightclub in Europe. His parents needed to get some perspective.

Nevertheless, he'd agreed to attend this evening's social and be on his best behavior. He was even now rehearsing his various speeches, in fact, having been instructed that he should be "warming the hearts of the people he'd be asking to follow him into the twenty-first century in a few short years." Great change could only come after great trust, his father had told him. It was time for him to start building that trust.

Too bad heartwarming speeches were *not* his forte. Everyone seemed to have conveniently forgotten that fact.

Kristos entered the room quietly, slipping into the back as his father was wrapping up his welcoming remarks to the families who had joined them here. Unlike tomorrow's ball, there were no foreign dignitaries present. It was a meeting intended only for the trusted allies of the royal family.

Despite himself, his heart swelled with pride as he looked at the group of aristocrats gathered within the salon. The men here were not the idle rich, though some had every right to rest upon their laurels. But they were men of business, first and foremost. Bankers to fishermen, restaurateurs to landowners, they'd made their living with their hands and their brains and their hearts.

"I give your mother three minutes before she spots you." The whispered voice at his side had him turning in surprise.

Dimitri stood with his hands behind his back in full military splendor, looking dressed for a parade. Even his shoes were polished.

"How did you get roped into this?"

"A friendly face for the Americans. Your mother's idea." Dimitri glanced at him, then raised his brows. "You didn't know?" He nodded toward the front of the room, and Kristos turned.

A man leaned over, and he had a clear view of Emmaline's friend Lauren, laughing with one of his father's closest friends. Between her and Emmaline sat an aide, while at the table opposite, Nicki and Francesca sat with their heads bent toward another aide. Interpreters. He frowned. Didn't Lauren speak credible Oûrois?

And more to the point...

"Why are they here?"

"Your guess is as good as mine. Stefan's in a lather over it—as much of a lather as he ever gets."

Kristos frowned. "Why?"

"Adds to the complexity of the story, he says. If the four American women were guests of the Crown, featured at the ball, and then whisked off to the American embassy with souvenirs and well wishes, the story dies. Put them at an event that is closed to the media, where they don't speak the language? Well, most of them don't. The party girl does, of course, though your parents are acting like she doesn't, which is also interesting."

"Party girl?" Kristos knew he meant Lauren, but—

"Hot blonde, bad attitude."

Kristos lifted a brow. "It sounds like you've gotten to know each other."

Dimitri grunted. "She wouldn't be that lucky. I've endured enough of her in one experience to last a lifetime."

"Yes, she didn't seem too impressed when she met you on the beach, if I remember correctly."

"Which is further evidence that she's a little slow. But she apparently has a fondness for *tsipouro*. She attempted a drinking game with it the night before you met your Emmaline." Dimitri narrowed his eyes and cast another look at the front of the room. "That makes her a fool. She could easily have come to harm, and it's not as if her friends would have known how to help her, with her the only one who can speak the language."

Kristos snorted. "I'm sure she would be very open to hearing your opinions on how she should conduct herself." He grimaced, his gaze finding Emmaline. "I'm inclined to agree with Stefan, however. Why present the women as part of tonight's gathering? At best, it muddies the water. At worst..."

His gaze was drawn inexorably to his mother, who wasn't looking his way at all but at a young woman Kristos remembered from his stacks of pictures. Catherine's intent regard was telling, and he could see the reactions in the girl herself as well as the women surrounding her, young and old alike. She was being singled out for special attention, and special attention meant favor.

But favor for what?

When he would have winced, Dimitri's words recalled him.

"Look sharp." And, as always, the bodyguard was right. His father's gaze was lifting even as Kristos straightened, and their gazes connected across the room. With a proud smile, King Jasen raised his hand and introduced Kristos loudly, inviting him to stand forward. The entire room stood and applauded, and Kristos bowed his thanks, already uncomfortable with what was required of him, but determined to do the job he'd set out to do.

There were only about twenty long strides that he could take to settle his nerves, but Kristos made the most of them, stopping to shake hands with the men gathered at the back of the room, nodding to Oûrois young and old. Then he was up the short steps and embracing his mother and father before turning grimly to address the crowd. *Just get this over with.*

In that moment, he met Emmaline's eyes. She stared at him across the room, her manner taut, expectant, and radiating support. In a single breath, with the wave of her emotion flowing toward him, something shifted inside Kristos. His heart seemed fuller, words that had eluded him in all his tortured practice sessions now coming to his mind effortlessly, demanding to be spoken.

"My friends," he said with emphasis. "My people, my allies. I am honored to be standing not just in front of you this night, but *with* you." He continued on, becoming even more assured, more passionate as he saw the spark of his words take light in the eyes of all who heard and understood him.

And even those who didn't.

Emmaline's gaze never wavered from his face, and neither did her outpouring of intense, positive focus. He knew she couldn't translate his words, but he spoke to her just the same.

The speech was an unqualified success.

It was another thirty minutes and four debutantes later before he could safely stop by Emmaline's chair. Unfortunately, while she didn't speak Oûrois, everyone at the table knew English. There was no way for him to speak privately with her, and he didn't trust his reactions even if he could, so he contented himself with bowing. "An unexpected pleasure to see you tonight."

"Your mother was kind enough to allow us to meet so many of your countrymen," Emmaline said graciously. "She also loaned us an interpreter so our fellow tablemates could speak at length on their work. I do wish I knew more Oûrois, though. It's a lovely language."

Her words arrowed through him, even as the words of Council Minister Cyril flashed in his memory. *Remember this above all else, Kristos. All eyes are upon you. And it will get worse before it gets better.* He wanted more than anything to take Emmaline in his arms right there, but that was madness. So he turned from her before his own face betrayed any emotion. The two women at the table he also knew—and had for years. His heart sank even as he glanced at the daughter, recognizing the interest lighting her face.

Cyril was right. It all *would* get worse before it got better.

He left Emmaline with another short bow, then rounded the table to do what was expected of him.

Thirty-Five

"They're totally talking about us again, aren't they?" Emmaline said the words between her teeth, her face practically frozen in place. She'd now cheerfully greeted no fewer than twenty charming older men, their less charming wives, and their positively predatory daughters. "If I hear one more comment about my 'robust' American accent, I might snap."

"Getting watched again," Lauren said in a light singsong, nodding at the sea of people who ebbed and flowed around them. Em didn't need to glance toward the head of the room to confirm Lauren's words.

The queen had been eyeing them like a hawk the whole night, even placing them in the line of attack. At first it had seemed almost cruel, because she and Lauren had been paired off, which had forced Em to stand in the shadow of her more attractive friend—and hear almost firsthand all the sniping, bitter, snide comments the young women thought they were saying in private about her, not realizing Lauren knew the language.

By the third round of princess-bride hopefuls, though, she got it. Got why they were here tonight, got why Lauren's understanding of the language had gone deliberately unmentioned.

They were part of the vetting process.

The more badly behaved a woman was, the less likely the queen would look positively on a match between said woman and her son.

A match with Kristos.

Just thinking about that made Em slightly ill. Kristos's speech had been the one bright moment in this evening. He'd spoken with passion and eloquence, his eyes on her in a way that made her heart soar, for all that she didn't understand the words. She'd not even paid much attention to the hushed translations of the interpreter, because it was as if Kristos wasn't talking about the future of Oûros, the lives they all might live, the possibilities that might be explored. It was as if he'd been talking directly to her about *their* future, the lives *they* might live, the possibilities that could be *theirs*.

Which was insane. She knew it was insane. *And yet...*

"I think I actually donated that suit to charity last season." These words were, even more brazenly, spoken in English, though the beautiful woman's gaze was filled with mock pity as she surveyed Em. "I did think the queen would take better care of you than that."

"She's been so gracious at every step, and we're just delighted to meet you all."

"*And* she decided to focus her efforts on tomorrow's gowns." Lauren delivered this line with the same blithe serenity with which she'd faced every round of women, only turning to Em to hiss their insults after they'd drifted on. But this statement made the bombshell blink.

"Tomorrow? So you *are* attending the Accession Ball?"

"She's been so kind." Em fought a sudden surge of triumph as all of the women narrowed their eyes. Lauren had essentially thrown down the gauntlet for a sartorial smackdown at the gala the following night. And at least she knew that Nicki, Lauren, and Fran wouldn't be wearing anything to poke fun at. As for Em, she'd already had her fill of attention. Whatever the queen saw fit to clothe her in, she planned on remaining out of the limelight, allowing Kristos to do his thing untroubled by her. She'd had enough scowls and sniffs and downright snarls from women who didn't even know her.

Of course, what if Kristos asked her to remain longer in Oûros, somehow? Would she be able to deal with it then? *Yeah, well...not a problem I'm going to have.*

"Ladies." The queen's sudden, soothing voice floated over them, chasing Em's thoughts away. As one they turned, and she saw Kristos standing with his mother, both of them appropriately regal in their formal attire. "You've been so gracious to join us. Have you found the evening enjoyable?"

Her words were for them all, but her gaze centered on Em and Lauren—the bait, Em thought grimly, and the hook.

Lauren remained strangely silent, so Em filled in. "It's been most educational. We have so many stories to share."

The queen's eyes glittered with satisfaction. "And I look forward to hearing them all. We'll be dismissing the families shortly, but I thought I would give you time to escape ahead of the rush. Dimitri will take you to your rooms." She turned and took a step, signaling to the back of the room.

"Who?" Lauren frowned and glanced to Dimitri, whom Em had never seen look more dashing. "Oh, great," Lauren muttered. "The knuckle dragger."

Em's eyes flashed to Kristos in horror, but his lips were pressed tightly together, his expression unreadable.

"Thank you again," she said to the queen, and tugged on Lauren's arm. "We'll be leaving now."

They made their final good-byes, but still, it seemed that Kristos would not look directly at her. He hadn't since his speech, really, his gaze sliding off her face like he couldn't bear the sight of her anymore for longer than an instant. She told herself he was following decorum, that they'd shared more time together than they should have already, and she needed to accept the reality of their situation. The necessary distance.

Nevertheless, it hurt.

They were halfway down the hall when Lauren poked an unusually surly Dimitri. "How's your English?" she asked, repeating the question in Oûrois.

He frowned at her, offering her a derisive smirk as he shook his head. He turned forward and kept walking, while Em stared. *What is he doing?*

"I think pretty much all those women should be kicked to the curb," Lauren said, loud enough for them all to hear—even Dimitri, though she'd clearly decided he couldn't understand them. "There was one, maybe two who didn't enjoy ripping apart Em, all of us, really, but mostly her. Those are going to be the only ones I recommend to the queen."

Em tried to warn her that the guard could understand them perfectly, but Lauren turned to her. "I'm right, don't you think? Pink dress and white suit with the gold cuff?"

"The Callas and Gerou families," Em nodded, recalling the introductions. "If I remember, their families are wine and honey producers, respectively. Their daughters would've worked with their hands, outdoors, at least at some part of their lives. They wouldn't have had time to develop their evil stepsister skills."

Dimitri glanced at her as they turned the corner, heading ever deeper into the castle's inner sanctum, but he offered no comment.

"Well, someone was paying attention," Lauren teased. "But tomorrow, we might need muscle head here to keep an eye on *you*. I only gave you the barest crib notes of what those girls were saying while we were standing in the belly of the beast. You don't just have a target on your back, you've got about two dozen machine guns aimed at it. They thought they had to beat out each other, but now they can be united against public enemy number one." She waggled her brows. "You."

"Yeah, right. I'm leaving in two days. How much of an enemy can I be?"

"There is apparently rampant speculation about what we've been doing here at the castle and how inappropriate it is that the prince and royal family has spent so much time on a group of diplomatically unimportant American women. That, of course, led to quite a bit of chatter about how things will change once the new princess-to-be gets installed. I swear it's 'Beverly Hills Housewives,' toga style."

Ahead of them, Dimitri began coughing, and Lauren shot him an annoyed glance before returning her attention to Em. "We need a plan."

In the end, of course, the only plan that seemed certain to work was to look fabulous and smile as if they had a secret. Even if they were walking into a ballroom filled with nasty women, what did it matter?

The queen arrived an hour after the party for her debriefing, and if they'd surprised her with anything they'd heard, she didn't show it. In fact, she had news of her own for them: their new passports had been approved and should be delivered from the US embassy in Athens within the next few days. After they'd received those, they could leave Oûros at any time. The next stop on their revised itinerary was Tuscany, where they could drown any slights delivered by Oûros's finest shrews in good food and wine.

And, Em had to admit when she surveyed her friends the next evening, Lauren hadn't been kidding.

The queen *had* put her greatest effort into outfitting them all for the Accession Ball, and the Americans would definitely be able to hold their own against their exotic counterparts.

Nicki looked like a Greek goddess of war in her toga-inspired sheath, gold glinting at her neck and cuffs—including a bracelet that snaked around her impressively toned bicep. Frannie looked almost regal herself in a mint-green gown that draped her body perfectly and set off her exotic eyes. And Lauren was radiant, her ice-blue Oscar de la Renta gown a shrewd choice both for its chilly beauty and its now-collector's item status.

Em's own gown was in the building, she'd heard, but was still clearing the various security checkpoints, a fact that had set them all giggling more than a few times, as their anxiety tangled together with their excitement for what lay ahead.

"Now remember," Em urged, "no fights. No scenes. No *tsipouro*. I need you guys on your toes if someone is going to pour wine down my back."

"Go get dressed." Nicki waved to the aide, who now stood at the door, looking expectantly at Em. "And if you have a clothing crisis, send someone to get us. Surely in this entire freaking castle, they can find something to fit you." She grinned. "Or we'll take out one of the dueling daughters who show up early for the ball, and you can wear her gown."

The journey across the castle to the queen's state rooms was brief, but the castle itself was unusually quiet. The Accession Ball was to be held in the Visitors' Palace, exactly the kind of event that the impressive glassed-in building was meant for. They would all arrive at the party via limo—after the fustier dignitaries, she was advised, but before the night's main stars, Oûros's native belles.

Em grimaced. It was too bad this night wasn't going to be televised. She could see the previews now: *Gowns! Glory! Backstabbing in Oûros!*

Her laughter helped settle her nerves, and by the time she arrived at the appointed door, she felt almost centered. She walked into the chamber with her head high.

Then her mouth dropped.

Hanging from a dressmaker's mannequin, with stuffed arms held out wide to give the full effect, was the most beautiful gown she'd ever seen. She didn't even realize she'd stopped midstride until the queen's bright laughter startled her and she almost stumbled.

"Exactly the response we were hoping for!" Catherine announced, and repeated the words to the dressmakers, who were also now looking at her with shining eyes.

"But it—it's custom-made," Em said, finally stepping forward, walking around the mannequin and seeing the pins and unfinished seams. The gown was crafted in layers of lush pink fabric, not so soft as to be debutante level, but a rich, dusky rose that she knew would look good against her skin—the shade of a dark blush. The gown's neckline was a low square, rimmed in a softer pink, and the bodice was tight and sleek against the waist. Its rose-pink skirts fell straight over the hips before blossoming into a sharply defined cascade of heavy material, caught up in elegant gathers. And the gown's sleeves dripped lace and beading, especially from the elegantly elongated cuffs, an unexpected detail that rendered the gown the perfect fusion of past and future, daydreams and reality. "It's beautiful," she murmured, then turned to the women, speaking the only Oûrois words she knew for certain. "*Absolutely beautiful.*"

"And so you will be, Emmaline," the queen ordered, gesturing to the women, who suddenly exploded in a flurry of movement. "The gods have blessed us with your visit to Oûros, and I should like very much for you to celebrate this night as the sweet princess you are. Life is short, is it not?"

Em blinked, but she had no time to respond to the queen's words, as she was surrounded by the fluttering hands and prodding fingers of a trio of laughing, chattering women.

Thirty-Six

Unlike during the social of the day before, Kristos could not slip in silently to his own Accession Ball. More was the pity.

Because all he wanted to do now was talk with Emmaline. Tell her the mad, insane idea he had formulated just last night, even as he was giving his speech, even as he should have been focused on his countrymen, his allies. Instead he'd only been able to focus on her, and from that had come the idea that had no preparation, no counsel from all who should advise him.

The idea that just seemed *right*.

He stood now with his parents at the front steps of the Visitors' Palace, his eyes long since blinded by the flash of photographers' bulbs. All the media they thought they'd shooed out of the country were now back in force, and with the arrival of every new limo or luxury SUV, the excitement seemed to mount. Though the families of Oûros they'd invited wouldn't be arriving until the very end of the procession, he'd already welcomed a half-dozen nobility or near-nobility from across Europe, and even the American ambassador to Greece and his wife, who warmly shook his hand and asked after the Americans staying with the family.

It was the question of the hour, in fact. His mother had just smiled and said they would be along shortly, and that was all the information she was interested in sharing.

Over her head, the king had shrugged. He'd been married to Catherine for too many years to second-guess her machinations.

Still, Kristos wasn't expecting the next dark SUV that swept up the drive to carry anything more than another aristocratic family. It had none of the usual markings of a royal transport, and the windows were tinted black. But when Dimitri stepped out from the passenger's side, Kristos straightened. Another doorman opened the double passenger doors, and a great, excited cheer went up.

The media went apeshit.

The Americans' names were suddenly all being called, none louder than Emmaline's. At a nod from Dimitri, the ranks of guards drew tighter, lining the red carpet as an honor barrier. No one carried obvious guns, of course, but at least their presence would give the women space to breathe.

Francesca stepped out first, and there was a moment of hushed silence before the photogs practically leapt forward, the flashes from their cameras becoming a light storm. Nicki stepped out to equal applause and quite a few more appreciative whistles. Kristos cringed at the comments, but Nicki seemed to take them in stride, offering him a broad wink as she and Francesca turned back to the car. Lauren emerged next, standing next to a slightly stunned Dimitri.

"Oh, lovely," his mother breathed. "Well done, dear."

Kristos could understand the dazed look on the bodyguard's face. While Lauren had always, arguably, been the most classically beautiful of the four Americans, tonight she was spectacular. With her sleekly styled hair, serene expression, and perfectly fit dress, she looked more like a reincarnation of Princess Grace of Monaco than a thoroughly modern celebutante. She waved to the cameras and smiled—radiantly—then turned back to the SUV as well, reaching up to help the last of their number into the spotlight.

Emmaline emerged with one hand firmly lifting her skirts high, so the first thing Kristos saw was her foot, clad in a dark pink shoe. Then a frothy dress in more shades of pink fell over that shoe, and she stepped out of the SUV and onto the red carpet.

A roar went up from the crowd, and Kristos found himself glad that their early guests were already safely ensconced inside the Visitors' Palace—and that the rest of the young women he was expecting tonight were in their own limos outside the palace and hopefully not online. The distant, rational part of his brain didn't want to deal with the fallout from the media's attention to Emmaline.

But he couldn't help but revel in it now.

In yet another way he'd never expected to see, Emmaline was absolutely breathtaking. The gown fit her perfectly from its plain square neckline to its almost theatrical sleeves, the folds and gathers of the dark rose silk molded to her slender body. Her hair was not swept back, like Lauren's, but hung to her shoulders in soft brunette waves, framing her face and setting off the blush that softened her cheeks. Her makeup was understated, and, unlike the other women, she wore very little jewelry —only a constellation of pink dangling diamonds at her ears.

"Catherine..." the king suddenly said, disapproval in his voice.

"Shh."

Emmaline nodded deferentially to the crowd and looked around, not even wincing at the flashing lights and shouted questions. The girls all then turned and glided up the red carpet toward the receiving line and mounted the steps of the Visitors' Palace, as if they had been born to royalty themselves.

Kristos greeted them all, one by one, but when Emmaline paused in front of him, her eyes downcast, her manner shy, he felt his heart give a sudden, ruthless tug. "Absolutely beautiful," he said in Oûrois, and she finally met his gaze. Her expression was filled with emotions he couldn't hope to sort out, but they were powerful, they were sure, and they were all intended for him. "Welcome to the ball, Emmaline. I am so glad you're here."

For some reason, those words seemed to unlock her reserve. She gave him an unguarded, delighted smile that almost brought him to his knees—well, one of them—right there, in front of everyone. Then she allowed herself to be urged along by Lauren. Kristos stared perhaps a moment too long as she disappeared into the archway, before turning back to face the cameras again, his face once more carefully neutral. He watched the next vehicle circle up the drive, recognizing the crest on the side of the limousine, and glanced at his mother.

"That was neatly done." His mother had been in charge of the order of guests, and she'd positioned the arrival of the American guests perfectly—after some of the most notable foreign attendees—and before the most discussed prospects for his royal hand. As much as the thought made him feel slightly sick, he had to admit the timing was masterful.

She lifted a sardonic eyebrow. "I didn't just start planning parties yesterday, Kristos. I've had a few years to prepare."

King Jasen's words were slightly more pointed. "Those earrings were a *gift*, Catherine. A gift I thought you treasured."

Kristos's eyes widened as he turned to look at his parents more fully. Catherine's smile was placating as she leaned up to kiss Jasen's cheek, but ever so slightly smug as well. "It's not as if she's going to keep them, Jasen, and I thought it would be a shame for them not to be on display again, given the event."

"God save me from a meddling wife." The king rolled his eyes. "If anyone notices those…"

"Then they can talk to me about it," Catherine said firmly. She turned to Kristos, dismissing the matter with a graceful flutter of her fingers. "Your father gifted me with those earrings on the night of his own Accession Ball, sweetheart. I rarely get the chance to wear them and—more to the point," she said sternly, looking back at the king, "they are *pink*. Now, I ask you, how much pink jewelry do you think I actually have lying around my jewelry boxes?"

"Not nearly enough, I see," Jasen said dryly.

"Not nearly enough is right."

They all turned to the fore as the media's interest was piqued again with the arrival of another limo. The next set of doors opened, and a gratifying swell of approval lifted from the photographers and reporters. The face of the young woman turned from slightly pensive to delighted, and Kristos breathed a sigh of relief.

It was never easy to sway the media to your plan, but despite her clear enjoyment of their American guests, his mother needed the focus to remain on the women of Oûros. Because, regardless of the outcome of tonight's nonsense, she needed to keep up at least the *illusion* that the family was continuing the tradition of the Accession Ball as some sort of sneak peek at the next Queen of Oûros.

Kristos shook his head, suddenly unsure about his own illusions. His heart had always been with the military, his head in the battle, his body eager and willing to be on the front lines, defending his country, supporting his fellow soldiers. But now he was a man divided. Ever since his visit to the solarium yesterday—and his speech last night when her emotion had swept him up in her gentle embrace—his attention seemed to center solely on Emmaline, his heart practically in his throat. He no longer knew what he wanted.

Well, that wasn't true. Not exactly.

"Kristos, your attention." His mother's words recalled him, and he straightened his shoulders, ready to face once more an illusion not of his own making, until he could sort through the ones that were.

Because unless *he* somehow made some kind of miracle happen tonight with Emmaline, the people of Oûros would be waiting a long time for their queen. He pushed away the ache in his chest to focus on the elegant, expensively gowned woman making her way toward him up the steps of Visitors' Palace.

A *very* long time.

Thirty-Seven

Em turned again on the dance floor, her gaze sweeping the impressive room. It was everything she'd imagined, really. The starlight twinkling far above, the women in eye-popping gowns, their partners either dressed formally or in military uniform. Dimitri once again looked extraordinarily handsome, working his way through an ever-expanding ring of admirers while still remaining close to her and her friends.

And Em had had no shortage of dance partners either. The men of Oûros—and Europeans, as well—seemed more than happy to overlook her lack of understanding of their native languages and instead spoke in English with remarkable fluency. Even now she was in the arms of Stefan, Kristos's half-cousin, and his command of the language was almost as unsettling as his cold blue stare, which currently was burning holes into the back of a very familiar figure.

"I take it you don't approve?" Em asked, drawing his attention back from Nicki. "I think she looks amazing."

"So does a third of the room. The third whose attention she doesn't want, trust me. She doesn't exactly *blend*."

Em choked out a laugh, drawing the curious gazes of the

couples nearest them. Stefan didn't have the reputation of providing much comic relief. "Blending is not high on Nicki's list, no. But you'll be finished with us after tonight, right? Kristos told me that they had increased the castle staff to deal with the 'influx of Americans.' Were you caught in that net as well?"

"With four of you, you'll agree that the net needed to be cast fairly wide. All the way up to Theodopolis Papalia's mountain home. I trust you found it comfortable?"

Her gaze shifted to him. Of course he would know that was where they'd spent the night. Dimitri had been there, and he'd been in communication with the castle. But how much did Stefan actually *know* know?

Em didn't want to think about that too much. "Will you help Kristos with his work now? Or do you still report to the king?" She wrinkled her brow. "Or is it the Council?"

"The king," he said summarily. "And, to a lesser degree, the queen and crown prince, should he have need of me."

"I wouldn't trust that crown prince guy. He's always been a pain in the ass." Em's heart did a tight little flip as Stefan turned her again, both of them breaking apart as Kristos stood there, alone. "May I cut in?"

Stefan bowed to him, his face a mask once more, betraying neither approval nor censure. Then Kristos was in front of her, his hands firm on hers, his grip steady as he turned her in his embrace. She could feel the wave of interest perk through the room, and she frowned at him. "I didn't think I was a candidate for your dance card."

"Given the givens, I should think you would merit multiple dances, if only to keep everyone guessing." Kristos's words were light, but his eyes were intent. "You are beautiful, Emmaline. You've never looked lovelier."

"Oh." Em slanted her glance away, knowing that her blush betrayed her anyway. She looked back and tried for bravado.

"And you look very dashing. Even if this is totally weird that you have to do this."

"Weird." The way he said the word made her think she'd overstepped, but before she could backtrack, he shook his head. "One of the sessions I sat through earlier today centered on the wartime truces that have been signed by Oûros throughout its history, from present time all the way back to the ancient world. Some of the agreements struck along the way...*those* were weird. This is merely a random, distant echo."

He gazed around the room then, his face set in an expression of relaxed camaraderie that probably was very effective if you weren't standing right next to him. At length, he sighed. "But, yes, it definitely is still very...odd."

Em laughed, and Kristos seemed to relax further, and she suddenly got an image of what it would be like to be partnered with this man for more than a dance. To be the one who could bring a smile to his face when the cares of his work wore him down, to be the one who supported him and his position without even being in the room, simply by pursuing her own projects and initiatives. To be the one who loved him with all her heart and soul.

Idly, she wondered which of the young women would end up catching his eye. Despite yesterday's Mean Girls Social, as she and the others had started calling it, there were a few women who'd seemed genuinely nice after the dust settled. Those women were here tonight as well, looking impossibly perfect. So were they the front runners in the Crown's estimation? Was "nice" important to being a princess bride? Or was it more about beauty, or refinement, or education, or being able to speak six languages?

And why did she care so much?

"Where are you heading after you leave our shores?" Kristos

asked, though his words seemed oddly stilted. "France? Farther north?"

"Tuscany," she said. "Some vineyard owned by friends of Lauren's father. She really does have the best connections."

"It's safe?"

She flashed a surprised look at him. "What do you mean, is it safe? Of course it's safe."

His lips pressed together in a thin line. "You should have an escort until you are settled there."

"We'll be fine. And your men are needed here." She tried to return levity to the conversation. "They've got a new crown prince to protect, after all."

She'd said the wrong thing again. Kristos glanced away from her and muttered something in Oûrois, but she didn't need to know the language to understand it was a curse. She tightened her hold on his arms, forcing him to look back at her. "I know you're not sure about this—that there are things you wish you could change about why and how you're here today. But you *are* here. And it's not such a bad place to be."

"Spoken by the woman who's about to leave."

His words were a sharp rebuke, but Em pressed on. "You've been preparing for this since you were a little boy."

"I've been preparing for the military. Which is where I should be."

"No." Em's quiet certainty made him look at her, really look at her, and the unexpected pain in his eyes almost made her stop. But she knew the words she needed to speak, what he needed to hear. "That's not true. You've been getting ready to serve your country, yes, to make sure every rock, tree, and blade of grass is safe, just as you said. But there are infinitely more ways to do that than by running around the forest with infrared goggles. Your fighting may be across tables instead of battlegrounds, and your truces might be struck with everyone wearing suits instead of uniforms, but what is the difference, really? Aren't you still doing everything you can to make sure your country stays safe? Is that such a sacrifice to you, that the manner of your service has to change to meet the needs of the people?"

"The people want things that are ridiculous."

"I know," Em said gently. "Like traditions. And continuity. And the security of knowing that, despite everything else that's changing all around them, a few things in their lives are going to remain the same." She squeezed his arm again, hearing her own words on a different level, one much closer to home. "They want a leader who respects that. Your father does, and now, you can too."

He glanced at her again, and something had changed in his face. His eyes seemed almost desperate now, his expression stark, and Em felt the fire of their attraction surge between them then, the need to fling herself against him so strong, so immediate, that she pulled up short—as did he. Kristos took a step back, then bowed to her, offering his arm, his words painfully clipped.

"I think we both could use a drink," he said. "Allow me?"

Thirty-Eight

Kristos felt a darkness rising up to clutch at his throat and willed himself to walk steadily to the side of the room. His entire world seemed to be crashing around his shoulders. When he'd stepped out to dance with Emmaline, he'd had a speech prepared. But everything she said, everything she did seemed to indicate that she'd already made peace with the idea of leaving him and Oûros behind.

And why wouldn't she? He'd met her, what, three days ago? He hadn't read her file—though everyone assumed he had—but he'd learned enough about her just by being around her to know that she had a life filled with obligations, hopes, and aspirations that had nothing to do with him. She needed to take care of her parents and, as soon as she was able, return to making music.

Music. He'd forced himself to compartmentalize that tiny shred of knowledge about her, to push away the wellspring of pain that had somehow opened up inside him at the thought of letting her go.

He'd only heard her play one composition, and yet what did the choice of a favorite melody say about a person? In that one brief piece of music was fifteen years—probably twenty years or more, actually—of practice, of failures and success, hours bent over a scrap of wood when others were out doing whatever children did in America. He'd been forced to endure his own rounds of musical training for a few excruciating years before his parents had relented. Ari had stayed with it longer, but he'd also had no taste for the tedium of the day-after-day practice that was required to excel. Far easier for them both to escape the music room and take on the world.

But not easier for Emmaline. She'd stayed the course, done the work. As she would with her own parents. He could see that in her eyes. As she was counseling him to do now. His grand, half-formed plans of suggesting something entirely different for them now seemed stupid, immature. He wanted her, God knew he wanted her—but he couldn't have her. Not anymore. She'd accepted that, so why couldn't he?

"Kristos." Emmaline's quiet words drew him back, and he realized they were at the refreshment table laden with the delicacies of Oûros. A quick review of the dance floor showed him his parents engaged in animated discussions at the other end of the wide space, Stefan scowling in yet another corner, and Dimitri—well, Dimitri would be wherever his hot blonde was, whether she wanted him to be or not. Kristos considered officially assigning his friend to the woman for the rest of her visit here. Surely there was a viable reason to justify that.

"You're smiling again. That's a good start." Em had freed her hand from his grasp and now offered Kristos a small glass of clear alcohol. "This is *tsipouro*, right?" she asked. She sniffed it. "I tried this the other night. It really didn't seem that strong."

"It sneaks up on you." Kristos took the glass from her and held it tightly, reveling in the bite of cold from its chilled surface. He toasted her, and she looked relieved. Then her expression faltered slightly when he downed his drink in one gulp.

"I think a lot would sneak up on me if I drank it so fast."

"Then I pray that you should never need to."

As Emmaline blinked her surprise at him, the music changed, becoming a traditional reel. The men crowded the floor, dragging the women into the center, even a laughing Lauren, Nicki, and Fran.

"Should you join them?"

"I don't know this dance, fortunately," Kristos said, but more to the point, his father wasn't joining in the frolic. Instead, he had pulled aside the queen and seemed to be talking with her intently, more than willing to ignore the crowd.

And what was good for the king... Another burst of hope had him turning to Emmaline. Perhaps he was just making this too hard. Perhaps he would just ask the question and let her make her response. He owed her that. He owed himself that.

"Do me a favor?"

"Of course." Em sat set down her glass and nodded, her gaze following his to the far door. "Oh. You want me to leave?"

He almost kissed her right then. His dear Emmaline, always assuming the worst. "No. I want you to go out that door and down the hallway to your right, until you find a room that isn't full of people. Hopefully, that won't take you too long. And then I want you to wait for me."

"But—"

"It's a favor, remember?"

He watched Emmaline maneuver through the crowd with delicate grace, quickly swallowed up by the throng. For once, all eyes were not on him but on the wild dancing at the center of the room, and after watching the dance himself for a few more minutes, he turned to the door opposite where he had directed

Emmaline. If anyone noticed him leaving, they'd note that he'd left alone.

Not that he gave a damn if they noticed or not.

Kristos broke into the coolness of the hallway a few moments later, his strides quick and purposeful. He nodded to the guards who were positioned along the corridor, both grateful and irritated to see them at the ready. When he found Emmaline, he experienced the same mix of emotions. She was alone, yes. But she was in the conference room that had started this odyssey this week, with its wall of flickering news feeds. She turned when he entered the room, her face intent with concern.

"What is it, Kristos? What's wrong?"

Kristos cut her off in three short strides and gathered her close. His mouth came down on hers, and, with a startled gasp that was almost a cry, Emmaline threw her arms around him, her hands clinging to his shoulders as her lips parted and she pressed close. In that kiss, he tasted desire and resolve and pain and regret, and something more, something he wanted to spend far longer than the next five minutes learning about.

He broke away and sighed as she drew in a deep gulp of breath, the two of them clinging to each other in the reflected light of the screens. "What was that for?" she asked, her voice shaky.

"Does it need to be for something?" He lifted his hands to her hair, grateful that she didn't have it slicked back into some impossible-to-touch hairstyle as he buried his fingers in it. He kissed her brows, her cheeks, then returned again to her lips, as if he was drinking from a cup that would too quickly be taken away. She curled her fingers around his hands, her entire body trembling, not unlike the way she had when they'd first met.

When he lifted his face, though, his heart gave another hard lurch. "Ah, no, *koukla mou*. I didn't mean to make you cry. "

"It's okay—it's okay," she murmured, standing back to wipe

her tears away. She offered him a shaky laugh and shook her head. "I'm being ridiculous. It's just this night, this dress, you—" She flapped her hand around, her voice wavering dangerously. "You really should put all this in a tourism brochure, because I'm telling you, you'd be completely overrun by hopeless romantics. Especially from Missouri." She pursed her lips, glancing away. Then she looked back at him.

"Thank you," she said. Her words were certain and firm, as if she was making a declaration to him, maybe to herself as well. "Thank you for rescuing me."

He lifted his brows. He should ask her now. This was the time. "Well, you weren't really in all that much danger—"

"Yes, yes, I really was." She closed her hands over his again, holding on to him as if he were some sort of a lifeline. "I think I'd given up on one too many things by the time I reached Oûros. My music, my life. Maybe even myself, a little bit. You made me see that all I needed to do was reach out for someone who might just reach back for me. Might just believe in me, see me as I couldn't see myself. I did, and you were there. I'll never forget that. I really won't." She glanced away again, toward the flickering screens.

That sounded an awful lot like good-bye. *Do it now.* "Emmaline, I want to make sure you won't forget." He drew in a breath.

"Wait, what *is* that?" Emmaline's gaze had sharpened on the screen. "Where is that coming from?"

"What?" He turned as well to see what she was looking at, then he frowned too. First one, then another screen was switching to breaking entertainment news, with Emmaline's picture featured prominently and the headline. "Princess Gold Digger" flickered across the screen in English and Oûrois.

He flinched. "Emmaline, don't look at that."

"Princess *Gold Digger*?" She repeated the words, her eyes

going wide as she read the captions. "Can you turn any of these up—oh my *God*."

"Your Highness." An aide rushed into the room, stopping short. "You are needed in the ballroom, sir," he said quickly, his gaze going from Kristos to Emmaline.

"Tell them I'm busy," Kristos snapped as Stefan stepped around the aide, coming to stand beside them. For the first time, Kristos noticed the thin wire trailing from his half-cousin's ear. A headset. He must have been given word about this newest media bomb.

"Go," Stefan said. He reached out and gripped Kristos's shoulder. "I'll translate for Miss Andrews—"

"You don't need to translate!" Emmaline's sharp words drew their attention. "I can read the captions easily enough. Oh my God—that's my house—where did they get those photos? How dare they! How is this even *allowable*!"

Stefan began to speak, but Kristos stopped him, anger and a gut-wrenching awareness sparking through him. He had done this. He had let this happen. "It's allowable because we have freedom of the press, Emmaline."

He knew his words were harsh by the way she jerked her attention to him, but he couldn't help it. Because he also knew what would happen next, as the media story got bigger and uglier and even more hurtful. The *only* thing that could happen next, given all she knew about him, and all she'd already experienced about what her life would be like if she remained. He'd been a fool to expect anything different. "This is simply part of being in the castle."

"Well, I want to *leave* the castle, then. Now. Tonight. I want us all out of here. I'm sorry, Kristos, I truly am. You've been nothing but gracious to me. But this—they have a picture of my *house*. We have to leave."

"*Emmaline*." He didn't even know if he'd spoken her name

aloud, but he must have, since she stepped sharply away from him, as if his touch would undermine her resolve.

"I have to go." Her words were absolute. "I don't want to be here any longer. I can't." She held up a hand, forestalling any response on his part. She glared back at the screens, and her face changed with each new image—first to anger, then to disbelief. Then to humiliation.

This was what he'd brought her by drawing her into his life. This was what he'd done to her. And now the last image he'd ever have of her would be Emmaline's stricken eyes as she stared past him, shock and outrage drowning out all the memories of laughter, of passion—and what he'd thought was even love.

His chest burned with cold fire beneath the secret he kept there. *What was I thinking?* Of course she'd leave. No one would stay for this—this life of constant scrutiny. He himself didn't want it, and he'd been born to it. Why on earth had he thought he could ask her to live it with him?

He straightened, feeling the cold finality of her decision like a slap, and forced his voice to be calm. "Of course, Emmaline. Dimitri and Stefan will ensure the safety of you and your friends."

She blinked, some of the color returning to her cheeks as she looked back at him. Still, he didn't want to hear her apologies, if indeed she was about to give them. He couldn't. Like a battle that couldn't be won, some things were better off being forgotten.

"Kristos—"

He drowned out her response with the memorized rhetoric of the speeches he was still expected to make tonight. The first of a hundred thousand speeches, he had no doubt, to cover over the emptiness in his heart until he could finally break free from this castle once more. He'd been a fool to think he might find a path forward as the crown prince.

He had only one path, and he needed to find a way to reclaim it. Alone.

Emmaline took a step forward, then stopped short as he bowed to her with excruciating politeness.

"Good evening, Emmaline," he said, not even recognizing his own voice. "May the gods keep you safe, wherever your travels take you."

Thirty-Nine

"Where did the captions go?"

Turning from the sound of Kristos's fading footsteps, Em glared at the screens, willing herself not to cry. Her words seemed sucked away by the enormity of the images flashing across the screen in front of her, the closed-caption translations having somehow disappeared. Pictures of her mother and father in their younger years, herself in her concert uniforms, bending seriously over her violin. They looked like benign pictures, positive pictures, but why were they being flashed across the screen at all, and what—

"What are they saying! Turn that up!" she demanded, uncaring that she sounded coarse, common, unwilling to look away as a new caption flashed up again on the screen below a sleekly blonde woman and her metrosexual counterpart, both of them looking serious and vaguely sad. The translator apparently was attempting to interpret the slightly slurred voice that now came streaming over the speakers of the conference room, as light as feathers falling in the breeze and so, so sweet.

"She always loved to read about princes."

Those were the words *she* heard, in her mother's voice, but her ears had grown used to interpreting the stops and starts, the broken whispers. The drifting voice that now made Dr. Honor Andrews sound so different to anyone else. Anyone who wasn't Em and her father. Because clearly, these were not the words the media station had heard. Below her mother's face, the caption read: "She always wanted to be a princess."

As the real voice of her mother finally assaulted her, she could hear every defect, see the images of her mother's slack face from the local newspaper coverage of the brave recovery of the local professor, a story that barely anyone had seen when the accident had first happened, but now...

"She's worked so hard," her mother said, the words so frail, so fragile. After that, she said something else that not even Em could decipher, but her statement ended once more with: "...a princess."

Given that those words could have been interpreted any way possible, the station went in for the kill, and the words "She'll stop at nothing to be a princess" flickered to life beneath her mother's face.

Em put her hand to her mouth, taking a step back as telecasters then flashed to images of Em getting out of the SUV that had taken them to the ball earlier tonight, her beautiful dress shimmering around her like a dream come true, her face beaming, juxtaposed against the heart-wrenching picture and fractured breathing of her mother.

My God. The woman on the screen—*her*—with her laughing eyes and perfectly styled hair... She was *horrifying*. She was leaving her mother behind to be cared for by hired help while she ran across the globe and tried to throw herself into some unsuspecting prince's arms, all for a chance at becoming something she was never meant to be.

"Why is she doing it?" the serious blonde asked her grim counterpart. "Who could do such a thing? Abandon her parents to go play at being princess. Does she really think she's going to land her prince? And then what? Where will the riches of Oûros go? To help care for Emmaline Andrews's parents so she doesn't have to, or into her own pockets?"

Em backed up another step, sharply.

"Only she can tell us." The male part of the duo turned to the camera. Somber. Sad. But with a hard glint to his eye as well, as if here was the news that the people needed to know. "And yet the Gold Digger Princess once again isn't talking. Royal spokespeople confirm only that—"

"What the hell! Turn that off! Turn that off now!"

There was a flurry of silks and rushing feet, then Em felt arms around her, pulling her back, turning her forcibly away from the screens as the pictures flickered. But she'd seen it all already. This was only the leading tide of newscasts, and they weren't even the American ones.

"I'm a *monster*," she said, and her vision swam as Lauren stood directly in front of her, her hands on her shoulders.

"You're the least monstrous person I know, Emmaline." Her words were sharp. "The story had died, and the media secretary here had done too good a job burying it. Am I right?" she demanded of someone over Em's shoulders, but Em was too sick to look. "But you can't just cut something off like that. That's not how it works. All the parades of the local women were great, but they were boring. They should have leaked something about our next location, or—"

A snort of derision that sounded too close to them went a long way toward calming Em's nerves. Dimitri stood watch beside her now, scowling at Lauren, but it was Stefan who spoke.

"The effect of stopping the story completely versus an approach that would have simply let a little air out? Worthy of consideration, but ultimately not any more likely to succeed.

The story was going to die or it was going to explode. It was a fifty-fifty chance no matter which way we allowed it to play out."

Em blinked at him. "You *knew* that? You knew this might happen tonight, and you still let us go in front of everyone like we did? Waving and laughing like we didn't have a care in the world, when my parents—my God, my *dad*. I have to call my dad!"

"I've already texted the nurse. She'll stay on-site for the next few days." Nicki's voice cut into Em's scrambling thoughts, and she held up Lauren's phone. "She's worked with Lauren before, and it's not the first time this sort of thing has happened. She knows how to handle the media."

Em's gaze swung back to Lauren, who shrugged. "You get used to it. It sucks, but you get used to it."

"And give your parents some credit, Em," Nicki said. "They aren't exactly fans of *E!* or whatever shows would carry this crap."

"Not only *E!*, unfortunately." Fran was at the computer set up at the base of the monitors, her fingers racing over the keyboard. Stefan immediately stepped toward her.

"You don't have access—"

"Just hitting the Internet, don't get your tights in a twist." Fran scowled at the screen. "The story's been cooking since about noon our time, looks like, gathering up a head of steam. It's been picked up by the *Guardian* in Britain, which will pick up anything that's bleeding, but it hasn't hit the AP yet."

"The AP!" Em felt what was left of the blood in her face drain away. "Tell me you're joking."

"I'd like to say I was, but it all depends on the current news cycle. If it's a slow day, this will definitely get noticed. Gowns and crowns are always an attraction." She frowned, her gaze tracking the scrolling information. "Unfortunately, where it's hit is bad enough. The *Guardian* has a direct feed into most of the tabloid sites in the US."

"This is insane." Em turned to Stefan. She already felt terrible for how she'd treated Kristos, but she'd been so horrified at the implications. *Princess Gold Digger. Who'd even come up with that?* Far better for her to just leave and stop the damage altogether. "There's no fallout for the royal family, is there?"

Lauren groaned. "Like that should be your concern."

"I'm serious," she said, forcing Stefan to turn his attention to her instead of continuing to scowl at Frannie, her fingers flying over the keyboard as she pulled up various search engines. "This newest round of stories, what is the net effect?"

"None, not in any lasting sense." Stefan shook his head. "The queen, or more likely the king and Kristos, will make a statement exonerating you of any intent, malicious or otherwise. It's not necessary, but—"

"Not necessary." Em stared at him, his callous tone grounding her further, yet swinging her right back into anger. "My parents are on *TV*. My mother's voice was played on international media. She's a respected historical scholar, and they made her sound like an imbecile!"

"And so the royal family will almost certainly make a statement about their shock and dismay over the entire situation, their plea for the media to report news and not gossip, and their deep apologies to you and your family." Stefan spoke the words as if he was checking off items from a PR list instead of discussing the defamation and embarrassment of Em's family on a global scale. "Once you've left Oûros and the ordinary state schedule is resumed, the story will be replaced."

"That's what everyone said *before*, and that didn't work out so well." Em waved her hand at the now-quiet screens. She glanced to Nicki and Fran, bent over the computer, and another flush swept through her. "This is going to be on the Internet forever. You realize that, right? After your royal celebrations are concluded and the prince gets married or whatever, *I'm* still going to be the one who goes online and gets to see my name splashed across the web as 'Princess Gold Digger.' And forget me and my stupid problems. Forget that every time I apply for a job or audition for an orchestra, I'm going to be looked at with curiosity. Forget that my association with you has resulted in an entire *lifetime* of whispers and punch lines and probably memes, for all I know. That's all beside the point. My mom was brought into this. And even if she's not the queen of Oûros, she's still *my mother*. And I've brought nothing but shame to her."

"Stop being melodramatic," Stefan said, his tone harsh enough that Nicki and Fran looked up from their computer, and Lauren sucked in a startled breath. Em took a step back in the face of his sudden, sharp irritation. "You've provided assistance to your parents for the past year and more, dropping out of college, deferring your scholarship. It's due, isn't it? And you're not going back, I suspect." He scowled at her, then moved on. "You're making your living now not by performing at one of your country's most revered orchestras but by teaching lessons to the children of your local school. Your parents are not idiots, Miss Andrews, to care about any of this. They will treat this situation for what it is and so should you and any future employers you seek. It is not a situation of your making."

But Em had stopped listening as the realization behind his words struck her. She stared at Stefan's cold aristocratic face openmouthed, knowing she was gaping, knowing that she probably looked the fool. But she no longer cared about that. No longer cared about anything.

"How did you know all that?"

But even as she asked the question, she knew the answer. Of course she knew the answer. Kristos had probably been given an entire file cabinet of information on her before she'd ever shown up at the Visitors' Palace that first afternoon. Their entire two-day "escape" probably had been vetted and approved as the least distasteful option to contain the story about her. And all the media coverage that had been generated had been carefully manipulated to the advantage of the royal family, since the very first photos had been taken.

She felt beyond exposed, beyond vulnerable.

She felt betrayed.

"I want out of here," she said, her voice gaining strength with each new word. "*Now*."

Kristos sagged slightly as the last of the guests left after lingering in the Great Hall for far too long. His mother looked almost as haggard as he did, at least when she thought no one was looking at her. His father also had become increasingly taciturn as the guests had somehow seemed to thwart their every attempt to end the evening.

But now they were alone, and he turned immediately to the far doors. He'd lasted over an hour here after leaving Emmaline, and he'd spent that time laughing—talking. Clapping people on the back. No one would know that his hands were nearly shaking with fury. No one *could* know that. He'd sent word to Stefan for reports, but nothing had come of that yet, much to his increasing irritation.

He nodded to his parents. It was far past time he—

"Kristos."

The king's voice carried the sharp crack of authority, underscoring his position not only as king but as father. It was the only reason Kristos stopped in his tracks.

"There's been another media surge. I am needed—"

"I know about what has been aired about Emmaline. It's out of your hands now."

That drew him up short. "What do you mean, out of my hands?"

Jasen drew a tired hand over his eyes. "You have to learn to think *strategically,* Kristos. You could have predicted that this was one of the paths the media might take after you'd read Emmaline's dossier."

"Her what?" Kristos shook his head. "I never read her dossier."

The king's raised brows were the only indication of his disappointment in that revelation, and he pushed on. "Her family is in debt. Significant debt. Emmaline may not have known it originally, but there was a reason why she needed to get a scholarship to pursue her studies. When her parents both left their jobs abruptly in the wake of the accident, their insurance covered only so much. Her father tapped any accounts he could find to pay for their care. Now their credit is compromised. Anyone with rudimentary skills of observation could see that, and suddenly here's a young woman halfway across the world, kissing a prince. It's not a difficult leap."

Kristos could only stare. "You *knew* about this story, that they were going to take this angle? You knew it was brewing and yet you let Emmaline show up and wave at the cameras?"

"No." It was his mother who spoke now, her voice cutting sharply across the conversation. "We didn't know they were going to stoop this low. We should have guessed, but we didn't know. The first broadcasts were only brought to our attention at the onset of the gala. The damage had been done. There was no point in changing course once everyone was inside."

"But she is being *vilified,*" Kristos gritted out. "Surely we could have stopped that from happening." He knew his anger was mostly directed at himself, but that didn't help matters. He could have stopped it from happening, yes. But he hadn't wanted to. In his selfish need to put his own life on hold, he'd compromised Emmaline's. Again and again.

His father shook his head. "When the media take hold of a story, it's no longer yours to change. It's not something one person can do. I'm sorry, but this is part of being a member of a public family that you are going to have to learn to accept and endure, or simply stay out of the limelight altogether."

Kristos bristled. Hadn't he just said as much to Emmaline? *Hypocrite.* "She doesn't deserve this. She didn't do anything wrong except run into me."

"Technically, it was the other way around." His mother's gaze was gentle, but still intent upon him, as if she was trying to see things that weren't there anymore. Could never be there. The weight in his chest seemed to grow, dragging him down.

"That is exactly my point. At every turn, I have brought her under more and more scrutiny—the Visitors' Palace—the chateau—the castle. She was living her life very well before I happened to her, and now she's a virtual prisoner behind these walls."

"Not a prisoner anymore."

Kristos turned, his fury stoked even higher to see Stefan's cold face as his older half-cousin sauntered into the room. "What are you doing here? I asked you to protect Emmaline and her friends."

"And we have." He nodded to Dimitri, who stood stiffly at his side. The bodyguard's face was also a mask of cool civility, but something dark and fierce swirled beneath it, something barely able to be contained. "They'll stay at the Grand Hotel Oûros tonight, and leave tomorrow for the airport. Given the additional scrutiny, I've arranged for a charter flight to Galileo Galilei, then private transport to their villa in Tuscany."

"At the Hotel—are you insane! We've already seen how inadequate their security is. That's unacceptable."

Stefan didn't honor this with a response. He looked to the queen. "They left behind their gowns and completely understand if you cannot ship them—"

"Of course we'll ship them," his mother said, waving tiredly. "I'll have an aide make arrangements for cleaning and transport. It's not as if we don't have their addresses."

Her words galvanized Kristos once again. "They figured it out, didn't they? Emmaline did, most certainly." He glared at Stefan, who stared back at him, unconcerned. "She found out about our dossier on her. That was the final straw."

"She made an educated guess that I didn't dispute." Stefan shrugged. "What did you think was going to happen, exactly, when the curtain came down on the charade you were playing with the woman?"

"Charade!"

"Stefan." King Jasen's tone held a warning, but Stefan's eyes were flinty as he glared back at Kristos. Demigods could be intractable in their thinking, and Stefan had the blood of the eternal strategist in him. He'd clearly worked all the angles.

"She's an American with a brain-damaged mother and a clinically depressed father who's barely able to bring himself back from the edge of ruining her entire family, after an accident he believes he could have avoided. You can't expect to swoop in and carry her along the tide of your largesse and expect she won't be changed by it in the aftermath. You made her into an overnight sensation with your juvenile posturing and swagger, and, like it or not, she is going to be the one to pay the price for that."

"Stefan, that's enough," Catherine said. "We'll provide every statement we can to help ameliorate the media's portrayal of Emmaline—"

"No, *we* will not. I will." Kristos seethed, his fists clenched. It was everything he could do not to launch himself at Stefan, but a part of him, once again, knew that his anger, his outrage was as sharp as it was because of the *truth* in Stefan's words.

The royal family hadn't done this to Emmaline and her friends.

He had.

In only a few short days, he'd managed to turn her life into a media circus. And in so doing, he had taken a sweet, caring, beautiful woman, and had transformed her into the horrified shell he'd seen in the conference room earlier this evening. The last sight he'd ever likely see of her was that of her shocked eyes, wide and disbelieving, as the reflection of a dozen news videos splashed across her face.

He refused to wish away the last three, perfect days he'd spent with Emmaline, though he knew she probably did. She had no reason to ever forgive him, and he would never ask that anyway.

It was finished.

Forty-One

Em and her friends had been waiting for hours in what had to be the most comfortable jail cell she'd ever seen, but it was still a jail cell. Dimitri had joined them a good forty-five minutes ago and had stood stone-faced, looking straight ahead. His only words were that they needed to wait until safe passage could be assured for them. As if they were criminals, or hostages. Or both.

She felt sick. She hadn't meant to incur the Crown's enmity with her sudden need to flee, but what else was she supposed to do? Sit around and eat chocolate-covered fruit while every television in the kingdom blared with accusations of her gold-digging ways? Her stomach plunged again, and she placed a balled fist against it.

"You need to stop obsessing," Fran murmured beside her. "Everything that's passed is unchangeable, and everything forward doesn't have to be tainted by it."

Em glanced at her. "Do you tell that to convicted criminals too?"

"Every time I get the chance. But you're not a criminal, Em —and you don't have to be a victim either."

"That's beautiful." Nicki rolled her eyes. "But that doesn't change the fact that some assholes are out there saying things they should be held accountable for. Em wouldn't even know how to *begin* going on a gold-digging expedition for a prince—a prince none of us had ever heard of before this week except Lauren, and Lauren doesn't count. She had to do something when she wasn't shopping."

"At least I have a decent wardrobe to show for it," Lauren shot back. "You spend every day in shorts and jog bras. And don't tell me you're pursuing your dream life in your work as an 'adventure blogger.' I'll throw up."

"I'm twenty-three!" Nicki shrugged. "A normal job will be there when I'm ready for it. And this isn't about me. How'd this get to be about me?"

Em smiled, knowing her friends were only trying to cheer her up. The fact that it was working wasn't the surprising part. The fact that she was letting them do it was.

Maybe Fran was right. Maybe she was worrying too much. The people who knew her, knew that she wasn't some needy, grasping harridan out to sink her nails into an unsuspecting prince. The thought was laughable. True, she still could barely make ends meet with her father's hospital bills and probably even more creditors that would start popping up when word went out that she was back, but she was making it work.

She had her job at the school and was giving lessons, just as Stefan had said. She also helped make doughnuts most early mornings at the shop her father loved, though that was more to be there whenever her dad came in to see his pals before his workday at the library began. It was the only time of day he really relaxed, really became the man she remembered before the accident.

The time stretched on another hour as they waited, and Em checked her phone for the millionth time. It was past three a.m.

now, and Nicki had already dozed off on the couch, Fran drowsing next to her, looking for all the world like they were teenagers at a sleepover kept up way too far past their bedtime. Dimitri still stood like a rock at the far end of the room, and Lauren followed Em's gaze, scowling at him. "What's his name again?"

"Dimitri," Em said. She glanced at Lauren. "I keep meaning to tell you. He knows English."

"I know the asshole knows English. The fact that he thought I was so much of an idiot as to not have figured that out is one of the many marks against his character."

"You knew?" Em lifted her brows. "But all that stuff you said—"

"Was going to make it to the queen's ears anyway. She showed up, what? Thirty seconds later? If she was using Dimitri as her messenger boy, who was I to keep him from his job?" She looked over at him now, raising her voice. "What are we still doing here, GI Joe? I thought we were going to a hotel?"

Dimitri's gaze shot ice across the room. "The hotels are being watched, and we've had difficulty finding an option that isn't overrun by photographers. It would be better if you stayed here."

"Yeah, no."

He shrugged. "Early scouts have reported photographers setting up camp along all driving routes. We can move you in another few hours when they lose interest, but for now, we wait." Dimitri's gaze flicked back over them. "The most viable option is to relocate you to one of the private condominiums owned by the Crown, to ensure your safety until you leave."

"How is that *anything* like what we asked—"

Lauren's words were cut off, however, as the door opened and several people entered. Em's heart lurched as she searched their faces, but she knew that Kristos wouldn't be among them.

Of course he wouldn't be. He'd left her to go deal with his royal duties hours ago, and he and his mother were doubtless already poring over The Girl Most Likely dossier, trying to pick his fiancée. The whole thing should make her sick.

It didn't, though. Now that the adrenaline surge of her disastrous television encore had passed, the hollow feeling in her chest felt nothing like sickness. Instead, it felt a whole lot like plain old grief.

Dimitri spoke in rapid Oûrois to the men, nodding several times. He turned back to Em, ignoring Lauren completely. "We're ready. Your bags have already been loaded and taken separately, so it's only the four of you that will need to be transported. We considered the possibility of taking each of you separately, but that would result in too many variables."

Em lifted her brows, remembering the last time she'd been separated from her friends. That really hadn't turned out so badly, had it? *Let it go, Em.*

But Dimitri was continuing. "We will have to take a circuitous route. It will take some time."

"Your country isn't that big." Lauren scoffed.

Dimitri looked at her, his gaze almost dangerous. "But it has many secrets."

He lifted a hand and signaled, and the guards came forward. None of them had guns drawn, of course, but their movements were far too exact for them to be simple tour guides urging them along their way. Em and the girls stood, then they all moved down one corridor and into another, the halls eventually giving way to familiar passages.

Em frowned. "We're in the guards' barracks."

"We're taking my vehicle." Dimitri gestured again, and a guard opened a door, several men exiting before them. "It is nearly change of shift, and the trucks won't attract attention. Not even mine."

He gestured to a muscled-up SUV that looked closer to a tank than a vehicle, though Em couldn't identify the make. "Why am I not surprised that's yours?"

"Get in and get comfortable," Dimitri said. "It's going to be a long drive."

He wasn't kidding. They drove so far into the mountains that Em was beginning to wonder if they'd end up at Theo's chateau again. All of the adrenaline and exhaustion of the past few days' events started to creep up on her, and she fought to keep her eyes open. She looked over at Dimitri, the other three girls now fully passed out in the backseat. "What's the delay?" she murmured drowsily.

Dimitri glanced at her with the first real smile she'd seen him crack since the gala had begun. Heck, possibly since they'd left the ATV in that tiny mountain town, covered in mud and branches. "Go to sleep, Emmaline," he said, his gaze returning to the road. "It appears our initial accommodations were not suitable for the Crown. Or the second one we suggested. Or the third. We've had to make adjustments mid-journey, and it has taken time to prepare. We'll be there soon."

It was almost dawn when they finally pulled up to a building with subdued lights. No one was on the street, and Em straightened in her seat, blinking as they turned into the over-hang that must lead to some type of garage. The vehicle purred to a stop and the other girls stirred—well, Nicki stirred. Lauren and Fran were still out.

Dimitri rolled his eyes and hefted Lauren's body, while another man stepped forward to pull Fran into his arms. Nicki fought off help, hopping out of the SUV along with Em, blinking around. "The mythical condo?"

"Looks like."

Dimitri explained the layout as they entered the elevator chamber. Their rooms were on the top two floors. The other building inhabitants on the lower floors would be notified, but they were used to staying away. Dimitri handed over keys to the main doors and to their rooms, then he and the guard left Nicki and Em staring owlishly after them.

"Why does this still feel like jail?" Nicki grumbled, eyeing the guard at the far end of the hall.

"Life of the rich and famous." Em pressed her key against the lock and heard the tumblers shift. "See you in the—well, soon," she said, as sunlight peeked through the shuttered far window.

"There better be sunshades." Nicki padded down the hallway to her own room, and Em waited until she unlocked the door and slipped inside.

Then she pushed her own door open, not bothering with the lights, though the room was shadowed and murky.

She hoped for just a moment that Kristos would be there, waiting for her.

He wasn't.

Forty-Two

Princess Emmaline Aphrodite Grace gazed out of her embattled kingdom from behind her prison walls, so desperately sad that she could barely move.

Okay, she was clearly going to have to work on her fairy-tale endings.

But there was not much to look forward to today, their second day in captivity in the condo, not even on this beautiful dawn as she gazed over the sandy beaches of Oûros. Even the Aegean Sea, glistening in the distance, seemed to mock Em with all her beautiful memories that had now turned sour.

Because for the second morning after the Accession Ball, she'd awoken alone, so terribly alone, that she hadn't wanted to move. She'd lain in her borrowed bed with its borrowed linens and borrowed pillows, thinking of her borrowed life that had brought her to both the heights of pleasure and the pits of dark despair.

Kristos hadn't reached out to her. She hadn't really expected him to, and yet these past few days had passed in a weird sort of limbo without him, and she'd found herself far more exhausted than she should be. Though both she and the girls had decided not to turn on the television yesterday, their mutual resolve had lasted only until about three o'clock. The moment they'd flipped the enormous television on, however, it had cut away to another story of the gold-digger princess, now disappeared once again, and the gleeful expressions of the entertainment reporters had resulted in a resounding cry from all of them to "turn it off."

After that, they'd found it easy enough to drown their sorrows in a bottle of smuggled *tsipouro* Lauren had bribed a guard to bring in, and an enormous fruit-and-cheese plate the condo management had seen fit to send up to their rooms.

And now they were waiting again, because the word that had come over this morning was that they still had more hurdles to jump over. They needed to wait to make the trip to a private airstrip late that night, ensuring they wouldn't be accosted along the way. Lauren was convinced Dimitri was doing it to be obnoxious, and that their enforced imprisonment had nothing to do with royal command.

Still, no matter what the reasons were, the result was the same. They were *stuck* here. Half hideaways, half outcasts, all of them suspended in time.

Em slumped back in her chaise, bringing her violin away from her chin. That was the ironic thing, of all of this. The queen had shipped the lovely gift violin to the condo—without a note, without an explanation—yet it was exactly that violin that Em had found herself turning toward, again and again in her isolation. She'd even tried her audition piece a few times. Once, she'd made it all the way through... and then she'd started crying.

Why had it taken her heart being broken, for her to find her way back to her music? That didn't seem remotely fair.

"Ugh. How can you stand the light?" Lauren stalked out onto the balcony, then squinted into the brilliant rays blanketing their sumptuous balcony. "I'm not even hungover, and I feel like death."

"Yeah, but it sure is beautiful." Em waved her bow at the view. Only the hardiest of beach lovers was lying out at this hour, but couples walked the edge of the water and several joggers traced their way toward the distant, craggy mountain path—one of them Nicki, who'd announced that one day of forced confinement was her limit and that this morning she'd free-climb down the side of the condo to get some exercise. In her ball cap, sunglasses, shapeless T-shirt and shorts, she could be any of a hundred tourists, she'd argued—and she'd been over the balcony before anyone could talk her out of it. Let the guards figure out how she'd made it past them when she walked back in.

"My idea of beautiful is generally less...bright. At least before I've had my coffee." Still, Lauren slung herself into one of the heavily cushioned chaises that overlooked the beach. "Pretty awesome views, though." She squinted at Em through slitted eyes. "It sure is good to be king."

"Yep." Em burrowed underneath her light coverlet. "I think most of the city is subsidized in one way or another by the royal family. They try not to talk about it."

"Too déclassé."

"One must keep up appearances." She smiled ruefully at Lauren. "Did you ever suspect this tiny little kingdom was going to cause you so much trouble?"

"Me? I'm not the one who's become an international celebrity. No, no, don't you dare wince." Lauren kicked at her with a sandaled foot. "I've been living with the Internet on my back since I was nine years old. You don't go anywhere or do anything in society without knowing that's part of the game. And let me tell you, people can say some absolutely awful stuff about nine-year-olds that will pretty much make you give up on humanity."

"I never knew."

"Of course you never knew." Lauren shook her head. "You had a life. You didn't Google your friends to see what creepy things were being said about them by total strangers. You didn't even know who my father was when I showed up in the Freshman dorm that first day. It took me half a semester to forgive you for that."

"Well, you were rooming with Frannie. I'm sure she explained you were being unreasonable."

"Unreasonable with borderline narcissistic tendencies, I think was her actual diagnosis. Not that I remember." Lauren sighed, stretching in the pool of dappled sunlight. "Speaking of..."

She turned and peered back into the suite. "Fran? You gonna join us out here, or are you the only one of us who couldn't hold your *tsipouro*?"

"Just a minute!"

"Right." Lauren rolled her eyes and settled back into her chair. She regarded Em more somberly. "You finally ready to tell me what your parents said when you called? You weren't exactly in a talkative mood about it yesterday."

"Yeah." Before seeing the latest round of newscasts, thank heavens, she'd called her parents. It hadn't started well. She'd been fine until she'd heard her father's voice, and then had come the tears, the humiliation, the apologies. She'd had to force herself to calm down enough so he could understand what she was saying. And then...

"He took it really well." Em shook her head, still surprised even now, almost a day later. "I mean, I don't know if he was still half-asleep, though he sounded alert enough, but he..." She sighed. "It was pretty much just the way Stefan said it would be. He told me it was going to be okay, and that Mom was strong enough and he was strong enough to weather a bunch of idiots talking about them online, and so I should be strong enough too. I was pretty much bawling at that point, and he told me I'd always be his princess, and that has never really been his thing, you know? The princess stuff. It was Mom's. So that didn't exactly stop the flood of tears." She brushed her cheeks. "And here I go again."

"Tears are good for you. They help release the emotions we can't process otherwise." Fran appeared in the doorway of their rooms, her glasses perched on her nose, her hair tied back in a loose bun. She carried her ever-present laptop in her hands and looked over the top of her glasses at Em. "But I wouldn't bother putting up the tissue box quite yet."

"Why, what's happened now?" Em frowned at her as Fran walked out into the sunshine and paused to drink in the light the way she did, as if there were answers in each individual sunbeam.

She squinted back down at her laptop. "Well, I wanted to show you out here, but it's way too bright."

"See? I told you," Lauren said. "They've got a critical excess of sunlight here."

"Show me what?" Em grimaced. "I don't know that I'm up for more episodes of Princess Gold Digger. It's way too early to break into the alcohol again."

"Oh, I think you'll like to see this particular twist ending. C'mon."

Fran led them back into the shadowy confines of the suite's living area, plopping down on the least comfortable seat, which was something she did. But at least here, that wasn't saying much. She turned the screen around so that it was facing Em and Lauren, who dutifully hunched forward.

"This is going to make me cry?" Em asked.

Fran shrugged. "Probably."

It was a YouTube video, and the first thing Em noticed was the name of the poster: "Mrs. Carvalis's Class." She reared back. "Oh no. That woman is the sweetest person in the world. Tell me they didn't say anything mean about her or about any of her students. They're third graders!"

"Is she like this when she watches movies?" Fran's question was directed at Lauren.

"The worst. Hit Play."

Fran moved the mouse and hit another button so the image expanded to fill the whole screen. It started with the kids all milling around, three little cherubs standing earnestly at attention with their tiny violins. "Class—class!" Em heard Mrs. Carvalis's voice. The class settled, and the three children played a short, rousing reel, their smiles filling their whole faces as they finished and bowed. "Who taught you that song?" came Mrs. Carvalis's disembodied voice.

"Miss Emmaline!" the kids sang out.

Mrs. Carvalis knelt in front of them, then, holding up the mic. "And what do you think of Miss Emmaline, Bobby?" she asked the first little boy, his hair messy and his eyes large.

"She's *usually* here on Wednesdays. It's fun when she's here."

"She makes me feel like I can play anything." Katie spoke next, her face shy under her fringe of red hair.

The third girl was small and thin, her hair tied up in tight braids. Little Mandy Su, who'd joined their class just that year and hadn't even spoken for the first four weeks. "She gave me her violin from when she was little," she said, her fingers spasming on the violin as Em pursed her lips. "She told me it would be mine for keeps if I played all year and made it feel special."

"There you have it," Mrs. Carvalis said, turning to the camera. "Emmaline Andrews really *is* a princess."

"What?" Em sat up sharply as Fran tapped another video. The screen filled with another teacher's class, then another. Then two parents waving at a camera. And the old men at the doughnut shop, and a student of her mother's who dropped off books every week, without fail, since Em had come home.

"Em reads to her, I know she does," the student was saying now. "She reads her mom the same fairy tales Dr. Andrews teaches in her class along with the other lit subjects. Because fairy tales have always been the professor's favorite." She glanced away, then looked fiercely at the camera. "Dr. Andrews deserves a princess for a daughter, and that's what Em is."

There was a graphic at the bottom of the screen that flashed then: #PrincessEm.

"Do not even."

Fran's fingers clicked another browser window, and #PrincessEm was scrolling, with pictures posted from her former schoolmates, college friends, festival competitors. The comments ran by too quickly to read, and Em didn't try. "This is terrible," she moaned.

"Are you nuts? This is amazing." Lauren was sitting up straight now too. "Facebook?"

"Stories of Emmaline are coming in from friends and former high school pals, and wonder of modern miracles, no one is being an asshole. I think because of the kids' videos and the YouTubes of Em's own concerts that are now up online.

"My what?" Em shook her head. "I don't have anything online."

"Well, you do now. Someone set up a Facebook page yesterday morning and has been boosting the posts. Marvin something?"

Em's eyes widened. "That's the church choir director," she said. "He's retired now. He taught at my grade school."

"Well, he's a fan."

"Show us more," Lauren urged. "What's the reach, any news pickup?" She stood and strode over to the TV, switching it on.

"Local so far, but it's an ABC affiliate, so you know it's going on *Good Morning America*." But Fran wasn't done yet. "Especially after this. It was actually the first thing to pop up, I think."

A shaky YouTube video screen settled, and Em's eyes went wide. "Mom," she managed, reaching out to touch the screen.

Settled in the middle of her favorite place in the house, the sunroom, surrounded by her books and seated next to her husband, her brilliant mother, Dr. Honor Andrews, smiled out at the camera. Still so thin and fragile, she was dressed in her favorite university outfit—a long, flowing dress with embroidered sleeves, black tights, and clogs.

Her hair was pulled back at her neck, and though it had gone nearly white in the aftermath of the accident, that simply served even more to give her the sense of being some otherworldly sprite who'd touched down to earth for just a short time.

"My daughter's name is Emmaline Aphrodite Grace," her mother said, each word pronounced succinctly, exactly, and clearly with great effort. Her hand was tight on her husband's as he beamed at her with love in his eyes. "And she already is a princess."

Em's hand flew to her mouth, but before she could even let a sob escape, Lauren's voice called to her from the center of the room. "Hey, what's wrong with Kristos?"

Her attention jerked from Fran's laptop to the large screen TV, and she blinked, trying to make sense of what she was seeing. For a second, she thought she was back in the castle again, watching the borrowed video of the royal family. Because Kristos was once again in front of a crowd of reporters, standing tall and rigid, his face devoid of all emotion. He was speaking in Oûrois, but the words didn't matter, couldn't matter. He'd gone hollow again.

"He's totally losing the crowd," Lauren said. "Is he sick?"

"He's something." Fran was leaning forward too, her brows drawn together in a worried frown. "He looks like someone died. Can you get those closed caption things to come up?"

Em could only stare at Kristos's stark face, his empty eyes. She'd never wanted to see him look like that again, not if she could help it. Which, if she was honest with herself... she could.

Her own heart was proof of that. Not twenty minutes earlier, alone on the balcony, she'd sat with her violin and tried not to cry, swamped with a feeling of isolation and abandon. Then she'd seen the smiles of the children, the teachers. Smiles intended for her. Then she'd seen her parents as they'd looked into each others' eyes, their love so full it made her ache.

And just like that, something had switched over in her heart, had come to life again. Not forever, maybe. Not completely. But something *had* changed.

She now knew firsthand the power of having the support of people who loved you...even if you didn't know how much they loved you. Especially if you didn't realize that.

And if she could do anything to help Kristos, help him show his true passion to his people, his dedication to their country and everything it stood for, how could she not do it?

Because she *did* love him. She'd known him for barely a heartbeat, but that didn't matter. He wasn't hers, he could never be hers, but that didn't matter, either.

She loved him, and that was enough.

She bolted upright, her eyes fixed on the TV. She had no idea where Kristos was right now, but his number one bodyguard would. A bodyguard who still guarded their condo complex, despite his clear distaste for the assignment. Well, that assignment was going to come in handy now.

"Lauren, I need you to get Dimitri."

"Him?" Lauren looked at her sharply. "Why?"

"Just do it."

"Your highness."

The aide stepped away from the microphone, and Kristos swung his gaze out to the crowd. They were restless, but at least they were quiet. He'd stopped all questions relating to the Americans within the first fifteen minutes of this press conference. He didn't want to hear about those four young women ever again, he'd said definitively. It was time to look forward.

Only, as he'd moved through the torture that was his speech, he found himself not looking forward, but back. Back to the first time he'd seen Emmaline's wide eyes and laughing face, back to when the mere touch of her hand on his had seemed to make everything in his body come alive. In the end, he had failed her, he supposed, but no more than he had failed himself.

Now he needed to move on. "We have much work to do," he spoke into the microphone. "Much work that will ensure that Oûros will claim its proper place among our allies, and that we will make new allies as well." He droned on, his thoughts a thousand miles away to where Emmaline and her friends would be heading next. Dimitri had told him that their passports had finally been delivered to the castle this morning. Emmaline might be on a plane even now, flying away forever, returning to—

Something jostled in the crowd, and he flicked his glance toward the movement, frowning, even as he continued his memorized rhetoric. "In the coming weeks, we will be welcoming to our shores the delegates of the special committee on financial stability, and—" he stumbled as his gaze caught on someone in the crowd. *Could it be? No.* "And we are very pleased to take on this topic so critical to the future of Oûros."

A gray-haired woman shifted to the side, and then he did see her. Emmaline. She looked more beautiful than he could have imagined. Her hair down around her shoulders, her body encased in a long, cream-colored sundress baring her arms. Her hands were clasped up her chest, her hair was uncovered and floating softly in the breeze, and she was looking at him like—

She was looking at him like she was a woman in love.

Kristos. Her lips moved as she spoke his name, but she was too far away for him to hear her, of course, too far away for him to see anything except that she was here. That she hadn't left. That she was staring at him with such naked adoration that anyone who turned to see would record it, and it would start all over again—the attention, the speculation, the questions, the furor. It would start over, and she must know it would start over, and yet she wasn't turning away from him. She wasn't hiding.

She's here.

A sudden surge of excitement coursed through him, and Kristos turned back to the cameras, the crowd. He could feel the buzz beginning at his change in demeanor, but he didn't care. He knew—finally—what he had to say. "But you know, there is time enough for me to tell you of those plans. Instead, allow me to tell you something else. Something of my past, and of Oûros. Why I am honored to be here, before you now, in whatever role you will have me. For I have been blessed to serve this country, and I have learned so much in doing so."

He blinked as someone shouted his name, then as another small cheer was raised. He spoke on, telling the reporters the same non-classified stories he'd told Emmaline about his experience in the military—had he really shared those stories only a few days ago?—and the crowd's responses got even bolder, a rallying cry going up as he explained the sacrifice of the soldiers he'd fought alongside. The Oûrois who had so boldly given their strength and their bodies and, in some cases, their lives to serve this glorious country. How could he not do the same?

Another shout sounded from the media, then someone called out Emmaline's name. Kristos stiffened, but Emmaline didn't. She stood forward, and her face remained as open and unguarded as it had throughout his speech. Radiant. Beautiful. She was so clearly in love that the weight in Kristos's chest suddenly seemed to burst into flame.

He would not hesitate now, he resolved. Never again, in fact.

"Emmaline. Would you join me?" The entire royal contingent around him devolved into excited chatter as he spoke the word, but Emmaline, though clearly surprised to hear her name over the microphone, didn't duck away, didn't resist as she was urged toward him, despite the flurry of flashing lights and shouted questions. She was smiling; she was gracious. And she still had no idea what was to come, he suspected.

He should feel badly about that.

He didn't.

"What are you doing?" she asked as she finally reached him, but he lifted her hand to his lips to kiss it softly, then continued holding it as he faced the cameras once more. This time, he spoke English.

"My countrymen, I now have the pleasure of introducing

you to a woman whom many of you think you know, a woman I have been lucky enough to welcome to Oûros these past several days. Much has been said about Emmaline Andrews. Some of it has even been true."

This last earned him a chuckle, and Kristos continued. "She came to our shores not expecting any special treatment, yet she has conducted herself with dignity throughout—at least when I wasn't mauling her in public. But, as those who know me well enough understand, I am but a man."

That made even Emmaline smile, and he turned to her. "I'm sorry for all that you have experienced while in our care, Emmaline. It's my fault, and I take full responsibility. You should not have had to endure it, and—"

His words were cut off as Emmaline lifted a hand to his face, turning it so that the back of her fingers rested on his cheek. The simple grace of the movement stole his breath.

"You don't need to apologize to me, Kristos," she said. "You and your people have been nothing but kind, and you've given me an adventure that I will remember the rest of my life. If that required my picture to be taken a few times, then it's more than worth it." She blushed, but she didn't waver in her gaze. "*You* are more than worth it."

She looked out over the photographers again, and it took him a moment to realize she was addressing them directly. "Thank you all, so much more than I can ever express. Without you, I would never have received the blessing of so many people's comments and good wishes, people I never realized I'd touched. Nor would I have had the memory of their caring to hold in my heart. It's a gift I can never repay. You have brought me that. Oûros has brought me that. And Prince Kristos," she said, a catch in her voice. "Has brought me that. Thank you."

She said these last words with heavy finality, nodding graciously as she finished, and he could sense her pulling away from him, feel her turning to look for the van, the cab, even a donkey that might carry her away from all the scrutiny once more—away from him.

Except he couldn't let her go. It had all come down to this, and he could now, at last, see his future stretching out for him. A future not of battles and glory, perhaps, but a future that filled him with excitement just the same.

He laid a hand on her arm as she tried to move away. "There is...one more thing, Emmaline."

Forty-Four

Emmaline blinked at Kristos, her inner resolve crumbling. Did he have any idea how close she was to bursting into tears? She hadn't realized what she was doing, walking up here. Now just standing next to him was almost more than she could bear.

Nevertheless, she forced herself to remain still as Kristos turned to her, his face achingly gorgeous, his golden eyes intent. And then she realized that the cameras were still on him, on both of them, and she forgave him in an instant. Because if there was a video of this somewhere, which surely there would be, it would be one more memento of him. One more gift.

One more memory of when, for the briefest, most magical, and most insane of times, she'd been a real-live princess.

"Emmaline," he said, and his voice wobbled in a way she'd never heard before. She tried not to frown, but his eyes suddenly looked almost desperate too, the conflict of emotions clear on his beautiful face.

What was wrong? What was upsetting him so?

She almost asked him outright, but he picked up her hands

in his and held them together, his eyes intent on hers. "Emmaline, I am in love with you."

The gasp that swept the crowd was loud and instantaneous, and Emmaline knew she echoed it. Her jaw dropped, and she could tell that she had tried to pull away from Kristos without realizing it, simply by the strength of his tightening hands on hers. "It's possible I fell in love with you the first time I saw you, but ever since then, I've simply fallen deeper. Your beauty, your music, and your kind heart have made you more of a princess than anyone I've ever met in my life. I would be honored if you would be my princess too."

She blinked at him, then froze as his words caught up to her, her eyes going wide.

"Kristos!" she said, the word wrung from her as if it was bursting out of her heart. "What are you saying?" Her mind raced to find a way to explain away his bizarre words, his completely unexpected declaration.

His face was infinitely tender, as if there was no one in the courtyard besides the two of them, no one watching but the bright Oûros sun. "I'm saying that I love you, Emmaline," he said, bringing her hands to his lips. "And that I hope you love me. In fact I hope that you'll—at least consider—something more between us. Perhaps much more."

"Of course, I...Kristos?" Emmaline gaped as Kristos sank to one knee, his left hand still grasping hers as he used his right hand to pluck off one of the official-looking emblems on his uniform, holding it up to catch the sunlight. "I regret that I am ill-prepared for this moment, but I can't wait any longer to ask this. So please accept this as my promise for now."

He placed the tiny pin into her palm, his touch calm and reassuring even as her entire body trembled. "Emmaline Aprhodite Grace Andrews, you will always be my princess." Kristos's words seem to ring out in the courtyard, and it suddenly felt like the whole world was holding its breath. "Will you also marry me?"

"But what, what are you—" Suddenly realizing that the time for explanations was not now, that now was only for words—one word in particular, one word that she never expected to be able to say, not and mean it like this, with her whole heart and soul, and with every fiber of her being. "Yes!" Emmaline gasped. "Yes, Kristos, yes, I will."

KRISTOS CLOSED Emmaline's fingers over the military pin, though her hand shook so badly that he suspected she'd lose the thing any moment. He stood and fumbled for his mic, turning it off as a roar of approval and excitement went up all around them.

Emmaline just stared at him as he stood. "Could you possibly explain to me what just happened?"

"For the rest of my life."

She blinked, and a renewed rush of emotions swept over her face. She didn't believe him, he realized. She thought this was another stunt, another step in the process needed to extricate herself from Oûros. But her expression when he'd proposed— her eyes... There had been no mistaking her reaction to him then. Her mind might not be willing to believe what had taken place between them, but her heart had.

Still, Emmaline clutched his hands, turning her face resolutely forward to the crowd with a smile before he leaned into her. "We'll need to go greet my parents. And I almost certainly need to apologize to yours."

"My—oh—" Emmaline blinked at him. "My parents are never going to believe this."

"Then we should start explaining it to them."

He turned and called an order, and it was Dimitri, of course, who took it. Dimitri who grinned fiercely at him, then turned away to commandeer the Crown's communications tech. Then Kristos glanced back to Emmaline's wide eyes, wanting more than anything to kiss her again. She was his. Or at least, she had the promise to be his. It was enough for the moment. There would be time for them to discuss the reality of what he had just proposed. The requirements of the Crown, Emmaline's own true desires. There would be time for them to learn more about each other as people from two very different worlds. For now, he had only his heart to trust. And that was more than enough.

Emmaline's natural caution surged to the fore, of course. As he knew it would, though he loved her all the more for it. "Kristos, even if you did finally read that dossier on me, you don't know me at all. We just met this week." She sounded like the words were being yanked out of her with pliers, but she pushed forward doggedly. "I am honored—truly honored—if this is what you want, but how can you know that? You didn't know I existed before you ran into me on the beach."

"I'm thinking of renaming that beach."

"That is not the point!" She brought her head up, desperation and confusion and that same deep well of sadness behind her determined eyes. "This isn't a decision you can rush into, you more than anyone. It's a decision that will affect your entire life! Your future—your people... You've known me three days!"

"Five, technically," he said. "I understand your confusion. I have often been told that time seems to pass more swiftly when I'm around."

Emmaline blinked at him, apparently shocked that he could joke at such a momentous time. And in truth, he should be as startled as she was, should be as nervous and unsure.

But he wasn't. Not in the slightest.

"I kept coming back to you, *koukla mou*. I couldn't stay

away. From the first time I met you, you seemed to draw me into your sway. I could no more stop touching you than I could stop breathing. I want to share your life with you, to listen to your music—and for you to pursue that music, however you wish to pursue it …whether that's back in your American university, or in any concert hall in the world, as long as you always return to me. At this point, I don't think I could bear this life without you."

"But that's… You're not considering everything. I need to make a list."

He smiled. "Then put this on it. When I saw you in the sea, fighting against the current, it was not my obligation to go and retrieve you—it was my right. When I saw you in the Visitors' Palace, it was not my job to find you, to pull you into my arms once more—it was my duty. Not to my country, but to myself. If I hadn't taken you away from your hotel and into the mountains, I would never have forgiven myself. I would have snuffed out the one light that has ever shone brightly for me. I would have lost my guiding star."

"But, *Kristos*."

"Emmaline." His words were firm enough that she glanced up to meet his gaze, her face seemingly transfixed for a moment, the two of them caught in time. "You said it once, but I need to hear again, before we take another step. Do you love me?"

Her eyes widened, but she nodded without hesitation. "Yes, I love you. I do."

"And when did you start loving me?" Somehow, he'd managed to move closer to her, the tide of photographers forgotten, the shouted questions, their urgent cries merely part of the backdrop now, falling away.

"I—I don't know," Emmaline said, biting her lip. "You weren't there, and then you were. In front of me, in the center of my mind. Like you'd been there all the time." She waved a hand nervously. "When you talked about your love for your country. Your dedication to your fellow soldiers, I loved you then. And I loved you when you laughed and raced down that mountain in that ridiculous—that ridiculous jeep..." She tried to laugh, but it sounded more like a sob. "And when I saw you for the first time, when you practically knocked me over. I probably fell in love with you then too."

"So many times you have fallen in love with me, and we have only just met."

"I know, but—" Emmaline sighed, and tears did slip down her face now, though her smile was tremulous, vulnerable. "That's different. I've been making up impossible stories for most of my life."

He leaned forward to kiss her in earnest, ignoring the renewed cheer that sounded around the courtyard. "And I have been waiting for you just as long."

EMMALINE ALLOWED Kristos to steer her toward the side, and suddenly there was a man in front of her with an enormous headset, smiling kindly as he slipped it over her hair, then adjusted the mouthpiece in both hands. "Your father!" he shouted as she stared at him, and Emmaline blinked at him.

How is that possible? "Dad?"

"We can hear you!" Her father spoke but he was shouting, and Emmaline heard the sound of clapping, and knew her mother must also be on the line. She couldn't stop her tears from falling then. Someone pushed a soft white cloth in her hand, and she nodded, the only action she could manage for a moment when no words would come. Her father shouted again into her continued silence. "Are you okay?"

"Yes—Yes!" Emmaline said quickly. "Ah...did they tell you? Do you know what just happened?"

"You just got *proposed* to is all I could make out," her father said gruffly. "Some woman who said her name was Catherine told us." He hesitated. "Those people over there are hard to understand, Em."

"I know." She half choked on the words, caught between laughter and tears. "You get used to it."

"Your mother heard the word 'wedding,' and she hasn't stopped smiling." His voice broke a little, and Em felt another surge of waterworks threaten. "So I guess we'll figure everything out eventually. But I understand from whoever that woman is who just spoke to us, your young man loves you very much, and that..." He sighed again. "Well, that's really all any of us needs."

They spoke a few moments more, then said their good-byes, Em promising to call again as soon as she could, and it was only with great effort she pulled the headset from her hair, her hands spasming on it as if she could touch her mother's hand across all those miles.

"Emmaline." The word was rich and full of joy, and Em turned in Kristos's embrace to see Queen Catherine before her now, holding out her hands. Em stepped out of Kristos's arms and placed her own hands into the queen's, reassured by their strong grip.

"I—I guess I don't really know what to say."

"Kristos was never one to wait when there was the opportunity to rush in full tilt. But in this case, I couldn't be happier for his haste—though perhaps his sense of decorum could use some work. It was clear to everyone that you didn't see this coming."

Em's eyes widened a little, her stomach tightening in concern. "Was that bad?"

"Bad?" Catherine shook her head. "It was probably the best reality TV stunt never scripted. If only we'd lined up advertisers beforehand, we could have made enough money to fund Oûros into the next century." She frowned at Kristos. "Still, I hope you don't plan on making such a public spectacle of your life going forward."

"Not even remotely." Kristos looked at Em. "Unless you would like to start a new series? She's right. It could be a windfall for Oûros."

At Em's scowl, Kristos's laughter rang out over the open air, which seemed to be some sort of signal. "Em!" Nicki came bursting down the path still in her running gear, Lauren and Frannie right behind her. They enveloped her in a monster group hug. "Oh my God, girl! What is going on?"

"You're getting married!" Lauren's eyes were wide, her brows climbing up her forehead. "How is it I didn't know this!"

"I didn't know it either!" Em gasped, as Frannie shook her head.

"Well, *I* knew it. You people are idiots."

"Shut up!" Nicki pounded Fran's shoulder, then they all seemed to turn as one to Kristos. Em immediately saw the problem.

"But what does this mean? Our trip, our plans—"

"It would give me the greatest honor if you would—all of you—agree to remain in Oûros as our honored guests for at least one more week." Kristos looked at Lauren. "I know you were planning on a European tour on your own, but we would be delighted to take you anywhere you would like to go while Emmaline and I ah...see where this road might take us. We can show you places that I guarantee are like nothing you've ever experienced."

Lauren looked at him with narrowed eyes for a moment before she nodded, unable to stifle her grin. "Deal. But this better be good."

"It will be." Kristos laughed. "I stake my reputation and my country's honor on it."

Laughter rose up all around them, and Em found herself watching the scene as if it really was a fairy tale, and she—finally—was seeing it all the way to its perfect ending. The friends she loved so dearly, the brilliant sunlight of a city that seemed created to make dreams come true...and the man who even now was turning toward her, his eyes intent upon her, a smile on his lips, holding his hand out as if to welcome her into a future that was filled with hope, with possibility—and with love.

Princess Emmaline Aphrodite Grace placed her fingers into the outstretched palm of the prince of the magical kingdom...and stepped into her life.

Epilogue

The sun was setting over the Aegean far to the west. Emmaline pressed her lips firmly together, willing herself *not* to ask the million and one questions she'd been storing up on the thirty minute drive from the castle to this remote outcropping up the coast of Oûros. Kristos and Queen Catherine hadn't explained where they were going, they'd only requested that she join them.

Since her and Kristos's engagement announcement, the kingdom had descended into joyful chaos—with celebrations, national holidays declared, media coverage from all over the world, and small, handmade Oûrois gifts flowing in from all corners of the country. This had been going on for well over two weeks, and things were only now settling down. The other girls had left to travel around Europe a bit more so Emmaline could continue to get to know the royal Andris family. Increasingly, however, Emmaline had sensed a tension in her new family, a sense of wound-tight anticipation.

So today, when Kristos had casually asked her to take a ride with his mother, she'd agreed almost breathlessly, not sure why she felt so nervous.

Kristos and Queen Catherine had made the sunset trip seem like a low-key jaunt along the sea, but when they'd set off in an off-road jeep without even a single guard in attendance, Emmaline had suspected this wouldn't be your ordinary guided tour.

She was right.

From the guarded gates at the mouth of the nature preserve, to the winding, increasingly unmaintained road that devolved into little more than a goat path, every new kilometer of this journey seemed to draw the three of them deeper into the ancient past. When they'd abandoned their jeep and begun a trek through the dense forest, Emmaline had been sure she'd seen dancing fairy lights in the distance, and that the wind had whispered through the heavy branches, murmuring in a long forgotten language.

Now, as Kristos gripped her shaking hand and tugged her out of the thick canopy of trees and onto a windswept ocean-front cliff, she could do little more than stare at the gorgeously carved white marble temple that rose up before them. With its deeply veined stone currently burnished by the gorgeous red-gold sunset that seemed to light the Aegean on fire, the temple extended maybe thirty feet across. It appeared perfectly circular and featured a dome ceiling supported by thick carved columns. To her eye, it looked like the ideal place to host a wedding, a murder, or a sacrifice to the gods...or maybe all three at once.

"What..." Her single, faltering word was all she allowed to escape her lips as Kristos urged her up the steep steps and beneath the dome. There wasn't much to see at first—mostly a smoking furnace in the center of what looked like a ceremonial maze, the whole thing no more than eight feet square. Then, at the front of the temple overlooking the ocean, she saw that three squat bowls of metal rested atop the waist-high marble wall that formed the outer edge of the building.

Kristos squeezed her hand more tightly and drew her forward as the queen entered the maze, quickly traversing the tight turns with what looked like practice ease. Meanwhile she and Kristos walked up to the hammered metal bowls—two of which were filled with what looked like items blown up from the cliff but couldn't have been. The first bowl had a small pile of dried out driftwood and seagrass, while the second held flower petals and dried twigs. The third was starkly empty.

"What is this?" she murmured, willing to accept nearly anything Kristos might say. Ancient traditions were the weft and weave of European countries, even if the beliefs that had created them were a thing of the distant past. "Some sort of... ceremonial site?"

"Oûros is a country of many contradictions, *koukla mou*," Kristos replied, his words weighted enough that she glanced toward him—then was held in place by the intensity of his stare. "We stand firmly in the present, yet are tied to a past that remains real, vital—alive."

Behind them, a rush of flame brightened the space with a whoosh. Emmaline glanced up, exhaling a quick "oh!" as she took in the richly painted ceiling of the dome.

Easily a hundred deities crowded in the curved space as if they were gazing down through the mists, from Zeus to Hera, Hermes to Apollo, Aphrodite to Poseidon to Artemis. Below them, frolicking through clouds, trees, and the open seas, were dozens of other gods and mythical creatures she couldn't begin to identify, though she suspected her mother probably could.

"It's beautiful," she whispered. She got the feeling nobody should talk above a whisper in this place.

"It's the communication portal for the gods," Kristos corrected her, speaking loud enough to make her jump. "And this is the heart of what we wanted to show you tonight. Oûros's own closely-held secret, that few people outside the royal family know. Since that family now is about to include you...it's time."

"Time," she echoed, hoping she didn't sound as clueless as she felt.

He nodded, still watching her closely. "Our country was first founded by one of Hercules's descendants, shortly after Athens fell to Rome in 146 BC. The Olympian gods retreated, and though they were worshipped by Rome after a fashion and co-opted into the Roman pantheon, they essentially never got over the fall of their beloved Greece. In 820 AD, they started talking about a victorious return, but by then, the world had changed. Humans had changed. The royal family of Oûros, with the advantage of nearly a thousand years of perspective, realized that at the height of their power, the gods had interfered too much with mortals. They treated Earth as their vacation home, and they couldn't simply let humans be humans. At that point, quietly, almost reverently, we built the barrier between our realms, with a solitary gate through Oûros."

Emmaline swallowed. Could this possibly be real? Yet, she knew it had to be. Suddenly, so much of this idyllic, fairytale-like kingdom made more sense. How special and separate it felt, like a country on a cloud. "And the, um, gods allowed you to do it?"

"At the time, they were content to have the most basic connection to Earth—a way to allow them to see what was happening, and even send out envoys to do their bidding on occasion. Most of the half-blood descendants of the gods had made their home in Oûros by then, and the gods' love for our country was great. Greater, in many ways, than their need to roam the wide earth again. They had their idyll in this world, and the promise of a way out...and that was enough."

"But you never intended to let them out again."

Kristos shook his head with a wry smile. "Not on purpose,

no. The royal family of Oûros pledged to maintain the gates to Olympus, to ensure that humanity could never be controlled by the gods again. We became the gatekeepers of the gods of Olympus."

"And—they're still out there? The gods? They're all still alive?"

"They are eternal," Queen Catherine answered, coming up beside him. She held a softly burning taper in her right hand. "And their human children walk among us still—not eternal, but very long lived."

"Children. You're talking demigods." Emmaline's eyes widened. "Who? Have I met any?" She turned to Kristos. "Are you...?"

"No," he laughed. "I'm content with my role of gatekeeper. But yes—you've met a few." His eyes were merry with the delight of a shared secret, and he shot a glance to his mother. "You think we can trust her to keep this sacred knowledge safe?"

"We can trust her to be guided by her heart." The queen's words seemed deliberately vague, which made Emmaline bite her lip.

"I don't want you to tell me anything that makes you uncomfortable," she said quickly. "I mean, you don't have to tell me...wait a minute. You're talking about Dimitri, aren't you? *He's* a demigod? Of course he is." She put her hands to her ears, shaking her head as she screwed her eyes shut. "Oh, my gosh. I'm not sure I can keep this secret from my friends. I want to, but..."

Another thought struck her, and she blinked her eyes open again, staring. "Stefan, too?" she demanded, picturing the impossibly suave aristocrat, who never appeared ruffled by anything—well, except Nicki. But..."They're *immortal*?"

"Extremely long lived," Kristos corrected, which was no

explanation at all. "And, in the nature of all demigods, unusually strong, charismatic, driven...and each connected uniquely to the attributes of their long-ago forebear. You'll get a complete list of the demigod rolls once, ah..."

"Once you're married," Queen Catherine finished for him, as Kristos met Emmaline's eyes, a deep fire burning in them that warmed her far more than the queen's slow-burning taper.

"Assuming you're still willing to take on such unusual in-laws," he said.

"I am. Of course I am," she said—meaning every word. She also noticed that he hadn't confirmed her guesses about Dimitri and Stefan, but he hadn't denied her either. And since he hadn't pushed her on keeping the royal family's secret from Fran, Nicki, and Lauren...

She continued speaking quickly, hoping to distract him. "And none of the gods ever escaped?"

He shrugged. "There have been rare occasions that a major god or his agent has escaped for a short time, and of course the lesser deities can slip through our defenses with a bit more ease. We haven't watched the minor gods so closely, though. They don't wish to draw attention to themselves, and generally stay out of human affairs."

"Or so we thought," Catherine said grimly. Stepping forward, she set the taper to the small pile of driftwood in the golden hammered brazier, and sighed. Her shoulders slumped, her mouth tightened, and she looked older than Emmaline had ever seen her. "Bring him home," she murmured, and there was no question who she was thinking of: her lost son Aristotle.

As the driftwood caught fire, the sound of waves crashing violently against the rocks far below shattered the stillness. Emmaline glanced up, startled. "Ah...is the *ocean* responding?"

Kristos shifted his now-worried gaze from his mother to

Emmaline. "Poseidon still has long reach into the Aegean. And according to the islanders and captains who form our surveillance networks, his sea nymphs have been unusually active this entire past year. If Ari is still out there, somewhere, Poseidon would be able to find him." He looked back to Queen Catherine, his gaze softening. "And if he had, he would have let us know before now."

"Maybe. But it can't hurt to remind him that we're still waiting." The queen turned her attention to the next brazier, her face clearing. A delighted, almost impish smile played across her lips, returning her to her usual youthful appearance.

"Thank you," she said simply, and she touched the taper to the offering of flowers and twigs, which crackled merrily in response. The sound of giggles seem to spring up from the water far below, and Emmaline glanced out over the ocean again, then back to Kristos, who now watched his mother far more warily.

"Mother, what did you do?" he asked. "You know better than to stir up Eros."

"I think Eros was ready to be stirred." Queen Catherine practically beamed at Emmaline, then handed the taper to her. Emmaline looked at it in surprise—it had barely burned down at all.

"Do you have any favor to request?" the queen asked her. "As our newest family member-to-be, your request would honor the gods with whom we are so entwined."

"I..." Emmaline blinked as she took the taper, then squeaked with surprise as a brief burst of wind flowed up over the sea wall, scattering the combination of offerings in their bowls and carrying their embers to the third vessel, along with tiny shards of driftwood and the honey blonde dried petals.

The petals reminded her of Lauren, and Emmaline's heart swelled with love for her friend. Lauren was the *only* reason she'd ever been able to come to Oûros in the first place, the only reason she'd been able to meet Kristos.

She owed Lauren...everything. She could at least offer her this.

Emmaline laid the burning taper against the dried bits of driftwood and flowers, and pictured her beautiful, sophisticated, ever-so-slightly uptight friend, always in control but never quite content.

"Please," she whispered almost silently to whatever gods might be listening, surprised to feel the scratch of tears behind her eyelids. "Please bring her love."

Another crash of waves from far below smashed against the rocks, and Emmaline flinched as a powerful bolt of lightning crackled down from the sky far off to sea, setting the ocean alight. A moment later, a powerful boom blasted her ears, practically shaking the temple.

"What the hell is *that*?" Kristos demanded, looking all around. "What did you ask for?"

But Emmaline merely looked at the radiant queen and grinned.

Queen Catherine clapped her hands together. "I think you'll fit in with our Olympian friends *perfectly*, Emmaline," she announced, her words brimming with delight. "Welcome to the family."

Thank you for reading COURTED! The adventures of Oûros continue with a Beauty and the Beast mashup in CAPTURED, as the demigod Dimitri and socialite Lauren go toe-to-toe...

Next to her beauty, I'm nothing but a beast. That doesn't change my job.

Lauren Grant, pain-in-the-ass celebutante and best friend of the future queen of Oûros, has a problem. She's caught the eye of a billionaire ballbreaker who won't take no for an answer, and the crown needs me to keep her safe.

I may be just a rough-edged demigod more comfortable with dive bars than diamonds, but I sure as Hades will keep this jackal from getting his claws into the icy blonde. Then I learn Lauren's wannabe boyfriend is actually a minion of the creeper god Typhon—avowed enemy of my own great-great forebear, Zeus. Yeah, no.

Even if I didn't have my orders, I'd take on this challenge just for fun.

Then, little by little, I realize things aren't exactly what they seem with the haughty American. She's hiding real terror behind her perfect façade, unwilling or unable to let anyone in. The more I learn, the more protecting Lauren Grant becomes my only goal. I'll tease her—tempt her—do whatever it takes to keep her safely by my side.

I just can't fall in love with her.

Purchase CAPTURED now—or turn the page for a sneak peek!

Keep the romance going! Sign up for my mailing list at my website, www.jenniferchance.com, to learn about upcoming books, giveaways and more. Or, connect with me at Facebook!

I appreciate your help in spreading the word about my books, including telling a friend. Reviews help readers find books! Please leave a review on your favorite book site.

Turn the page for an excerpt from CAPTURED...

Excerpt: Captured

Tonight wasn't about doing everything perfectly. Tonight was about letting go.

Flipping the *tsipouro* glass over with a flourish and smacking it down onto the table, Lauren Grant smiled with the first surge of honest pleasure she'd felt in days. She'd had to work way too hard to find this dive bar in the seaside paradise of Oûros, and harder still to ditch her friends and the persistent tagalongs from the palace security. But it was worth it.

She'd spent most of her life under the careful watch of others, and that hadn't kept her safe. For safety, she'd had to rely on herself. Same for having fun.

Two men and one woman were left facing her across the table. The woman listed to the side, supported by her husband, who kept shaking his head and grinning. The pile of cash in the center of the table was barely enough to buy a pair of shoes, but cash was never the goal anyway. It was simply a way to keep score.

The goal was to be the last woman standing.

"Another!" Lauren called out, and a cheer went up from the crowd circling the tiny table, along with laughter and catcalls, the usual fare of late-night drinking contests. The waitress moved forward instantly, a new round of *tsipouro* at the ready, but the husband waved her off as his wife slumped fully against him.

That left two.

Lauren smiled saucily at the duo. She was almost certain they were brothers, which didn't bode well for her. They were big men, swarthy, their Greek heritage not a distant echo but evident in every line of their sun-worn faces and thick, dark hair. These were the true backbone of the Mediterranean, not the people living in the vaunted castle on the hill, where her dear friend Emmaline was being courted by an actual prince. Hell, not even courted. She was going to marry the guy. And that was cause for celebration.

"*Yamas!*" She raised her glass with the word to another round of applause. Close enough to the Oûrois equivalent of "cheers," her lapse into Greek made her competitors eye each other smugly. The three of them tilted the *tsipouro* back, and the potent grape liquor washed down Lauren's throat in a fiery line of absolution. The distilled spirits might have been made of the dregs of the wine-making process, but it definitely packed a punch.

As she crashed her glass down on the table and more money changed hands, however, she saw him.

It didn't take much. A shift of the crowd in exactly the right way, the right-dodging face that should have dodged left. She didn't squint into the gloom surrounding their table to make sure, because she didn't have to. The man was Dimitri Korba, ranking captain of the Oûros National Security Force. Kind of a high-rent shadow, but that didn't improve her mood.

Dimitri Korba was everything Lauren didn't need right now, here in this tiny little bar in Oûros on the one occasion she'd been able to break free in days.

Granted, the man was mouthwateringly gorgeous in a big, iron-fisted kind of way. Six foot four if he was an inch, he wasn't built like the guys she knew back at home, their lean muscles and sinewy bodies honed with miles on the bike and the treadmill. Dimitri Korba was a giant. Heavily muscled legs, powerful arms, granite-set jaw beneath his dark, flashing eyes. Everything about him angled dark, actually, from his richly tanned skin to his black hair to his obstinate scowl. He was the quintessential bull, determined to tromp into any china shop in his way if it blocked him from his goal.

But in the end, he was simply another babysitter.

And she knew how to handle those.

Want to read more? Check out CAPTURED now!

Acknowledgments

The Gatekeepers of the Gods series would not have been possible without both my friends and fellow authors (who are often one and the same!) Special thanks to my original editor, Linda Ingmanson, who took on this romantic tale with enthusiasm and immense skill, and Toni Lee, who is a ninja proofreader. New thanks to the lovely and talented editors at Oliver Heber Books, especially Holly Thompson, who helped make the new edition of this book shine.

To Sabra Harp, you have been an amazing support through this new re-imagining. Thank you for being here for me! To Liz Bemis, huge thanks for creating a lovely set of covers and your endless patience and skills in helping my books look their best. You deserve every good thing. To Kristine Krantz, thank you for your ideas, insights, and invaluable critiques...even when you didn't realize it, I was storing up your every comment. To Cathy, Laurie, Fran and Sandy... thank you for the laughter and your friendship (and for being great romance heroine models!)

And to every reader who thought—just maybe—that ridiculously romantic dream might somehow come true... keep believing. Sooner or later, in ways you can't now imagine, it will.

About the Author

Jennifer Chance is an award-winning author of magical modern romance and romantic fantasy. She is also the urban fantasy and paranormal romance author Jenn Stark. For free reads, news, and a magical escape from the ordinary, connect with her at jenniferchance.com.

link: https://www.jenniferchance.com

fb: https://www.facebook.com/authorJenniferChance/